ALSO BY ZACH FORTIER

NON-FICTION
CurbChek
Street Creds
CurbChek Reload
The CurbChek Collection
Hero to Zero
Landed on Black

BIOGRAPHY
I Am Raymond Washington

FICTION
Baroota: The Hunting Ground
Cachibaché: Book II in The Director Series
Izadi: Book III in The Director Series
Chakana: Book IV in The Director Series

SCIENCE FICTION
The Overseer Series

 Scan the QR Code to the left to purchase Zach's other books.

IZADI

BOOK THREE OF THE DIRECTOR SERIES

BY AWARD WINNING AUTHOR
ZACH FORTIER

Published by

Steeleshark
press

ISBN-13: 978-0692064504
ISBN-10: 0692064508

Visit the author at:
Website: *www.zachfortier.com*
Goodreads: *www.goodreads.com/author/show/5164780.Zach_Fortier*
Blog: *www.authorzachfortier.blogspot.com*
Facebook: *www.facebook.com/authorzach.fortier*
Twitter: *www.twitter.com/zachfortier1*
Instagram: *http://www.imgrum.org/user/zachfortier/505378433*

CONTENTS

"The most dangerous person is the one who listens, thinks and observes."

~Bruce Lee~

"There is a beast who has taken my blame
You can put me to bed but you can't feel my pain
When the machine has taken the soul from the man
It's time to leave something behind."

~Sean Rowe~

PRELUDE

Sondra woke up to the sound of the dog barking. It was her husband's dog, Günther, a sleek black German shepherd that rarely barked. It wasn't her husband's dog, not technically. The dog belonged to the *Landespolizei*, the state police department they both worked for in the state of Hesse. She looked out the window and saw the dog was barking randomly, not directing its attention to any one specific thing or direction in the backyard, where its kennel was kept. The dog was bored, and its bark was based in anxiety. Her husband, Börn, was gone for the day to a training class in Wiesbaden, the capital of Heese. Sondra had to get up and let the dog in before the neighbors complained. Sometimes she wondered if his being in K-9 had been worth the constant work and attention the dog required. She was glad Börn was in training, it gave her some time to plan for the request that had been made. If she were honest with herself, it wasn't a request, it was a demand. They usually needed fresh product for the new clients. She was running out of places to pick up the new girls and not get caught. When she tried to explain that, they replied this was a specific request from the client who only paid cash and had requested a specific girl. She was warned about the consequences of not completing their latest demands. She had one small window to complete for their most recent demand. Worldwide cops have a saying: "You don't shoot a skunk on your front porch." She was about to shoot one inside her own home. But if she did it right, no one would ever suspect she was involved. Not even Börn. There was a knock at the door; Svetlana had arrived. It was time. Sondra's eyes hardened as she answered the door.

"Now I know you need the dark
Just as much as the sun
But you signin' on forever
When you ink it in blood"

~Jim James~
in State of the Art

CHAPTER ONE

I t had been several weeks since The Director's death. Nick was healing, mentally and physically. His trips to the gym had become a routine that made the day have some meaning and brought some purpose to the day-to-day boredom. One day on the way back from a particularly tough back workout, it occurred to Nick, what about Morticia? He hadn't thought of her or about her since seeing the video Arthur had sent of The Director's painful last few moments. Nick pulled into the farmhouse and stopped. He looked at the barn and wondered why hadn't he seen Morticia on her daily walks. He hadn't heard any conversation around the fire about her—nothing at all. It was like she just ceased to exist. He got out of the truck and walked to the barn. He expected to find her there, sitting in a chair, wearing some ridiculous business outfit she seemed to like to wear. Probably looking at herself in the small stainless steel mirror the Asgarda had provided her. As he approached the stall, he heard nothing—no movement, no unintentional sounds of her breathing or talking to herself, which she did a lot.

The stall was empty. It showed no indication of her ever being there, no sign at all that a human had been kept there against her will for several weeks. No body odor, no hairbrush, nothing.

"Hmm," Nick said out loud. "I wonder where she went? Wonder where they are keeping her now?"

Nick left the barn and headed back to the farmhouse. The Driver was in the kitchen by himself, making a ham sandwich. He looked up and saw Nick and said, "Hey, brother, can I make you a sandwich?"

Nick replied, "Thanks, but no. Just finished my workout and had a couple of *Muscle Milks*. I'm good."

The Driver said, "Your loss, brother. The girls dug a pit and roasted this pig last night. You wouldn't believe how good it is!"

Nick nodded. He had missed the pit/pig roast. He was in Bexx's room reading the latest book on his list, *1491*, by Charles Mann. To most of the Asgarda, it wasn't weird how he still saw and referred to the room they shared as her room. It was hers. He shared it. Nick said, "Hey man, did you know Morticia isn't in the barn anymore?"

"No? where did she go?"

"No idea. I just realized I hadn't seen or heard from or about her since Arthur sent the video of The Director's last moments. I went out there, and she's gone. No sign of her—nada, zero, zip."

"You think Bexx let her go free?"

"Don't know, man. Guess I'll have to ask her. Where is everyone, by the way?"

"I, um, think they are out... um, doing some workout or something." The Driver made no eye contact with Nick as he spoke.

Nick nodded. "Uh huh, working out. Thanks, man."

Nick knew from The Driver's body language he was hiding something. He honestly knew nothing about Morticia's absence, but then when Nick asked about where Bexx was, he changed. He knew something and had been told not to discuss it. Nick imagined the Asgarda forcing Morticia into some exercise regime that would make her hate the day she was born. He smiled, imagining what she would look like after a 5-mile run. All that facade of superiority would fade quickly. Miles on a trail run tend to remind you you're not all your résumé suggests.

That night after the Asgarda returned from whatever training event they had been on, they were quiet. It was something that would have been noticed by Nick even before The Director had been dispatched though he'd been singularly focused. He had one mission, one thought that absorbed all his life force like a black hole absorbs matter and energy. He was still acutely aware of the patterns of behavior around him. It was a requirement for his survival. Awareness mattered always. Now he sensed there had been a change. The rest of the household had been included in the reason for the change. He hadn't. There could be only one reason for that. Bexx had required it... demanded it. Nick sat and listened to the silence of the team as they washed up and changed clothes. Some washed their clothes, others showered, and sooner or later they all went downstairs to the kitchen. He got up from the bed where he had been reading and walked downstairs.

Nick saw the Asgarda had all gathered in the kitchen. Bexx wasn't present. "Where is Bexx?" he asked. No one answered. "Hello, Angels, it's me, Charlie. I asked a question. Where is Bexx?"

Nothing. No one made eye contact. One of the Powerpuff Girls said something in the language they shared, which he called Russian. He hated the sound of it. It reminded him he was still very much an outsider here, and there was also the small matter of years of mental conditioning when he was in the military. Russians were the enemy. The sound of their language still set him on edge. Remarkably, however, when Bexx spoke it, the edge disappeared. It sounded melodic and pleasing.

Still no one spoke, and another commented in Russian. Nick was approaching redline overload much more quickly than he should have. It'd been weeks since he'd been angry, but he was still unpredictable. For a microsecond in his mind, he saw himself flipping the kitchen table and then grabbing the nearest Asgarda by the throat and demanding an answer. He imagined the outcome in his mind and examined it from several different angles. Not a good idea. He was calm enough to see that. Redlined, yes, but not boiling over. Not yet. He turned and walked from the kitchen, thinking maybe it had finally happened. The Asgarda have all synced menstrual cycles and are a single homicidal organism hell bent on ending male domination of the world. He smiled at the thought of them all watching television one night and eating gallons of ice cream. Yeah, that's never gonna happen! If anything, they will beat each other bloody in some female version of a testosterone contest.

Now that he was sure something was up, Nick decided to wait and watch.

That night, the Asgarda made a fire and the team gathered around. They spoke to each other while Nick listened. He did not understand a word they said but watched and listened anyway. It was obvious from the back and forth from Bexx to specific members of the team they were planning something. Nick watched Special K specifically. Out of the entire team, she was the most animated and emotional. Whatever they were planning, she had a stake in it much more than she'd had in the hunt for The Director. This was personal for her, whatever "it" was.

3

That night after the team went inside, Bexx and Nick sat by the fire alone. Nick said nothing and just stared at the fire for some time, waiting. Finally, Bexx said, "Well? Are you going to ask, or shall we pretend you haven't noticed things have changed around here for another couple of days?

Nick said nothing for a while and finally spoke. "Where's Morticia?"

"Who?"

"The forensic proctologist, Queen Bavmorda, Elvira, the Bene Gesserit psycho bitch you had chained up in the barn."

"Queen who?"

"Oh my god, you've never watched *Willow*?"

"No. What is it... a movie or a TV series?"

"Okay, you seriously need to have the team take a day off now and then and watch some movies. The Driver and I can make the list, although I'm not sure you'll like his list now that I think about it. Anyway, quit avoiding the answer. Where is she?"

Bexx said nothing for a while and then finally after a big sigh said, "I made an agreement with her at *Cachibaché*. She broke it when she lied to us about The Director's name. You pointed that out, remember? She's been removed from the farm and will not return."

"That's it? No details? Did you at least play with the food before you killed it?"

Bexx said nothing.

"I see. So, I need to be glared at for the mere mention of humiliating that inhuman piece of shit, but you have the higher moral ground here and can do what you wish?"

Bexx shrugged but said nothing.

"Just know this, Mz. Bexx, Almighty Commander of the Asgarda. I'll only be kept in the dark for so long. Pretend all you like that nothing is going on, that I need not worry my pretty little head, but eventually this will come to a head one way or another. I'd prefer we survived this. That choice is yours. You said you understood what this meant. Show me you aren't like every other woman I've known. Prove it by your actions, not words. Otherwise, my ass is gone down the road. Glare at me all you want. I don't care. You only hold sway over me because of who I see you are. Change that, and you don't hold dick." Nick rose slowly, predatorily, and walked off into the farmhouse and left her there staring into the fire.

An hour later, Bexx walked into the dark room and got into bed. She could tell by Nick's breathing he was still awake. She whispered quietly, "The reason I haven't told you about what we're doing is not to exclude you. Remember at Cachibaché, I followed you into what felt like a suicide mission—just the two of us. We left the team behind. I followed you with no idea of where we were going or what the plan was. When you finally did tell me, I admit I thought you were insane. But guess what? You were right. It worked. You took the entire facility with very little help from me. Back then when you didn't realize I understood you, you told me you couldn't think for the entire team... that you functioned best alone. I agree, but we don't function like that. You're unique, and when the time comes, I'll include you. That time hasn't come yet. Trust me now like I trusted you then."

Nick listened and realized she was right. She was always right, it seemed. She had a grasp of the entire team and its function. He saw the world through his own lens. As distorted as it was, it worked. "I'm sorry. Too much baggage to carry, I guess. It felt like I felt when I found out Joanna had set me up. That isn't your burden to carry... or answer for. Thanks for explaining it to me. What about Morticia? Is she gone?"

"She's gone. I warned her never to lie to me. She did."

Nick smiled. "Adieu, Princess Leia."

CHAPTER TWO

The next few days, Nick watched and waited. Bexx may have wanted to wait to let him in on her plans, but Nick had no intention of sitting back and waiting to be spoon fed details. He went to work on Special K almost immediately.

One morning, he went to the kitchen and found Special K there sitting at the table alone. She was deep in thought, obviously upset and preoccupied.

"You sleep well last night?" Nick asked

She shook her head no and then said, "I'm distracted. Hard to sleep when I have so much on my mind."

Nick said, "I bet. Bexx told me a little bit about it. Wish I could help. If you need to talk, let me know. You know I do have some experience with this. I've worked a few of these cases."

Special K nodded and said nothing.

"It is different when it's personal, isn't it?" he said.

She nodded, and he left the room. *The seed is planted, he thought, let's see what grows.*

Nick left the room and headed out to the 'Yota. Starting up the truck, he started to back out of the driveway. He was nearly out of the drive when Special K came running down the driveway. He stopped the truck and waited for her to catch up. She went to the passenger side of the truck and opened the door. Nick said nothing. He hadn't expected her to respond this quickly. Special K got in the truck.

Nick raised his eyebrows and said, "Headed to the gym. Want to go?"

Silently, she nodded yes.

When they arrived at the gym, Nick nodded to Ali and asked, "Can I bring a friend today? Maybe a one-day pass? She needs to blow off steam."

"A friend, huh? Jesus, Nick, she is barely old enough to be your youngest daughter! What the hell?"

Nick smirked. "When you got it, you got it."

Ali grimaced. "Yeah, you can have an all-day pass, free, on the house. Just don't get all old-man creepy in my gym."

Nick nodded. "No creepy shit. Got it."

Nick sat down and started his warm up while Special K watched. When he was ready for the bench, he asked her to spot him. He didn't press her. He just waited. He could tell she was in an internal conflict, trying to decide how to begin. After a couple of sets, she finally spoke.

"You said you've worked these cases before?"

He'd been vague on purpose. He had no idea what was going on, so he threw out a wide net. Nothing specific. Just random, nebulous statements to hint that he'd worked on similar issues. Let her fill in the blanks to guide him closer to the secret Bexx and the Asgarda were keeping.

"Yeah, I've worked a lot of everything, ya know?"

She nodded. "So, what do you recommend I do?"

Nick, more serious now, replied, "I can't make recommendations to you until I know everything. We had a saying, 'You never give advice to someone unless you're willing to face the consequences with them.' I'm not willing to give advice until I know all the details... everything. I'm sure you noticed I think differently than Bexx. I'm what's referred to as a global thinker. Bexx is a sequential thinker or linear thinker. She sees the world in what's next and what needs to be done to get from point A to point B. She follows the bread crumbs, so to speak, to reach an outcome. That's not how I think. I have to have the entire picture... all the details. Imagine a juggler juggling an ever increasing amount of balls. That's me. I look at every ball. I juggle until I see where they fit in the big picture, and then when I understand that, they all fall into place and a plan emerges. It's very difficult for me to recommend anything when I don't have the whole picture. Does that make sense?"

She nodded yes but said, "No, not really."

Nick laughed. "Yeah, no one gets it until they see the results. It's up to you. You can tell me what you're comfortable with. I'll ask questions. Let's see where it goes. Okay?"

Special K nodded and started to tell him what had her so upset.

Nick stopped lifting and sat down and listened. The more he heard, the more focused he became. An hour went by, and then another. Finally, Special K had finished.

Nick stared at the floor. It was a lot to absorb. He finally looked up and said, "Let's go get a drink. I need to drive and think." They stopped at a small convenience store and went in to get a couple of drinks. When they came back out, Nick asked, "How long has your sister been gone?"

"She was reported missing two weeks ago by her husband."

"Do you trust him?"

"Yes, they have been together a long time. Since they were fifteen. I trust him."

"Why? In ninety percent of these cases, the spouse is responsible. How sure are you that he isn't just looking for a way out of their relationship and doesn't have the balls to admit it? You know my story, right?"

She nodded. She'd heard the story of Baroota many times.

Nick continued. "So, what makes him so different? People are screwed up. They betray the ones who trust them the most, often for no other reason than they're the easiest to betray. It doesn't have to make sense. It just has to be."

She nodded and said, "I understand that. Just trust me. It isn't him. I can't explain how I know it. I just do. It's a gut feeling."

Nick nodded. "That I understand. Some things you know at a visceral level. Okay, let me think on this. I may have a few questions to ask as I go down this road. Some of them will be ugly and are bound to piss you off. It isn't personal. It's part of the process, leaving nothing to chance, no stone unturned. Okay?"

Special K nodded.

"Let's go back now, and I'll start looking into this incident with your sister. No promises, but I'll look."

They returned to the farmhouse and went their separate ways.

From the upstairs window, Bexx watched as Nick and Special K got out of his truck. Smiling, she thought, *I knew there was no way you'd let this go. A dog with a bone, he wasn't letting go.* Her plan was working perfectly. Let Nick be Nick while she and the team went on their own path. Somewhere down the road, they may need him.

Bexx walked to the Bat Cave to speak to The Driver and Buffy. "Nick will be coming to you eventually for information. Whatever he asks for—and he'll be asking soon—give it to him. Just keep me in the loop. Let's see what he learns. But keep this just between us, understood?"

The Driver and Buffy nodded. They understood. They looked at each other, smiling, after she left. Finally, the entire team was in on the mission.

It wasn't long, and Nick was in the Bat Cave himself.

"Brother, I need a favor," Nick said to The Driver

"What's that?"

"I need a police report from Hesse, Germany. Can you do that?"

"Sure thing, Nick. I can slip into Interpol like a sixteen-year-old slipping into his girlfriend's bedroom window late at night. Silent, aroused, and ready for action. What case do you need?"

"It is a missing person case, and I need you to keep this just between us. No need to let the ladies in on this. They have their little secrets. We have ours."

"Sure thing, brother. What's the perp's name?"

"Dude, too much *Dragnet*. The missing person isn't a perp. They are considered a victim. Oh, and by the way, speaking of television, can you add Willow to the list of movies the Asgarda need to watch? No one has heard of Queen Bavmorda! Can you believe it?"

"Who?"

Nick rolled his eyes. "Jesus, you too? Yes, definitely add *Willow* to the must-watch list. The victim's name is Svetlana Kusina."

"On it, brother. I should be able to get the report in about ten minutes. Do you want to wait?"

"Yeah, I'll wait."

A few minutes later, the report was downloaded and on a thumb drive. The Driver handed it to Nick and said, "I didn't know you read Deutsch."

"Huh, what? I don't. The report is in Deutsch? That won't help. I need to be able to read it!"

"Lucky for you, I'm fluent in Deutsch, brother. Would you like me to read it to you?"

"Yes, please. Seriously, man? Interpol is multinational. All the reports can't be in Deutsch. Isn't there a translator program on the site?"

"There is, but it's tracked. No need to go there. The Driver is here!"

"Okay, man, but I need you to translate it word for word. Leave nothing out."

"Can do!" The Driver began.

When he was done, Nick had made a list for The Driver. "I need any and all information you can find on the person who reported Svetlana Kusina missing. That's where I'll start."

CHAPTER THREE

A couple of days after Nick had taken Special K to the gym and started to check into her story, he stopped in the Bat Cave again to ask The Driver a question.

"Hey man, do you still have that burner phone we used to communicate with Arthur?"

"Yeah, it's around here somewhere. What's up?"

"Just thinking maybe Arthur might have some connections that could help out with this investigation. I know it's a long shot, but who knows. If you find it, lemme know, okay?"

"Sure thing, man. I'll look around."

Nick turned to walk out of the Bat Cave and noticed a phone on the shelf near the door. "Oh, here it is. Never mind. I'll charge it and see if Arthur answers the office number." Nick took the phone and walked out of the office.

The Driver raised his eyebrows and whispered, "Oh shit."

Once Nick had left the Bat Cave, The Driver waited a few moments and then went out to find Bexx. Best to give her a heads up of the drama that might be headed her way once Nick spoke to Arthur.

Nick charged the phone and checked the phone log. There were no calls and no messages. Fortunately, The Driver had deleted the message Arthur had sent describing the wine bottles. Nick started to doubt that Arthur would be of any help in the current situation, but still there was this gut feeling that he may. Nick decided to call Arthur's office number.

"Arthur Look. How may I help you?"

"Arthur, how's the wife, man?"

"Nick?"

"Yes, sir! Just wanted to see how things are going."

"Things are good, Nick. I'm still working in the same office. I guess that's obvious since I answered the same phone. My new boss is a lot easier to work with. Not a surprise to you, I'm sure, given the last boss, but it's a welcome change."

"That's good to hear, Arthur."

"So, Nick, look, I would like to talk you but not now. I'm here at work, and it would be best for me to call you from a different line. Maybe I could call you tonight? I have some things to tell you that may be of some interest. Would that be okay with you?"

"Sure thing, Arthur. I'll keep the phone charged and wait for your call. Good to talk to you, man. Talk tonight!" Nick hung up.

Later that night, the phone rang. It was Arthur calling from home.

"Hey, man. What's new?"

"Nick, I'm home now, and I can talk more openly. First, remember what you told me about The Director having plans for me once my wife dropped off the list for bone marrow donor? You couldn't have been more accurate. I found out after his death that he'd set me up to take the fall for Camp Cachibaché."

"What do you mean take the fall for it?"

"He had a quitclaim deed made up and backdated. You know he was less than ethical, so he cultivated contacts who owed him favors. When you took down Cachibaché, he called in one of those favors and had the entire facility deeded to me and the paperwork dated for a year prior. That way, he was no longer liable should the secret be discovered. Can you believe that?"

"Yes, I can. The Director was an evil prick."

"No doubt. No one knows that better than us, huh? Anyway Nick, after all the drama settled, I found out I'm the owner of a missile facility in Dresden, North Dakota. Don't have a clue what to do with it. I can't sell it. It'd been for sale for a very long time before The Director bought it. Anyway, I was thinking, would you want it? All it requires is the taxes paid every year. I can quitclaim deed it to you, and I was thinking you probably have other missions in the works. Seems like a sweet place to work under the radar, so to speak. You know what I mean? No one around to notice a thing. Close to the Canadian border. No one would know if you came or went etc. What do you think? Would you be interested?"

Nick almost said no and then thought, *Damn! What better place to set up a second base of operations?*

"Arthur, I need to think it over. I'm interested, but I have to ask the rest of the team what they think. The place isn't filled with good memories for us. One of our own died there, and you know there're a few dead bodies we left there. How was that not ever brought back to you? Didn't the sheriff find the place?"

"Apparently, The Director had the entire place scrubbed. At least that's what I found in a file when I cleaned out his office for my new boss. The file referenced clean up and sanitation of Cachibaché and disposal of all incriminating evidence. I've no idea what he did or what the current state of the facility is, but I do have the keys to all the high security locks and all the information on the water and power systems. The facility is yours if you want it. Nick, it's the least I can do for all you've done for me and my wife."

Nick was about to refuse. The more he thought about Nõn's death and the water tower, the more he disliked the idea. Then he remembered how remote the area had been. The post office had been in the same building as the general store. It was that small. They'd be able to conduct training and practice tactics with no prying and questioning eyes.

"Arthur, how would I get the keys? Would it be okay to come to D.C. and pick them up and maybe treat you to dinner again? Meet the wife?"

"That would be great! I look forward to it. Will your friend be coming with you? I do remember she mentioned she was here to protect me on your last trip." Arthur laughed.

Nick thought it over. "I'll let you know. I'll call you when we've made plans."

"Sounds great, Nick. This time, dinner is on me!"

Nick hung up and sat for a long time motionless, deep in thought. The missile complex would make for a nearly perfect set up for The Driver and for the team. Once it had been brought up to living standards and furnished, it'd be habitable. The Driver would have an uninterrupted power source that was off the grid and more than enough room to house his beloved server room, the Bat Cave II. The more Nick thought about the idea, the better it felt. He decided to run it past Bexx and see what she thought before running it past the team. When he was done explaining the options and the benefits as he saw them, Bexx agreed to let him present it to the team.

That night, Nick made a fire. Bexx called the team to a meeting. She explained that Nick had asked that everyone show, including The Driver and Buffy. He had an opportunity that concerned them all and wanted everyone's input.

Once the group had gathered and calmed down, Bexx asked Nick to begin. He explained he had spoken to Arthur and detailed their conversation. "Basically, he offered me the missile complex and said The Director had scrubbed the facility of any evidence and placed it in a quitclaim deed to Arthur should any fallout occur. None had, and now it's Arthur's."

The team was silent. They had spoken amongst themselves about the incident with Schidel and Bexx, and the thought of his now-dead and rotting body in the facility didn't make it appealing. However, if what Nick had been told was accurate and the facility had been scrubbed, it'd make an excellent base of operations. The Driver was the most enthusiastic about the idea. He'd be able to have an impenetrable location to set up his hacking ventures. The team talked it over, and Bexx decided she and Nick would travel to D.C. and meet with Arthur. They'd see what shape the facility was in before the decision to move was made. Bexx asked The Driver to secure two round-trip tickets from Spokane to D.C. as soon as possible and then asked if anyone had anything further to bring up at the meeting.

Nick cleared his throat. "Um... yeah, I do."

Bexx raised an eyebrow. He hadn't mentioned anything else to her, and she was reluctant to have him speaking to the team without her vetting his thoughts first.

"Can it wait?" she asked apprehensively.

"It can," he replied.

"Let's wait, then. It's been a long day. The team is tired and needs to rest."

Later that night, she asked Nick what he wanted to say.

"I just wanted to let you all know I was working on your mission from another aspect—a fresh set of eyes. I've been watching Special K, and I could tell this mission had special meaning to her, so I spoke to her privately. Don't be mad at her for talking to me. I may have lied a tiny bit and told her you'd spoken to me about it, insinuating it was okay to talk to me about it. I didn't mean to go behind your back, and I'm sorry if that upsets you, but I'm not going to sit by with my thumb up my ass and do nothing. I can't do that, Bexx."

Bexx smiled. "Thank you for telling me. I'd already surmised what you'd done, and Katerina told me she'd spoken to you."

"Katerina?"

"Special K. That's her name. Katerina. You didn't know that?"

"Oh yeah, I did. Guess I was more comfortable with Special K as her name."

"Does it bother you that I don't call you by your name?" he asked.

I prefer Bexx when we're in front of the team. They're comfortable with it now, but in private, if you prefer, you may call me by my name. Actually, now that I think about it, I would prefer that."

"Okay, um... Tamriko, I have been asking The Driver for documents and to conduct searches in Interpol's database for Special... er, I mean, Katerina's sister. So far, nothing jumps out at me."

"Thanks for letting me know. Now, let's talk about the missile facility. What do you think about that idea?"

They talked late into the night about the facility's strengths and weaknesses. It had some serious potential, and some drawbacks as well. There was no infrastructure in the immediate area, but that was also a plus. They agreed to wait and see how it looked when they finally checked it out in person.

The next day, The Driver presented them with their itinerary for the trip to D.C. They'd be leaving the following day and then depart for Fargo, North Dakota. The ticket was open-ended from there. They could return when they'd made a decision. The Driver had made a reservation for a hotel and a rental car if they needed it.

CHAPTER FOUR

The next day, Nick and Bexx were headed to Spokane and then on to Salt Lake City. There they made a connection to Flight eight-thirty-two on Delta Airlines and continued on to the Ronald Reagan Washington National Airport. They arrived at the airport and let Arthur know they were on their way to their hotel and would meet him at Masala Art at five thirty. On the way to the hotel, Nick was quiet, mulling over the idea of the missile launch facility as a base of operations.

"I'm not sure about the missile facility being a good idea. What're your thoughts?" he asked.

"I don't know. The thought never occurred to me that we'd ever be going back there. I don't know how you saw it, but I always looked at it from the point of view of how to get in and disrupt The Director's operations, never how to make the most of what it had to offer," Bexx replied.

"Exactly, and I'm a little bit concerned that the facility will be booby trapped. The Director was a devious bastard. No way we're just going to walk in the front door and take it over. Just so you know, I've no intention of doing that. When we do go to the facility, I'll go in through one of the vehicle tunnels and check for any trip wires or bombs. You're just gonna have to wait outside. Okay?"

"No, it's not okay. If you go, I'm going. If you like, I'll follow you inside, but I will not wait outside and do nothing," Bexx said, irritated.

Nick sighed. "Yeah, I thought so. Always have to be the pointy end of the spear, huh? Just can't stop throwing yourself in front of the train. Jesus. I can't think for you, and I can't be distracted by you. You do understand that? Just by you being there, you'll change my frame of reference. I work better alone. You know this."

"I do, and as I remember, we did fine together the last time we came here. I'll follow you, and I'll not distract you any more than I did then. Remember we took this facility together? You ended up needing my help to accomplish that, as I recall."

Nick winced. *Jesus, she is always right,* he thought. "Yes, you're right. Okay... together, then."

Nick was silent for the rest of the drive. After they checked in and unpacked, they left for Masala Art.

Arthur was waiting for them when they arrived. He had a leather satchel bag that contained the documents he'd recovered from The Director's files and the keys and codes for the various locks—both mechanical and electronic. Also included in the files were the original blueprints and specs for the facility. Everything Nick would need to access and understand the facility's capabilities.

Nick and Bexx approached the table, and as he and his wife stood up, Bexx said warmly, "Hello, Arthur."

She hugged Arthur and then his wife and introduced her to Nick.

Arthur introduced his wife, and they all sat down.

"Long time, no see, Arthur," Nick said. "How's everything? Life better now?"

Arthur smiled and looked at his wife and said, "Yes, much better. We have some good news. It appears the last bone marrow transplant was effective, and she's on the road to recovery."

Nick asked, "And your work? Has that improved as well?"

"Yes, definitely. I have a new boss, and she's much easier to work for. I enjoy work again, and I'm more hopeful now than I've been in years, thanks to you two."

"Good! That is great to hear. So, let's talk about the facility. Do you have any idea who cleaned it and what their ties are to the previous owner?" Nick spoke carefully, not sure of what Arthur had told his wife about The Director.

Arthur began. "From what I can see, the facility was 'sanitized' from top to bottom by a professional disaster cleaning business based out of

Fargo, North Dakota. The company he used was named *Accent*, and from what I've found out, it was a one-time clean-up deal only. I found no other record of The Director using their services. He paid them twice their going rate for their guaranteed silence about what they discovered at the facility. The Director had no idea what had happened inside and apparently made up a story about an employee that had been hired and had been a heavy drug user.

"Nice story," Nick replied. "Covers all the bases and answers all the questions in one statement. You have to give the bastard credit. He was a slippery one."

"Apparently not slippery enough." Arthur smiled.

"Apparently," Nick returned. "So, everything's here? Power supply, water, sanitation, specs on the walls and locks. Any back taxes owed? Any chance of some locals showing up and having a claim to the property?"

"It's all there, and no chances of that. How about we order food now?" said Arthur.

Nick said, "Sure, let's eat. But before we order, I'm going to hit the little boys' room." He looked to Bexx and said, "Excuse me for a minute?"

She nodded, and he got up and walked across the room to the hallway marked "Restrooms."

Once Nick was out of earshot, Bexx spoke quietly to Arthur. "Arthur, while we have a moment, I have a favor to ask."

"Of course. Anything. Name it."

"You sent a picture and referenced four more wine bottles in The Director's liquor cabinet if I remember correctly?"

"Yes, I thought that'd be information you and Nick would like to know about. I assume that means there are more camps. Was I wrong?"

"No, I do appreciate the information, but well, I'm going to be blunt. Don't mention it to Nick. I've kept the information from him. It wouldn't be a good idea for him to learn of it now. We're currently tasked with a different mission, and I need Nick focused on that alone. He's much calmer now with The Director out of the picture and, to be honest, much more tolerable. I need this favor, Arthur. Please?"

"Of course! Consider the matter closed. Mum's the word."

"Thank you, Arthur."

"You're most welcome. Please, anything I can do to help, don't be afraid to ask. I'd be happy to do what I can."

"I may take you up on that offer, Arthur. I see Nick is on his way back now, sooo..."

Arthur smiled. "So how long will you two be staying in D.C.?" he asked, changing the subject discreetly.

Bexx smiled as Nick sat down and said, "I don't know. How long will we be staying, Nick?"

Nick shrugged as he sat down. "I guess we'll play it by ear. I'd thought we might leave tomorrow unless something comes up."

Nick looked around the table. "So what did I miss?"

Arthur said, "Not a thing. Just talking about the facility and what a surprise it was that The Director so graciously deeded it to me."

"Yeah, he was such a thoughtful guy!" Nick said sarcastically. And then he said, "I'm starving. Let's order!"

The two couples ordered food and sat waiting for the waiter to return with their drinks. Meanwhile, outside on the sidewalk, people were walking past on their way home from work. One man walked past the restaurant and casually looked in through the window. His eyes locked on the table where Nick, Bexx, Arthur, and his wife sat. He didn't stop walking. He'd seen all he needed to see in that one glance as Arthur had handed the leather satchel to Nick.

That night, Nick sat in bed and read all the documents Arthur had provided about the missile facility. He read late into the night. Something wasn't right. He could feel it. He kept rereading the documents about the clean-up of the facility and the story The Director had fed the clean-up crew about an employee who had been on a bad drug binge. It worked, technically. The facility had been scrubbed, but then he went and put it into Arthur's name. Why? It made no sense. Why would The Director risk Arthur being caught when Arthur was the one person who could detail everything he had done? Every single dirty detail. Nick sat staring at the wall, deep in thought, thinking through every detail... every nuance. Something wasn't right. It was three a.m. when Bexx woke up and reached over to the empty side of the bed that should've held Nick's sleeping body. She was up in a heartbeat. Where was he? She looked around the room, silently searching for something to indicate where he'd gone. On the desktop near the laptop and charging station for their phones she found a note.

Tamriko, hopefully you won't find this note and have slept through the night. If you do wake up, don't worry. Something isn't right about the paperwork Arthur gave us. I can't figure out what, but I can feel it. Something is very wrong. I have gone out for a drive to work it out. Be back soon. N

Nick returned to the room quietly at five a.m. and snuck into bed. Bexx spoke. "Did you figure it out?"

"No, but everything in my being says we need to be careful. It feels so close, like if I could just stop looking, it'd be in plain sight. I can almost see it. Something is very, very wrong. We have no choice now but to go to the facility. The answers will be there. Seriously, Tamriko, listen to me. Tomorrow, we'll go very slowly through the facility. I need you to stay back from me. Let me at least have the illusion that you're safely away from there. I need to be able to see it with no distractions. If I need your help, I'll ask for you by name. Otherwise, ignore me. Anything I say or do, just sit back and watch but don't talk. This feels very wrong now. It feels like a trap."

Bexx asked, "Do you think Arthur is a part of it?"

"No, he wouldn't have been able to pull this off. Someone... something else is behind this. I don't know who or what. I can feel it. I have to go with that. It just feels wrong. That's all I can say. I'm going to try to rest now while I can. Tomorrow, we fly to Fargo and then drive to the facility. When we get to Fargo, I'll need to pick up a few random things. Then we can go to the facility."

CHAPTER FIVE

They had boarded the plane, and it took off. Nick sat by the window, staring out at the Earth thirty-two thousand feet below. He had a dark look on his face and was unaware Bexx was watching him.

Finally, she spoke. "Tell me what this feels like."

He sat silent, frustrated. Then he spoke. "It isn't easy to describe. It is a feeling—an awareness just outside of what I can verbalize right now." He laughed. "That sounds so stupid and cheesy like some spirit guide bullshit Nõn would have said, but it isn't like that. It isn't a spirit. Maybe this will help. When I was a kid, my family..." He laughed again. "Well, I use the term family loosely. The people who raised me were very dysfunctional. I swear at one time or another each of them tried to kill me. They were very subtle about it—nothing direct was ever done. They'd just put me in a situation that was dangerous, and then when I needed their help, they withdrew. Passive aggression is the term, I guess."

She looked at him, confused. Her father had been extremely protective. She had no frame of reference for this.

Nick continued. "For example, one time my father took me and my brother into a field to help a farmer retrieve some cattle that had gotten loose. I was maybe ten. Everyone else who helped was much bigger physically. I was just happy to be included. My father rarely included me with anything he and my brother did. I should've known then something was wrong. Anyway, we surrounded a full grown and aggressive bull, and he stopped and looked at all of us one by one. Stupid now that I think about it all these years later, but we had left him nowhere to go. He was cornered. What did the older men expect to do with him? He couldn't get away, and he wasn't going to be led out by a lead. Does that make sense?" She nodded it did. "Anyway, he did what any animal would do when it was cornered. He fought back. It sized each of us up, and of course, I was the smallest and youngest. So it charged me. I had nowhere to go. I was ten years old, and this two thousand pound bull was running at me, running at full speed. Oh, and by the way—small detail here—the farmer hadn't cut its horns off. So it had a full year's growth of horns bearing down on me as fast as it could run."

Bexx now, wide-eyed, asked, "What did you do?"

"I waited until the last second, and he dropped his head. I reached out and put my hands on the horns as he flipped his head and used the momentum of his body to push me over him. I landed on my feet, unharmed and dazed. I spun around to try to find him, and there he was again. He was bearing down on me. This time I ran for the fence. He picked me up and tossed me in the air just as I jumped. I came away from the whole thing with minor scratches. But later, what occurred to me was that it was weird how my father reacted. He was angry I'd let the bull past. He chewed my ass for letting him past and told me to go back to the house if I wasn't going to help. Do you see what I'm getting at? It was subtle. He didn't care about what could have happened to me. He cared about what didn't happen. I didn't get hurt. That is what I mean when I say I can almost feel it. I knew then there was something wrong with the situation. I just didn't know what. I was in the moment and couldn't see the entire situation. Bottom line was, my father included me to get me hurt. He wanted me to be hurt. That's what I believe now. He didn't care about what could've happened because that was exactly what he wanted to have happen, and then when it didn't, he made it my fault. I know I was drunk that night in front of the fire when I told you I have a knack for survival, but I meant it. My father wasn't stupid. He was lethal. Does that make sense?"

"It does. I see what you mean. If you weren't watching everything and understanding every possible outcome of every scenario before it happened, then you'd be at risk. And this is how you grew up?" she said, eyebrows raised.

"Pretty much, yes. My whole life people have told me I'm paranoid and see conspiracies that don't exist, but my reality was very different than most. I survived in spite of the situation, not because of it. That gave me a very different vantage point of the world and people. When I became a cop, that experience worked for me, to my advantage. I saw things differently. I'd learned to examine them from many different angles at an early age. So, when I tell you this doesn't feel right, it doesn't. I just don't know why yet, but I will soon enough. I just hope I see it before the bull charges."

Bexx sat in her seat, looking at him, letting the story sink in. If this was a typical day in this ten-year-old boy's life, no wonder Nick was who he was. The reality of living like that every day of his life, and then here he was as an adult and his wife sent him to Baroota to die. Bexx was having her own moment of clarity. Now she understood what Nõn meant when she said, "He sees things differently." He had to. He had learned to as a means of survival. These weren't hunches or some paranoid delusions. They were honed observation skills that couldn't always be put into words.

She said, "I understand now. Whatever you need me to do at the facility, tell me. But don't ask me to leave you in there alone. I won't do that."

Nick nodded. The steward came over the plane's intercom and made the standard announcement that "We are making our final descent into Fargo, North Dakota. All passengers should start preparing by moving the chairs into an upright position, and all tray tables should be secured to the backs of the seat in front of you."

After they landed, Nick and Bexx secured a rental car and then headed to a sporting goods store. There, he purchased a Leatherman, a Streamlight Waypoint flashlight, and some road flares.

They then went to a pharmacy and bought some tongue depressors. Once they were in the car, he said, "That should do it. Let's go see how well they cleaned up the facility."

They had some lunch at the Smoking Moose Rocky Mountain Deli and then began the three-hour drive to Dresden, traveling north on Interstate twenty-nine past Grand Forks until Google Maps told them to take the exit at mile marker one-hundred eighty-seven and then turn right on eightieth Street N/E. A few more lefts and rights, and they arrived at the front gate of the facility.

Nick stopped and looked for a moment, turning off the car and just looking at the gate. It seemed like a lifetime ago that they'd been there. The Director was dead now. So was Nõn. He and Bexx were speaking English to each other and sharing the same bed. Arthur was now an ally. It was an amazing change of events.

Nick laughed. Turning to Bexx, he said, "Ready?"

Nick got out and punched the code into the cipher lock at the gate. The gate just opened.

He returned to the car. "One down... who knows how many left to go."

Bexx asked, "What does that mean?"

"The gate. It didn't blow up."

She realized he was serious. Deadly serious.

Nick continued. "Okay, here's the plan. We go into the facility through one of the tunnels—not through the front door—because that's exactly what some dirtbag like The Director would expect us to do. From here on out, I need your eyes open, looking at everything, seeing what isn't there and what is. No talking to me unless you see something. If you do, call me by name. Say 'Nick'. Otherwise, ignore me. I'll be talking out loud to myself. It helps me to process what I see and what I should be seeing. Got it?"

Bexx nodded.

Nick walked to the large, steel doors and unlocked the high security lock. He motioned to Bexx to get behind the car, and he carefully opened the door slowly as he stayed behind it. If the door was armed with a bomb of some type, it would protect him from the blast. Nothing happened. He sat down the bag of items he had purchased and opened up the road flares. He lit one and let the smoke flow into the tunnel. Then he turned on the flashlight and slowly walked inside. Bexx followed from a discreet distance of about ten feet.

Nick stepped and scanned left to right, up and down. He mumbled to himself, "Well, thief, I smell you. I can hear your breath. I feel your air. Where are you?"

"Where are you?"

Nick slowly walked into the dark tunnel. "Bexx, stay in my path, don't walk right or left of me. Directly behind me. Understand?"

She said, "Yes."

Nick crept forward at a painfully slow pace. "Come out into the light. Don't be shy."

"Ahh, finally," Nick called out. "Tripwire." He called back to Bexx. "Stay down."

He'd located a strand of fishing line barely visible in the smoke, invisible without it. It was about eighteen inches off the ground and traversed the entire width of the tunnel.

"There you are, thief!" He smiled.

He didn't cut the line and instead followed it to the sides of the tunnel. There he found the trigger device. It was a spring-loaded trigger, armed by the tension of the line. It was attached to a detonator buried in a large block of C-4 explosive. He left it there and followed the line to the other side of the tunnel. There he found the line tied to a pin. The pin was attached to a detonator again, buried in a block of C-4 explosive. The pin would be pulled by the line should someone walk past and snag it. The other side of the tunnel was armed with a detonator that would only arm if the line was cut.

"Tricky motherfucker," Nick whispered. He went back to the opposite side of the tunnel and removed a tongue depressor, then carved a small piece off of it and wedged it between the spring-loaded pin and detonator. "Bexx, lay flat. Cover your face and head with your arms." She did as he said. Nick said, "Are you ready?"

Bexx said, "Yes, ready."

Nick cut the line with the Leatherman. The line fell harmlessly to the floor. "Two down," he said.

He pulled the line out of the tunnel and wound it up near the wall. Then he carefully removed the detonators from the C-4.

He sat down and called to her, "Tamriko, it's safe now. Come here."

She walked to the light he carried and sat down next to him. He took a drink from a water bottle he'd brought with him. "So, what disaster cleaning crew leaves trip wires armed to C-4 explosive booty traps after they have completed the job, Arsenio Hall wonders, *hmmm*?" Nick said as he put his forefinger to his head. Nick continued. "It is going to be a long day, I am afraid. But once we have the place cleared, I believe it will be ours. Someone left it this way for a reason. Logically, it implies they wanted no one sneaking in and that only they would be aware of the potential danger. Trespass, and you die. I'm thinking once we have cleared the facility, it will be safe—safer probably than anyplace else we would could possibly ever find. Does that make sense?"

Bexx nodded it did.

Nick smiled. "Okay, one by one, we take them down, slowly, methodically. Eyes open now, looking everywhere. The booty traps won't all be this easy. Once more unto the breach, dear Bexx, shall we? Let's go find some more Booty traps!"

Bexx nodded, smiling. "*Henry the Fifth*? Seriously?"

They continued to clear the facility of booby traps, Nick laughing insanely every time he said "booty traps." Once he nearly blew them both up, he was laughing so hard as he disarmed another booty trap.

Finally, Bexx asked, "What is so funny about booty traps?"

Nick laughed harder. "Oh man, you are so missing out on the humor here. You've never seen *The Goonies?*"

Bexx looked at him, perplexed. "What?"

"*The Goonies?* Stephen Spielberg? Data... the little Oriental kid in the Goonies? Seriously, you've never seen it?"

She remained motionless, irritated.

"Okay, so this little Chinese kid is a Goonie and a wannabe James Bond and calls booby traps, booty traps, and everyone corrects him. It's a classic!" Nick looked at Bexx and saw no recognition of anything he'd said. "Match dot com screwed the pooch on our match, Tamriko. You got it going on like no one ever has, but your pop culture skills leave me feeling all alone and needy."

Bexx, so even more confused, said, "Can we just get on with it and find more booby traps?"

"Booty traps," Nick blurted out at Bexx. He hunched over laughing until he fell down and then nearly threw up.

Bexx sat down and rubbed her fingers against her temples, her eyes closed. Here they were in a very serious life-and-death situation, and Nick was laughing hysterically. In the back of her mind, she heard Nõn saying, "His sense of humor is so juvenile and annoying. He drives me insane!" Bexx whispered to herself in Russian, "Amen to that one, girlfriend."

Nick finally recovered from his laughing fit and continued clearing the facility of C-4 and detonators. While they cleared, he asked Bexx if she'd ever used C-4 in her team's training? She replied they hadn't.

Nick smiled. "Well, you'll have a free and probably large supply of training material if we make it through this in one piece. One thing you pay attention to is the smell. I knew charges had been placed when we came in the tunnel. I could smell it. It smells quite a bit like motor oil. I don't recall the smell being down here in the lower levels when we were last here. Then, of course, there was the clean-up crew. The building has been sanitized, and yet if you're paying attention, you can smell the distinct scent of motor oil in the air. The type of blasting caps we've found so far tells me a lot about who set the charges. There are two types. One is the *pyrotechnic fuse-blasting cap.* It's very reliable. The other is called match or *fuse-head electric blasting caps* and are the single most commonly used in the world. The first type is an older design and is safest around any electrical interference. The second is newer and very reliable. Anyway, they tell me whoever set these charges wanted them to be reliable for a very long time and more likely than not never planned on coming back to the facility. The explosive itself is definitely military grade C-4. There's no mistaking its shape and look. My guess is someone with some prior military experience and demolition experience set these charges."

They continued and collected the blasting caps and blocks of C-4. Finally, they'd cleared the lower levels and made their way to the upper levels.

When the entire facility had been cleared, they opened the doors and let the smoke from the flares escape. Nick looked at his watch and smiled. "Guess how long we've been doing this?"

Bexx shrugged. "I've no idea. Seems like several hours."

Nick laughed. "That would be correct. We've been purging the facility of explosives for twenty-one hours straight. We came into the tunnel during the early evening. It's now afternoon—the next day. Intense, huh?"

She just nodded.

"Okay, we'll rest for an hour or two and then collect the C-4 and blasting caps and put them in the armory. Then we can check out the facility to see if it's a viable option for our needs."

CHAPTER SIX

A couple of days later, Nick and Bexx were on a plane heading back to Moses Lake. They decided to take cell phone video and pictures of the facility and ask The Driver to set up a presentation of sorts for the entire team to look at and evaluate. Moving most of their operations would be simple, with the exception of The Driver. The Bat Cave was an extensive set up and would require his specific skills to determine if the missile facility in North Dakota would be up to his requirements.

Somewhere over Montana, Nick turned to Bexx and stopped before he spoke. She waited, listening, watching while he worked out in his head what he had to say.

Finally, he spoke. "I need to interview Special K about her sister and the mission you and the team are training for. I need her to feel like she can speak to me openly for as long as I need her to, whenever I need her to. As it is now, she's told me about the basics of what's happened, but I need more than that for it to make sense in my head. I just don't have enough information to even have a feel for where to begin. I know it makes no sense, but I have to see it all before I can begin to make a plan. So what I am saying is, I need you to give her permission to speak about anything I ask about."

Bexx nodded and said nothing for some time, looking out the window at the ground below. After a few minutes, she turned and said, "I'll tell her to answer anything you ask. I just need you to do your thing and let us do ours. Can you do that?"

"Yes."

"Fine, and one more thing. When you think you understand whatever it is you understand, I don't pretend to understand your process, but I see the results. Can you brief me—specifically me? I don't need you melting down in front of the team if they don't understand or ask the wrong question."

"I can do that, yes."

When they arrived back in Moses Lake, Nick sat down one morning and began to speak with Special K. They spoke for several hours. Mostly Nick listened and asked questions here and there. Finally, that night Nick was finished.

"If we can find her, it won't be pretty. You know that, right? I'm not going to blow smoke up your ass. She'll be in bad shape. She may not even want to come with us. You have to be prepared for that. She may be in very bad shape. She'll probably be so high, she doesn't even remember you."

Special K nodded. "I know. Do you think you can find her?"

"We'll see. There are no fairytale endings in this world. If they have her somewhere public, we may get lucky. If not, she could be anywhere—underground... maybe even dead already. But if we can find her, we will. She does have some things going for her. Her education is one. That makes her more valuable—a higher-priced commodity. Her appearance as well. Being fit helps. Her age isn't a good thing. She is going to be older than the rest of the women. It all depends."

"Thank you for trying."

"Don't thank me now. I was born for this. Thank me when it is over. By the way, are you fluent in German?"

"Yes, I am."

"Good. I may need your help."

Nick got up, left the room, and went to the Bat Cave.

"Brother, I need your best and as fast as you can do it. I need all the police reports, every witness statement, photos, and anything else on this case. Before, I wanted the information on the person that reported Svetlana missing. Now, I want everything on anyone involved with the case—the husband, Pieter, the people the *Hessen Polizei* interviewed if any, statements from Pieter and Svetlana's neighbors... anything and everything with their names on it. I want to know who Svetlana worked for. She was a student at the Goethe Universität in Frankfurt and was pursuing her masters in finance and money. I want her schedule, grades, attendance, financial records, medical records, everything—as fast as you can get it. Time is critical."

"On it, brother, like a twelve-year-old on his daddy's porn collection," The Driver replied.

"Let me know when you have it. I need to be able to understand it, so if you have to read it to me or Special K has to read it to me—either way—I need to be able to go over it detail by detail. In some kind of organized fashion. And I need it in paper—documents—not a thumb drive. I need to see it spread out in front of me."

The Driver arrived in the kitchen a short time later with a stack full of reports and photos.

"Do you have time for this, or should I ask Special K?" Nick asked.

"I'm really busy, man. Many calls for The Driver's immediate attention, but only one me! It would be best if she read them to you."

"Thanks, man. Do you have access to facial recognition software? I mean the high-end stuff, Homeland, NSA quality software?"

"Seriously? You ask The Driver a question like that? Would you ask a gigolo if he..."

Nick interrupted. "I get it. Sorry, my bad. Okay, take this photo and upload it. I want a search of everything the Web has to offer, and when you're done with the mom and pop daytime Web, go deep. Search the sites only you know about. Get low, fast, dark, and dirty. If she's on the Web, we need to know where and when. Every hour that passes matters."

Special K walked into the room and sat down. Nick looked at her grimly. "This won't be easy. I need to you read everything, every comment, word, and note in the margins, hunches, etc.—all of it. When we're done, we'll start over and then again. I need to know this case backward and forward. Okay?"

Special K nodded and then began.

They worked through the night, going over every detail and cross-referencing the statements and reports with school records and medical records. Nick sat quietly when they were done.

"They have done a pretty thorough job, the *Hessen Polizei*. I've heard the German police were world class. After seeing the size of this village, Darmstadt, I had my doubts. They crossed every T and dotted every I. They left no stone unturned and looked under every rock except the obvious one."

"You have an idea of where my sister is?"

"No, not yet. First, I wondered if she had left on her own or maybe had just left your brother-in-law. Those don't fit. I can't explain why, but trust me, she didn't leave him or have any intention of leaving. Someone has taken her. I don't know to where yet, but I have a hunch on who set this up. Nothing solid yet... just a hunch. I'll be right back."

Nick went down to the Bat Cave and woke up The Driver. "Wake up, man. Anything new?"

"Not yet. Still searching. The underbelly of the Web isn't as fast and easy to search as the top side. It is kind of like looking for that favorite scene in your favorite porn and not knowing the movie's title. It takes time."

Nick grimaced as he rubbed his neck. "Okay, thanks for the visual. I need you to search Hessen missing persons and cross-reference them with the two cops' work schedules, Sondra and Börn. When you have that, check the missing person reports against their names. I want to know how many of the cases they were involved with since they started working for the *Hessen Polizei*. I also need to know how many total missing persons cases Hessen had per capita and compare those with the other German states. Can you do that?"

"Okay, on it, brother, like the lead cheerleader on the high school quarterback's rock hard..."

Nick left the room before hearing the rest of the details of The Driver's fantasy.

When Nick arrived in the kitchen, Special K was asleep, head down on the table. He woke her up and told her to go upstairs and get some rest. He gathered all the documents and his notes and put them in a pile and then took them to Bexx's room.

She woke up as he entered the room and watched him. "Did you find anything?"

Nick didn't answer and instead asked, "How soon until your team is ready? I mean, can they leave on little or no notice?"

"Yes, of course. Why?"

Nick didn't answer. He walked out of the room and down the stairs.

She heard the front door open and close. Bexx got up and looked out the window. Nick was walking down the road outside the farmhouse, head down. Bexx watched him walking and thought, *Well, he's back. For better or worse, he's back.*

Nick came back several hours later and went straight to the Bat Cave. "Do you have the cases and documents?"

"I do. Some interesting facts there. I checked the missing person cases for Hessen and crossed them with the other states. Hessen has more than its share of missing persons per capita, which isn't odd in itself. They do have a Turkish slum of sorts in Darmstadt. What is odd, though, is I went back through the Polizei records and found an oddity."

Nick listened to The Driver's information and made sure he'd cross-referenced it all with the other officers' records.

"Okay, this might be an anomaly. Cross-reference what you've found and see if there are any matches in the surrounding states to what you have found in the *Hessen Polizei*. I'm going to get some sleep. If you get a hit on the facial recognition software, wake me immediately. Don't wait, and don't let anyone else but Bexx hear about it. If and when you find anything, it won't be pretty. Special K doesn't need to see this. Are we good? You understand?"

"On it, brother, like peanut butter on a..."

Nick cut him off. "Where the hell is Buffy?"

"She's in training with the rest of the team. They're on a run with Bexx."

"When they get back, get her down here. This has to be top priority. If Bexx disagrees, let her know I requested it."

Nick left the Bat Cave and went up to sleep.

Bexx and the team had reached the halfway point in their morning run, and they stopped. It was a custom they'd started long ago. Running cleared their heads, and at the halfway point in every run, they stopped and talked as they walked. Special K had fallen behind, which wasn't normal. Normally, Special K led their runs. She was the fastest runner in the group. They all hated she was so fast on the days she'd been eating Chinese food. They all turned and watched as she came running up, sweating more than usual and obviously winded.

As they turned and walked down the winding dirt road, Bexx asked, "How late were you and Nick up last night?"

"We were up all night and most of the morning. He finally told me to get some rest about an hour before you woke me up for the morning run."

"And?"

"And I don't know. He has this weird grasp of details. I swear he knows the reports inside and out. I read everything out loud to him, and he would listen and make me go back over a detail sometimes two or three times. He would say, 'Are you sure this is the correct translation? It's written exactly as you are speaking it?' I would reply yes, and he would mumble under his breath. He cross-referenced everything, and we went over it all time and time again. I swear he has the reports memorized now. I know I nearly do!"

"How is his demeanor?"

"What do you mean? Like, was he angry with me? Or rude?"

"No, how did he seem?"

"It's Nick! How do you think he seemed?" she said, frustrated and tired. She thought for a minute. "I guess at first he was okay—sort of normal for Nick—and then he became more and more focused... intense. At first, he would look at me when he asked questions. Later, he wouldn't look at me at all. He stared at the floor and rocked back and forth in his chair as he listened. Then he got up and paced. He paced for hours—back and forth, making me go over everything again and again. Weird too, he had change in his hand—quarters, I think. He kept them in a loose roll, taking the top quarter and rolling it to the bottom over and over. It reminded me of how my grandmother used to work her prayer beads over as she looked out the window when I was a girl. I didn't think he was even aware of anything but the quarters most of the time. And then he would ask a very specific question, and I knew he was there... just deep in thought."

Bexx listened, and then the group went silent, letting what Special K described sink in.

Someone said mischievously, "Great! Sounds like someone is about to be disemboweled again!" They all laughed nervously.

Bexx said, "Make sure you all will be ready to go on nearly no notice. When the time comes, I want to be able to move immediately. I don't think it will be long now, so be ready mentally and physically. Understood?"

"Yes, Commander," the group said as one.

"Okay, let's finish the run." And they started off running back to the barn as a group.

When they arrived at the farmhouse, The Driver was waiting. He briefed Bexx on everything Nick had requested and especially that he asked that Buffy be detailed specifically to the Web search for any signs of Svetlana, using the facial recognition software.

Bexx asked, "Where is Nick now?"

"Asleep, I think."

She nodded. "Do as Nick asked. I'll go upstairs to speak with him."

Bexx went upstairs and found Nick lying in bed, eyes closed but obviously not asleep.

"You need to rest," she said.

"I know. I can't right now. It's all there. It took a while to see it, but it's all there," he said.

"Now we just have to hope we can find her." He opened his eyes. "It may be too late. You know that, right? We may never find her. And if we do? Well, you saw Nõn and what her captors did to her physically, torturing her to break her. You don't want to know what they did that left no physical scars. This is going to get really ugly. You understand that, right?"

Bexx nodded and sat on the bed. "You have to rest. You are no good to me worn out and frazzled. How can I help you sleep?"

Nick sat and stared at the ceiling. "Read to me... anything. Just read in Russian or whatever it is you speak. Read out loud. I just need to hear your voice."

Bexx's eyebrows raised. "You're serious?"

"Yes, whenever anyone else speaks it, it sets me on edge. Your voice is different. Just read. Don't ask why or how. I need to disconnect just for a while. Please?"

"I'll tell you a story. I don't have anything to read that's from Georgia, so lie back and listen." Bexx began. "Well, first you should know I do speak Russian, but my native language is called Kartvelian. Most of Georgia speaks it." She began to tell him the myths of the pre-Christian Georgian belief system in how the universe was formed and organized.

Minutes later, Nick was asleep. Bexx kept talking quietly as she watched him.

CHAPTER SEVEN

Nick woke up a few hours later. Bexx had left the room. It was still light outside when he swung his feet over the side of the bed and stood. He dressed and went down the hallway to the old wooden steps that led down to the kitchen. No one was in the farmhouse. It was uncharacteristically quiet. He looked out the window of the kitchen at the old barn and stared alone with his thoughts. He had a pretty good idea from the interviews and witness statements Special K had read to him who was responsible for her sister's disappearance. Proving it, if that mattered at all—he wasn't sure—was another thing. Finding Svetlana, that would take a miracle or some amazing luck. Still, he'd try. He had no choice, really. The course was set. Like a heat-seeking missile that had been launched without a target, he was searching for the right heat signature. There was no going back now. He took a deep breath. The rest would be up to The Driver and Buffy. They'd have to make a nearly impossible connection, or the girl would disappear and never be located. She'd live a life no one deserved. Nick glared at the barn, deep in thought, lost in barely describable images flitting through his mind. The thoughts were dark and feral. Thoughts most people refused to acknowledge they had, Nick embraced. If he had the opportunity...

"Best not to get too wound up," he said out loud to no one but himself. "This is such a long shot—rescue one woman kidnapped halfway around the world and taken to who knows where." Nick took down a glass from the cabinet and filled it with water. The lack of direction was disconcerting, and uncomfortable. He preferred a clear target to focus on and pour all his energy into... to obsess over. He felt lost.

While Nick slept, The Driver and Buffy worked in shifts accessing files and databases and cross-referencing them, making sure every detail was examined. They were each focused on the task when Nick walked into the Bat Cave.

"What's the latest, brother?"

"We've found most if not all of the information you asked for. There are some interesting irregularities in the missing persons' cases, which I'm sure you expected to find; otherwise you wouldn't have asked for them, yes?"

"Yeah, I have a hunch. I'd prefer not to say what it is. There's a rule in investigations. You never go into an investigation with a theory of what happened. Let the evidence lead you. If you go in with a predetermined idea of what happened, you'll either consciously or unconsciously make the facts fit your theory. We don't have a lot of room for mistakes in this case. The clock is ticking. Every day we look but are unable to connect the dots, Svetlana suffers."

The Driver was quiet, watching Nick. "Brother, the weight of this—year after year—how have you done this for a living? When I attack a site or a business, it's sheer joy. It's like a child stealing cookies from the cookie jar. If I don't succeed, no worries. There's always tomorrow. This feels different. I feel the pressure already."

Nick looked at him, silent and stoic. "The weight is what matters. You have to feel it and own it— make it personal—or you won't do what needs to be done. Let's see what you found."

Nick and The Driver looked over the information for the next few hours, each talking to the other over what the details could possibly mean for the potential to locate Svetlana. It looked bleak, to say the least. They knew it, but neither spoke the words. The possibility of failure was not an option to be spoken out loud. Best not to breathe life into that idea.

Buffy sat and listened to Nick and The Driver as they poured over the information. The conclusions Nick came to seemed implausible and unrealistic until he described what he saw and the implications of what wasn't being said. Then it made sense, sort of. He saw things through a different lens. The Driver had a skill set she understood. He made sense to her in the way he looked at programs, information, and operating systems. She didn't always immediately see what he saw as a backdoor or point of attack. But afterward, when he explained it, she understood. Nick saw information in a lack of information—a lack of detail he thought should have been there. It was an uncomfortable thing to wrap her head around. Finally, they were silent.

The Driver looked at Nick. "Is this what you thought you would find?"

Nick said nothing and just nodded, yes. "Okay, man, we know what we know. Now focus on one task only. We have to find her. Use whatever rabbits are up your sleeve. Search porn sites—every damn one of them—with your facial recognition software. Limit the search to posts and sites that have been up since Svetlana disappeared. This is going to be some ugly shit. You'll have to dig deep and go into dark corners you may not want to. It will be there somewhere—a pic of her, an ad offering her up to the highest bidder, a video. It may be hidden in chat rooms or in some gamer chat room. I don't know. These people hide in plain sight. Just like our abductor did, right out in the open for all to see and yet observe nothing at all."

"We're already on it, brother. If she is out there, we'll find her."

Nick nodded and placed a hand on both of their shoulders. "No pressure, but... well, it's up to you. I can see what happened but not where she went. Too many blanks there to fill in. We have to hope she didn't end up in some sick fuck's private collection. Pray he or she likes to show off their collection."

Nick left the Bat Cave with The Driver and Buffy silently watching him. When he was gone, The Driver turned to Buffy, raising his eyebrows. Each took a deep breath and started on running the search for Svetlana.

Nick walked back upstairs and found the day had turned to night. He'd been in the Bat Cave a lot longer than he realized. The formerly quiet farmhouse had come back to life with the sounds of Bexx's team talking and laughing over the day's training.

Bexx turned as Nick walked into the room and asked, "Did you sleep?"

"I did, thank you."

"Is there anything new in the search you want to share?"

"There is some news—nothing about where Svetlana is yet, I'm afraid—but yes, there is information it would be wise for all of us to know."

"Do you want to tell us now, or should we wait until tonight?"

"Let's wait. I'm still processing it. It'll be hard to explain if I can't wrap my head around it in a way that'll make sense. I had a hunch, and The

Driver has come up with enough evidence that I'm comfortable it's accurate. It doesn't get us closer to Svetlana, but it lets us know what happened."

Later that night, Nick had built the customary fire in the fire pit as the team gathered around. Bexx, The Driver, and Buffy all sat as well.

Nick's eyes locked on Special K's for several moments. Then he looked into the fire and began. "First, you were right. Svetlana's husband, Pieter, doesn't appear to be involved in her disappearance. From the interviews and witness statements, his comments and reactions feel true. So, there is that at least. I'm not saying I like what I've found out about him. He's a musician, a flake, and a piss-poor excuse for a husband. But I don't think he had anything to do with her disappearance. Let's go back and call this what it is. She was abducted. The *Hessen Polizei* are calling it a missing person case. Not accurate at all. She was taken—kidnapped. Not that I think it matters how they classify the case. They could call it a kidnapping, and they would be no more successful in finding her. The people who took her are practiced at their craft. They left very few clues. I can go through the details and explain what I think happened. Basic details are these: Svetlana was studying at Goethe Universität in Frankfurt. Her major was in finance and money. She was in Germany on a student passport, and her husband had been allowed to accompany her. The night she disappeared, she had told Pieter she'd been offered a modeling job that would pay cash. She was working as a housekeeper to help make ends meet."

"She told him she could make more money with this one modeling job than an entire month of cleaning homes. Pieter was suspicious and said that in his statement to the police, but not suspicious enough to accompany her and make sure she was safe. His band had a gig in a bar that night, and he didn't want to miss it. Outstanding husband, like I said. Anyway, that was the night she disappeared. Pieter felt sure one of her house cleaning customers had set her up with the modeling job. She cleaned three homes in Schneppenhausen, a small village outside of Frankfurt. All of the occupants of the homes have been questioned. One couple is a U.S. Air Force Lieutenant and her husband, Tina and Lindsey. Another is a couple both employed by the *Hessen Polizei*. Sondra and Börn are their names. The final couple is very litigious. They like to sue their landlords to get out of paying rent. They are continually running scams and suing anyone and everyone they can. Astrid and Martin are their names. At first, they seemed slimy enough to be involved in something like this. Their constant manipulation of the legal system was on one hand a red flag, but then on another, it draws attention to them immediately."

"They're the obvious choice. I went over their statements several times, looking for anything out of place. There was nothing. They seem too good to be true, you know? Like yes, obviously, it must be them. They are native Germans and speak Russian as well, as does Svetlana. Just like Pieter, they seemed to be the most likely place to search. The *Hessen Polizei* incidentally agree. Their interoffice communications show they suspect either Pieter or Astrid and Martin if this is something more than a missing persons case. They list them as persons of interest, which in police speak is 'suspects.'"

Nick looked up from the fire to make sure he hadn't lost anyone. Scanning their eyes, he saw they were all still with him.

He continued. "Next is the Air Force lieutenant. She's too busy at work and doesn't speak enough German or Russian. She had a hard time communicating with Svetlana but spoke enough to get the general idea that she liked Svetlana. Her husband is questionable like Pieter but honestly not bright enough to speak enough German or Russian to communicate anything more than simple ideas, like how to order a drink or pick up a prostitute. So, they're out as well."

"That leaves Sondra and Börn, the Polizei officers. On the night Svetlana was going to do the modeling job, Börn was at work. He is a K-9 handler and was tasked with mandatory training at the same time Svetlana was leaving her and Pieter's small apartment in Darmstadt. By the way, they lived in an area in Darmstadt that's known as a Turkish slum. That made me wonder as well, but after talking to Katerina here, I understood why they chose to live there."

The Driver asked, "And why was that? Seems like you live in a bad area. Bad things are going to happen."

Special K spoke up. "Our father was Russian. We grew up in Russia, but our mother was a Turk. We have family in Darmstadt. We visited them often when we were young, so when Svetlana was awarded a position at Goethe Universität, it seemed wise to her to live close to family."

Everyone nodded in agreement. It made sense to be near family. Their economic status was irrelevant.

Nick continued. "So Börn is at work the night Svetlana disappears, and that leaves Sondra."

CHAPTER EIGHT

Special K jumped in as soon as Nick said 'that leaves Sondra.' None of this made any sense to her.

"You're saying a woman abducted my sister? You have that three men who are involved and easily could have set her up with this alleged modeling job. What makes you think a woman would do this to another woman? This makes no sense to me! Were you listening to the witness statements I read over and over for hours?"

Nick said nothing and let her vent. She went on and on and threw out a few insults as well, calling Nick incompetent and his conclusions ridiculous. Finally, she was quiet—fuming and angry, but quiet.

Nick continued. "Svetlana's relationship with all three of these families begins with Sondra. She hired her first, she and Börn have a son, and Sondra felt she needed help with the housework since she worked full-time with the Polizei. When Astrid and Martin moved in, she introduced Svetlana to them. Astrid introduced Svetlana to Tina. Tina said she needed a housekeeper because she was working fourteen to seventeen hours a day at her job, and when she was home, her husband's children sometimes lived with them. She couldn't keep up with the house and work. She described Svetlana as a 'godsend,' and additionally, she liked her immensely. They shared a love of learning and school. Both women were pursuing a master's degree. Interestingly, when asked if they had any idea of where Svetlana may have gone or with whom, both Astrid and Tina had no idea. They both said she was happy at home as far as they knew and devoted to her schoolwork. Tina said she thought Svetlana had a year left of school, so she was nearly complete with her degree."

"Sondra, on the other hand, made comments to the Polizei in her statements that she had noticed Svetlana was flirting with both Martin and Lindsey more than she felt was appropriate. She was suspicious of them having an affair with Svetlana. Pieter also mentioned Svetlana was uncomfortable with Lindsey and his comments to her when she cleaned the house. Pieter did not like Lindsey but doubted he had arranged any modeling job because Svetlana really didn't like him or trust him. Also, he barely speaks any language outside of English. It is a process of elimination, really. It all comes back to Sondra. I asked The Driver to do some checking into the *Hessen Polizei* and their statistics when it came to missing persons. I wanted to know about women only, dates, times, officers who handled the most calls, and the favorable clearance of those calls. I'll let him tell you what he found."

The Driver detailed the information and how he had broken it down and also that he had no idea beforehand what Nick was looking for; just that he asked him to specifically look at missing persons and how many had been found and cross-reference that with officers named in the cases.

He stopped and looked hesitantly at Special K. "Hessen has over fifteen thousand sworn police officers. Only one has such a negative clearance rate in missing persons, meaning this one officer has located the missing person and favorably closed the case less than any other in the department."

He didn't say her name, but everyone knew it must be Sondra.

He continued. "Additionally, I did a historical search, and this fact wasn't always so. In the past, she had the highest rate of clearing missing persons favorably in the entire department until four years ago. Then her clearance rate in missing persons only does a one hundred and eighty degree turn. Why four years ago? I don't know, but it's a very drastic change. So, I cross-referenced that with her other case clearance rates. All have stayed the same—burglaries, thefts, shoplifts, assaults... all high clearance rates. She appears to be an exceptional officer in every way except being able to locate missing persons."

The group was quiet, processing all The Driver and Nick had explained.

Special K spoke up again, her tone getting louder and more agitated as she went on. "What was the point of all that witness statement reading I did, going back over the details again and again? Explain to me why we did that? To me, this all sounds like you've made your mind up that a woman is guilty of abducting my sister, period. We all know you have issues with women. You made that clear from the start. You barely even know our names, and aside from Bexx, you treat us like we have no business being here. How do we know your own point of view isn't tainted? Meanwhile, whoever *did* abduct my sister is still free and doing who knows what to her."

Nick tried to explain. "I had you reread the statements over and over again to get a feel for how they spoke, the way they voiced their ideas, and the way they answered questions. It's hard to describe what I look for, but the best way I can think of is to say I look for what isn't there—what they don't say—and is that consistent with the way they speak and answer questions? It is much easier to do in person. But we can't do that here, so I had you re-read them until I could recognize the patterns."

Special K screamed at Nick, "What the hell does that mystical garbage mean? You look for what isn't there!"

The team was quiet, listening to the exchange. None of them knew what Nick meant, and most felt the idea that a woman had arranged for or facilitated Svetlana's abductions was ridiculous. Their entire lives, they had been harassed by men, pinched, groped, and solicited for sexual favors by men. Nick's theory just didn't ring true to them.

Nick spoke again. "Do any of you know how many keys a modern piano has?"

No one knew.

"It has eighty-eight keys. Older pianos had 85, but now all have 88 keys. Fifty-two of those keys are white. Thirty-six are black. Basically, every piano player in the world can play the same notes. Do you agree?"

They all nodded yes.

"Okay, so what is it that makes Mozart's piano playing different from anyone else? Everyone can play the same keys as many times as they want, but there is only one Mozart. What is it that makes him different?"

Someone said, "He had a gift."

"Yes, he did, but so did Bach. They used the same piano but made different music. Mozart made the piano do what others couldn't. Would you agree?"

They all nodded.

Nick could see Special K was getting more impatient. He looked directly at her. "You of all the people here should be able to understand this, so listen! I heard once the only difference in a gifted player of any instrument and the less gifted was the understanding of the space between the notes. The 'nothing' that was there. Musically, there are silent spaces that fill the gaps between notes. If the timing is off, it sounds wrong. If the scale is off, it sounds wrong. Press the keys too hard or too soft, and it sounds wrong. I can tell Mozart's work from Bach's because the tempo, sound, and cadence in-between the notes are different. That's what I look for when I listen for what's missing. That's the only way I can think of to describe it. I listen until I hear what isn't there. What doesn't fit."

Special K fired back, "And why would I of all people understand this garbage?"

"Because you can hear and speak so many languages. Each has its own cadence and tempo. Sounds you make in one language more than another. You listen for the sounds and the spaces in-between. The way they roll their Rs, for example, to know if someone is speaking German or Czech... French or Spanish. It's all the same noise, but the way it's done and the empty space in-between sounds changes."

Finally, the light came on; Nick had reached her. He could see it. She understood what he meant. She just nodded and looked back into the fire.

Nick continued. "Anyway, none of this really matters. Knowing who it was doesn't tell us where Svetlana is. The fact that Sondra is Polizei makes it even harder for us. She will have contacts a normal person wouldn't... understand things about criminal behavior a normal person wouldn't. She's made a couple of slips, as you've seen. Her clearance record changed drastically for only this type of case, and she's the only one of the women interviewed to have anything negative to say about Svetlana. Everyone else—neighbors, classmates, and people whose homes she cleaned—all liked her and had nothing but praise. Not Sondra. That's significant. It's like listening to a symphony of praise and in comes someone who plays a kazoo. It doesn't fit."

Finally, one of the girls said in Russian, "Nick likes Mozart? Who would've believed that?" That broke the ice, and they all laughed—even

Bexx. Nick had no idea what was said but guessed it had been about him.

"One more thing," he added. "Yes, a woman is involved, and probably more than one. Think about it. How else would you coax a smart, educated woman into a modeling job? Have a man ask her to pose for other men? Or have a woman, someone she trusted, someone in a position of authority she's been conditioned to trust ask her? Think about it. Who would each of you trust more—a woman or a man? Who would you use to lure her in? It's the exact same principle you used in the Asgarda in Ukraine. You sent women to infiltrate the Russians because they expected men to be the threat. How is this any different?"

Nick looked up at the group, his eyes searching for someone to answer the question.

The laughing stopped. The seriousness of Nick's observation hit them hard.

CHAPTER NINE

The fire had died, and the team had dispersed. Nick still sat staring at the deep red coals as the fire gasped its final breaths. He hadn't responded to Bexx when she had called his name. He hadn't heard her at all. Finally, she reached out and touched his shoulder. He jumped back, disoriented.

She stepped back as well, startled by his sudden and immediate drop into a fighting stance. Her hands up at her shoulders, she calmly said, "Whoa, it's just me, okay? It's just me. Welcome back."

Nick scanned the area instinctively. Seeing no threat, he felt stupid and embarrassed. "Sorry, I guess I checked out for a bit. What's up?"

"I was talking to you. When you didn't respond, I wondered if you were all right."

"Sorry... just thinking. This whole thing with Svetlana takes me back. Memories that have long been quiet are letting me know they're still there. Things I'd rather not remember, you know?"

Bexx nodded. This was the exact reason she had tried to keep him out of the mission. Most people have a safety valve in their memories—something that allows them to forget and shut off access to the most damaging memories. She realized Nick was missing this. He functioned by feeling his way through life. He survived by using intuition. When a situation brought on certain feelings, his memories were lined up in a queue and one by one came up to be replayed, relived, and relearned.

She spoke. "How does this feel to you now?"

"Like trying to win the lottery for someone dying of cancer. If The Driver and Buffy find her—and that is a huge if—she's likely to be so damaged, dying might be a better option than survival. I have no sense of who she is from my conversations with Katerina. I do sense she's proud, and they'll use that against her. She's also intelligent. They'll use that as well. It's a reality check to have people use your better qualities against you."

"How does someone survive when their better qualities are used against them? When the good becomes a weakness?" Bexx asked.

Nick's face grew dark. He took a deep breath. "Are you asking how I survived or how someone else survives?"

"Both."

"Most people are taught to accentuate the good in themselves—the strengths, the things that make life worth living. To survive, you do the opposite."

"What does that mean to you?"

"Depends, I guess. Point is, what does that mean to her? Does she have the ability to put her pride and intellect on the shelf and survive the moment—something I knew before I ever put on a uniform or set foot in the street. When life goes to shit, you survive the moment—break it down into small, manageable pieces and survive. Don't think long-term. Don't remember where you were. Think now, and only now."

Cryptic as ever, Nick had answered her and not answered her at all.

Nick continued. "You need to be prepared for the possibility that we never find Svetlana. Special K needs to be prepared. It feels like such a long shot to me that we will. I've done all I can do for now. The rest is luck and being in the right place at the right time. I'm going to go back to the gym tomorrow and go back to my routine. I'm worthless without a target. We have no target. When and if we ever do, I need to be fresh—not worn out from banging my head against the wall trying to make something happen. I can't make this happen. It will, or it won't. Simple."

"I agree. Can you do that? Go back to the routine until we need you?"

"I can. Especially when there's no target. I can see that... feel it. It's different than when we hunted The Director. I could feel him just beyond my sight... moving, plotting. I feel nothing now."

Bexx nodded.

They sat quietly—neither speaking for some time—Nick lost in his memories and Bexx lost in the things they'd discussed, digesting and understanding what was said.

Finally, they went to sleep.

Nick woke the next morning and got ready for the gym. Teeth brushed, gym bag in hand, he hit his beloved rust bucket, the 'Yota, and fired up the motor.

Halfway to the gym, he remembered the missile facility and the trip wires set there. C-4 detonators, clearing the facility, the smell of motor oil in the air—something was there nagging at him. He played it over and over in his head. What was it? What had he missed?

Nothing came. No answer. He rolled it over... juggled and examined it. Like a kid looking for the solution to a Rubik's Cube, Nick went to work mentally on what it was that bothered him about the silo. He liked the idea of staying there. Loved it, actually. It'd be like living in Fort Knox. About as safe as you could be once it had been cleared of booty traps. Nick laughed out loud. Some things never got old.

Walking in the door of the gym felt good—the sound of the iron banging into iron... the smell of sweat.

Nick nodded to Ali. "What's up?"

Ali replied, "Usual. Another surgery... this time a rework of an old surgery. I swear, when they say doctors practice medicine, they mean it literally—they practice. They seem to have no idea what the hell they are doing when it comes to my injuries. Idiots... very expensive idiots!"

Nick nodded. "Good to see you too!"

Ali gave him the finger. "Suck this, asshole!"

Nick laughed. She was surly as ever. That, he could always depend on.

Nick walked to his bench and realized it was new. He smiled. "Hey, what happened to the old bench?"

"Some old asshole sweated all over it so much, no one else would use it, so I had to replace it!" Ali fired back.

"Great, but what happened to it? Did you sell it?"

"Yeah, I sold it. I bring in new stuff all the time and sell the old."

"Good to know. Guess I better get busy sweating on this one. Never know when I might need a bench at home."

Ali waved him off and said nothing.

Nick tried to step back into his old routine at the same level and pace. He was left with a rude awakening. He had lost a lot of strength in the couple of weeks since he had been in last. Weight that used to be manageable no longer felt safe. He felt frustrated. Then he laughed. He thought to himself, *That's why I like it. Take too many days off, and the weights will let you know it. They never get lighter. They don't care if I'm tired, old, or had a bad day. Every moment of every day, they stay the same. Two hundred and fifty pounds today will be two hundred and fifty pounds tomorrow, no matter what.*

Nick finished the workout and headed for the door. "See you tomorrow," he said to Ali as he walked out.

"Thanks for the warning. I'll call in sick!" she quipped back.

Nick walked to the truck and stopped. He hadn't checked the parking lot. He looked around, stunned. *I'm getting soft,* he thought. *When was the last time I checked the parking lot?* He leaned against the truck, thinking, muttering to himself. "Slip up just once, and you know the rules—the street has no mercy. You can't relax just because you think the threat is gone. The threat is never gone. Remember that, asshole. It's never, ever gone! You're either aware and ready, or you're a victim waiting for the slaughter to begin." Nick punched his head lightly, "Stupid, stupid, stupid!"

Nick threw the bag into the truck and scanned the parking lot. Starting from scratch, nothing looked wrong or suspicious. No one was sitting in their car watching. He made a mental note of the cars that were present and jumped in the truck.

"Getting soft, old man... getting soft! What else have you let slip? What else have you forgotten to do?" he whispered to himself as he drove out of the parking lot.

When Nick arrived back at the farmhouse, Bexx asked, "How was the gym?"

"Good. Made me feel good and made me realize as well I need to keep at it. I have lost a lot in the couple of weeks since I was there last. Also, I remembered the missile facility. We haven't talked about that much since we came back. Seems like a good idea the more I think about it. I had an idea today. What do you think about using some of the space for gym equipment? I may have a line on good used equipment."

"Sounds like a good idea to me," Bexx answered. "I didn't see a lot of infrastructure in the area surrounding the facility, so it's probably a good idea to have our own gym on site, as well as a lot of other things." She noticed he had completely shifted gears after going to the gym. He was no longer locked on finding Svetlana, at least not entirely. Now he was thinking about the future and the possible move to the missile facility.

Nick laughed. "The woman who runs the gym is surly as ever. I swear she never lets up. Being married to her must be like marrying a badger."

"Is she married?" Bexx asked.

Nick thought and said, "Hmm, I don't know." Silently, he thought, Another obvious sign I'm too relaxed. He had no idea if she was married. What else had he missed? The idea started to fester in the back of his mind. He sucked in a deep breath, let it out, and grimaced.

"Could you ask Special K to go back through the files again with me?"

Bexx looked puzzled. "Can I ask why? You said there was nothing more you could do."

"Because going to the gym, I realized I wasn't doing the things I used to do before..." He was silent for a moment.

"Before?"

"Before we killed The Director. I stopped. I relaxed. I can't do that. Ask her. Please just make it happen."

An hour later, Nick was pacing the floor and Special K was reading the statements. He carried a handful of quarters in his pocket and worked them furiously top to bottom in his hand as he paced. Every so often, he would ask her to stop and go back over a statement.

She did, and finally she said, "I need a break. I have to get a drink and go to the bathroom. We've been at this forever."

Nick stopped and said, "What? How long have we been at this?"

She rolled her eyes and said, "Seven hours now! Maybe you should read out loud for seven hours at a time, and I'll listen and ask redundant questions. By the way, what the hell is the deal with the money in your pocket? Can you be any more annoying?"

Nick ignored her. "Go drink... pee... come back when you're ready."

Special K started up the stairs to the bathroom and nearly ran right over the top of Bexx, who had been sitting on the top stair, listening. She motioned to Katerina to be quiet, placing a finger to her lips, and let her pass. She didn't want Nick to know she was there.

When she returned, Nick pulled the quarters out of his pocket and showed them to her. "I roll them top to bottom. Top one comes off the pile and goes to the bottom."

"Yeah, I know. You showed me before. The question is, why?"

"When you were learning languages, what was the best way for you to learn? I mean, did you listen to them or write them, or could you only do it through speaking them? Or all three?"

She replied, "A little of all of them, I guess. Once I understood the language, I could speak it nearly perfectly by reading, and then I could correct the mistakes I made by listening to someone else. Languages came naturally to me."

"Okay, well, I learn by doing... touching. I like to build or make things. I can't make these statements make sense by building it or touching it. So, I have to do tactile things while I listen. I pace and roll the coins because I'm a 'hands on' learner. I need the physical sensation. Make sense? So while you need quiet to read and write a language, I need the physical sensation to wake my mind up and keep it engaged."

"Wow, really? School must have been difficult for you. You can't pace in a classroom."

"No doubt, it sucked. I barely made it. Try to explain to the teachers you can't remember anything from lectures and books, and they think you're stupid. No, I just learn differently, so when I pace, I listen, and process, add the quarters, and bam! I'm laser focused on what's being said and how. All four of my brain cells are firing at once!"

She laughed. "Okay, makes sense. This is your equivalent of a quiet room with no distractions."

"Exactly. Please keep going. I just want to make sure I didn't miss anything."

Special K started reading again, and Nick continued to pace. The coins began their endless journey in his hand from the top of the pile to the bottom.

CHAPTER TEN

The next day, Nick headed back to the gym. The efforts of the nighttime rehash with Special K had proven to be fruitless. But at least he was relatively sure he hadn't missed something there. Still, the missile facility nagged at him. He'd missed something there. He was sure of it. What he'd missed, he wasn't sure, but he felt it. Maybe more time spent in the gym focused on physical activity would make it clear. He didn't know. When he arrived at the gym, he made a point of checking the parking lots, made a mental note of the vehicles that were there, and then went inside. It was back day, deadlifts, one arm pulls, pull-ups, lat pulls, and then twenty minutes on the *VersaClimber*. When he was done, he stopped to catch his breath. It felt good to be back in the routine. If they did move operations to North Dakota, he definitely needed to set up an in-house gym. He looked at the new bench and thought, *Why not?*

Ali, as usual, was at her station, monitoring the door and making sure the patrons cleaned up their messes after they finished on the equipment.

Nick stopped and smiled. "I thought you were going to call in sick today?"

She responded, "I'd hoped you might be too tired to come back, so I took my chances. Guess I was wrong."

Nick smirked. "Sorry to disappoint. Hey, when you do get new equipment in next time, let me know. I may be interested in buying some of the old stuff."

"Gonna cancel your membership, then?"

"Not likely. Just want to have some stuff on hand. I might be moving. Don't know yet, and if I do, I want to set up my own gym for private use. So, keep me in mind."

Ali nodded. "I can do that. Got a business to run, so I always have new items coming in to replace the old. Write off the loss and then sell the old for cash. That way, I make money on both ends, coming and going. Claim the new on taxes as a business expense, depreciate the old, and then sell it for cash off the books. Always have to be looking for ways to make money."

"Makes sense," Nick responded

"Where are you thinking of moving to?"

"North Dakota, maybe. Don't know yet."

"Good, that'll work. Just don't want you setting up shop a block away and becoming a competitor."

Nick left the gym, walked to his car, checked the lot, and drove back to the farmhouse.

This was his daily routine for several days as he waited for The Driver and Buffy to make some kind of miracle connection on the Web and locate Svetlana. Every day, he went down to the Bat Cave and checked in. The response was the same—nothing yet. There were a lot of sites to search, and so far none had provided even a hint of the missing woman. It was discouraging to say the least.

A week passed, and nothing. The Driver came to him finally and said, "If she's out there, I can't find her. I don't know how the hell you could do this for a job for so long. I've never felt so inept. I used to pride myself on the kill, hacking into some alleged fortress of a corporation and destroying their security. It was a high to pursue my prey and dive in for the kill. This is just depressing."

"I get it, brother. It's hard. Stop for a while. Both of you, stop. We need to reassess... look at the problem with new eyes. Tell Bexx what you told me and mention that I think we need to rethink this. Ask her if we can have a meeting tonight at the fire."

The Driver nodded and slowly walked off, dejected, to find Bexx.

That night, they sat by the fire. Everyone listened as The Driver and Buffy detailed their search. When they finished, the group was silent, staring at the fire. Bexx looked around at her team. She felt their frustration. They looked to her for leadership, a direction, and guidance. She had none. They were at an impasse. Nothing was working. They'd tried every avenue—every suggestion that anyone had come up with, no matter how far-fetched—and still had nothing. Nick watched her as she watched them.

Finally, she looked at him and raised her eyebrows with a questioning look as if to say, "Any ideas?"

He nodded.

Nick cleared his throat and began to speak as he stared at the fire. "We've done what we could. I hate to say this, but we may not be able to make this happen. Sometimes doing everything, working every angle, refusing to give in is not enough. Sometimes you lose. I hate it, but it's a fact. I'm not saying we give up. I'm saying we need to rethink this. We're all so focused in one direction. We need a break, all of us. Our minds are locked on this. That's a bad thing sometimes. We need to let things settle and then come back at it with a fresh perspective. Let's call it a night."

They let the fire die and quietly went into the farmhouse to try to sleep.

Much later that night, lying in bed, Bexx spoke quietly in the dark. "It is so odd to me that after all my team has been through in Ukraine—to come here with Nõn, to help you hunt The Director, one of our own suddenly has a family member abducted. I was thinking back on all the missions we've run. Our people died sometimes. We knew loss, but I've never felt this helpless."

Nick listened as she talked, decompressing. It wasn't intentional, but her voice calmed him. He listened as his mind wandered, and eventually he dropped off into a deep sleep.

Nick woke up. Opening his eyes, he had a hard time remembering where he was. He was in his apartment, and the cell phone was ringing. He picked it up.

"Hello?"

"Nick, it's Nõn. Where have you been? I've been calling and calling."

"Sorry, I was asleep. I had the weirdest dreams. We were hunting The

Director, and you went to the Ukraine to do some reporter job. You came back with a team of Russian Amazon women. We finally had a lead and went after The Director at another camp. He set up another camp in a missile silo."

"That's weird." She laughed. "Anyway, the reason I called is, I need a ride to work. Can you take me to the diner?"

"Sure, I'll pick you up in a minute."

Driving to Nõn's, Nick kept thinking about the dream. When he arrived at her apartment, he honked the horn, and she came walking out. He unlocked the truck's passenger door and let her in.

She smiled and said, "Thanks for the ride. I was in a bind."

"No problem."

"So tell me more about your dream."

"Okay, so we were at a missile silo. The leader of the Amazon women and I took the whole thing by ourselves. She was amazing, seriously hot, and lethal. You were pissed off at me as usual, telling me I was off the rails and you couldn't do this anymore. And then..."

"And then?"

"Some hidden sniper was watching and shot us both with one shot."

"Wow, that was a bad dream. Did we die?"

"You did. I was grazed by the bullet and knocked out."

"Nick, listen to me."

"Sure, what?"

"That wasn't a dream. I did die."

Nick laughed. "Sure! Right!" He gazed at her, and she said, "Nick, this is the dream."

He looked at her, uneasy. "What?"

"Remember when you told me there are no coincidences?"

"What?"

Nõn's head exploded in the truck.

Nick came out of the dream, screaming. Bexx was shaking him. "Wake up. Wake up. It's a dream."

Nick jumped out of bed, disoriented. "Jesus! Fuck!" He looked around the room, bewildered. He wiped his face where he could still feel pieces of Nõn's brains and blood had covered him. There was nothing there. He turned on the light and looked in the mirror.

Bexx watched him. "It's just a dream. You barely nodded off and then started twitching. Then you started to scream. I couldn't wake you up."

Someone knocked at their door and asked if everything was okay.

Bexx said, "Yes, we're fine. Just a bad dream."

Nick shook his head. "No, it wasn't a dream. I could feel her. She got in my truck. We talked. I was driving her to work and then..."

"Who got in the truck?"

"Nõn. She asked me for a ride and got in the truck."

"And then what happened?"

"She said, 'Remember when you told me there are no coincidences?' I turned to look at her, and her head disintegrated. It just blew up. Just like at the missile facility. Her blood and brains all over me. I felt it! I saw it!"

"It was just a dream. Come back to bed."

Nick checked his face again in the mirror. He could still feel pieces of Nõn on him, sliding down his skin, but when he looked in the mirror, there was nothing.

Slowly, Bexx calmed him down and coaxed him back to bed. She talked to him about the missile facility and what they would do there, and soon he fell back asleep. She watched him immediately start to twitch and jerk. He was dreaming again.

Nick was in the gym, sitting on the old bench. He liked the way it felt. I wish I could have bought this piece, Nick thought. He looked up, and Nõn was talking to Ali. They were smiling and laughing.

He got up and walked over to the counter. "What's so funny?"

Nõn said, "See, he has no idea."

Ali said, "I told you. He doesn't listen."

"I don't listen to what?"

"It's a business, Nick," Ali said.

"What?" He turned to Nõn. "What?"

"Nick, you're off the path. It is time. There are no coincidences. It's time, Nick."

"Time for what?"

"I have to go now. I hope you heard me, Nick."

And she was gone. The gym was empty except for Ali. Nick looked around. No one was there.

Ali shrugged. "I told you it's a business. I have to make money on both ends."

Nick woke up. He looked over at Bexx, asleep, breathing regularly. He looked at the ceiling and whispered to himself, "There are no coincidences. That I know. It's time, and it's a business. What the hell does that mean?"

Nick got up carefully and got dressed. He went out of the room and closed the door quietly behind him, then he walked down the hallway to the stairs. There was a light on in the kitchen. He went downstairs and found The Driver sitting alone.

"Can I sit?"

"Sure, man. It's a free country."

"Can't sleep?"

"No, this isn't a feeling I'm used to. Before you came, I never even knew what it meant to get sloppy seconds. You out-scooped me with Jay and the information at the hospital. That has never happened. Now this. I don't like how it feels."

"Sorry, brother."

"How about you? Why are you up?"

"Weird dreams."

The Driver nodded.

"Look, I'm going for a drive. I need to think. Try to get some rest."

"Drive safe."

"Thanks."

Nick left the house and jumped in the 'Yota and backed quietly out of the drive. It was dark, so he waited to turn the truck's lights on until he cleared the driveway.

Nick returned later that morning. Pulling into the driveway, he got out of the truck and went into the farmhouse and then down to the Bat Cave.

The Driver was asleep in his chair, snoring.

"Wake up, man. I need a favor."

"Huh, what?"

"Wake up! Where's the phone we used to call Arthur?"

"What?"

"Snap out of it. I need the phone we called Arthur with... now."

"We got rid of it. Why?"

"I need his number, then, ASAP. Come on. Let's go. Wake up!"

"All right, all right. Here... here's the number." The Driver wrote down the number and handed it to Nick.

"Do you have a phone down here?"

"No, not at the moment."

"I need a phone. Who has one?"

"Bexx does. So does Special K."

Nick turned quickly and left the room. He went up the stairs quickly, taking two stairs at a time, and opened the door to their room. Bexx was still asleep.

"Wake up!" he said loudly.

Bexx was up instantly. "What? What's wrong?"

"I need your phone quickly."

She nodded and leaned over to the other side of the bed and retrieved the phone from the end table. "Here it is."

Nick took the phone from her hand and dialed the number. He started to pace in the room, waiting for Arthur to answer.

"Hello?"

"Arthur? Nick. Hey, man, I don't have time to explain. Just listen."

"Okay, shoot."

"The Director sent a sniper to the facility as an extra measure of security, right?"

"Yes, he did it after the facility was up and running."

"Great. Arthur, snipers rarely work alone. They almost always have a spotter. Did The Director hire a team or just a sniper?"

"He hired a team, a two-man team."

"That's what I thought. I need you to talk to him. I need you to ask him a couple of questions."

"I can try. I have no idea if he'll answer anything. He was pretty shaken up when he called."

"Shook up? About what?"

"I would guess about you. He said he saw you go down and saw the mist from the impact of the shot. He said you were dead and then got back up."

Nick's eyes were closed, and he was silent for a while.

"Nick? Are you there?"

"Yeah, when you call him, tell him I need answers to my questions. If he answers you truthfully, I'll let him live. The choice is his. This is what I need to know." When Nick was finished explaining to Arthur what questions he needed to be asked, he stopped. "Arthur, if he answers the way I think he will, you know what this means, don't you?"

Arthur cleared his throat and after some difficulty managed to say, "Yes."

"Be careful, brother. Make the call and get back to me ASAP. Call me back at this number."

Nick hung up and gave the phone back to Bexx

"What is it?"

"We missed someone at the facility. After the shooting and in all the chaos, he got away. Nearly every sniper has a spotter. The spotter got away."

CHAPTER ELEVEN

Nick was ramped up after the drive. He was pacing and mentally turned inward. Bexx could see something had changed after he went back to sleep. When he woke her up, it was morning and he was wide awake. Apparently, he had gotten up and left sometime during the night.

Nick left the room and went back down to the Bat Cave.

He went straight to The Driver. "I need you to make something happen as soon as possible."

"Sure thing, brother. Name it!"

"I need four cords of hardwood for burning delivered here. I don't want it split. Got that? It will do me no good if it's split, so don't bother. Repeat it back to me."

The Driver spoke slowly as he stepped back from Nick. "Um, four cords of firewood... hard wood, not split. Right?"

"Yes. Delivered as soon as possible. Pay the fee. Get it here."

"Nick, we don't have a fireplace inside the house. And the fire pit outside, well, we don't need wood split for the pit. What's going on, man?"

"Just do it! Make it happen! Now!"

"Okay, okay, Jesus! Calm down. I'm on it."

Nick turned and left the room. The Driver turned to Buffy and said, "Maybe you should..."

She nodded. "I will go talk to Bexx."

A short time later, she returned. Bexx said to make it happen just as Nick asked.

"Okay." The Driver started to search for firewood delivery in the local area, muttering under his breath. "What's the crazy bastard up to now?"

Meanwhile, Nick was back in the truck and headed down the road to Moses Hole. He had to find a hardware store.

The word had traveled around the farmhouse and among the Asgarda. Bexx called them together and briefed them about Nick's phone call to Arthur, his request for wood, and that she had no idea what was up. Until she did, she asked them to stay away from him. Whatever Nick was up to, she wanted them to avoid him. The team was more than happy to comply.

Nick returned to the house a short time later with a heavy splitting mall and a large seven-pound hammer. He pulled them out of the truck and took them to the barn.

Bexx met him there.

"The wood is on its way. What are your plans?"

"I plan on splitting it."

She looked at him, puzzled. "Okay, why the sudden urgency for fire-wood?"

"It isn't the wood. It's the labor. Look, I know you'd be a lot happier if I sat and meditated in some damn yoga pose, calm and serene. Lion pose or maybe Dog, right?"

Bexx didn't know what to say. She did like Nick calmer and tried to protect him.

"Listen, this has to stop. You are turning me into a damn neutered cat. If you want to find Svetlana, let me have this. I need to be me. Think of me splitting wood as my way of meditating. Okay? I'm on to something. I don't know what, but I need to think. Let me think."

Bexx nodded. "Just don't shut me out."

"I won't. Thanks." He paused for a minute. "Really... thank you."

She nodded.

An hour later, the wood arrived. The truck backed up and dumped four cords in the area between the barn and the house.

Nick started in on it immediately.

It had been ten hours since the wood was delivered, and Nick was still at it. His pace had slowed, but he kept at it. Bexx went out to offer him a drink. When she arrived at the pile of wood, she saw Nick's face was splattered with blood.

"Are you bleeding?" she asked.

"Don't think so," he replied. "Why?"

"You're covered with blood spatters."

Nick stopped and looked. He was covered, and the splitting-maul handle had blood smears on it as well. He looked at his hands. What had been blisters had become bleeding wounds. He smiled. "It's my hands. No worries. The blisters broke, and the skin is raw. No biggie."

Bexx didn't agree. "I want you to stop, now."

"No, I won't. I told you I need this. I know it looks crazy. But let me be. Trust me, please."

Bexx shrugged angrily and said, "You're no good to me dead, Nick!"

He nodded. "I'm no good to you as a neutered cat either. I have to work my way back. I need my edge. Trust me."

She turned and angrily walked away.

The team lay in bed later that night, all of them listening to the slowly repeating sound of the splitting mall hitting the logs. They could hear Nick muttering to himself, swearing angrily.

One of the Powerpuff girls said to another, "He's lost it! Now he's talking to himself."

Bexx listened as she lay in bed, trying to convince herself this was exactly what he said, his way of meditating. She had entire conversations with Nick in her head, trying to reason with him. The conversations always ended in an argument. As she thought about what she would like to say to him, she was barely aware the sound of the splitting maul hammering away at the wood had stopped. She got up from the bed and looked out of the window to where Nick had been. He'd stopped. He was looking out into the darkness, his head turned toward the barn and then down to the ground. He dropped the maul.

"Everyone out here, now," he said. "Hurry the hell up. I know you're all awake. Come here now! Come on! Bexx? Let's go, get them out here now."

Bexx called out through the house. "Come on. Let's go see what he wants."

The team stumbled out to the woodpile.

"Where's The Driver?" Nick yelled. "Driver? Get your ass out here. Let's go, man!"

When they were all there, Nick began. "We have been doing this all wrong. I see it now. I went at this from the wrong perspective." Nick spoke to The Driver. "I'm sorry, brother, but she won't be where I told you to look." Then he turned to Special K. "I'm sorry. I was blind. I was hunting the wrong person. Listen up. I screwed up. I went at this like I was looking for the victim. Of course we won't find her that way. I don't have a clue how to do that. I always went after the suspect... the bad guy. I used to say it took a wolf to catch a wolf. I haven't been hunting a wolf. I have been looking for the wolf's prey. I can't do that. I don't know how."

He turned to Bexx. "Do you understand me?"

She nodded. "What do we do, then?"

Nick spoke again to Special K. "I'm sorry for how this will sound. Just listen.

"We need to look at this like a business. They wouldn't throw a woman like Svetlana on the Web to do cheap porn flicks—webcam bullshit any eighteen-year-old with a smartphone can do. Blow job flicks are a dime a dozen on the web. Svetlana is a thoroughbred, not a plow horse. She can make them big money and not in porn. Not as some cheap-ass streetwalker in Czech. She's high-dollar ass, smart, fit, and has a Russian accent. We're looking in the wrong place. I aimed too low. We need to look at high dollar escorts—top tier, Elliot Spitzer types, ten thousand a night girls. Like the Olympian runner who was in the news. That's where we'll find her. Driver, make it happen. High dollar escort sites, Russian, blonde, etc. Plug in Svetlana's physical appearance. Go site to site. She'll be there, the sooner, the better. Let's go!"

No one moved. Nick clapped his bloody hands together. They made a sick, sticky clapping sound, the blood splattering out into the air with each impact. "Come on now! Let's go!"

Bexx was up when she saw he meant it. In Russian, she told her team to move to the house. The Driver was up and headed to the Bat Cave. What Nick said was starting to sink in. Buffy was a few steps behind. The Driver looked back at Nick with a curious look. The things Nick had said made sense the more he thought about it, but the process he used to reach this conclusion was slightly distressing.

When the team had left, Bexx walked to Nick and said, "Are you done for the night, or do we need to have more wood delivered?" She smiled.

He smiled as well. "Done for now, I hope. I'm beat. It took a lot longer than I thought. I need a shower and some food."

Bexx smiled. "Good. Let's go get you cleaned up and get those hands bandaged."

An hour later as they sat at the kitchen table, Nick was cleaned up, hands bandaged. He was making a sandwich while Bexx sat and listened. "Listen, Svetlana isn't all I've been mulling over. There's a lot more we need to talk about. I'll know more when Arthur calls back. I just wanted you to know."

"Do you want to let me in on it now or wait?"

"I can tell you now, but it's just a feeling. It'll sound insane, and probably it is. All I ask is that it stays here, between us. If I'm right, life is about to get really interesting—like supposedly the Chinese wish upon their enemies—that kind of interesting."

"It's that bad?"

"It may be, yes." Nick nodded as he started to explain to Bexx the conclusions he'd reached. When he was done, Bexx was no longer smiling. "Are you sure?"

Nick nodded. "I wish I wasn't. Maybe I'm wrong. I hope I'm wrong. We'll see what The Driver comes up with, and that'll tell us beyond a doubt if I'm right."

Bexx nodded.

CHAPTER TWELVE

The next day, the team went out on a run early in the morning. Nick woke up and could barely move. He crawled out of the house and painfully managed to drive to the gym carefully, cursing angrily the entire way. Every corner he turned was agony. His arms were protesting the previous day's activities with murderously painful screams. Not only did his arms hurt, his hands, which had been numb the night before, felt like they were being gently licked by the flames of a blowtorch every time he shifted the 'Yota's gears and turned the ancient steering wheel.

When he walked into the gym, Ali shook her head and started in on him. "What the hell is wrong with you? What did you do now? Start juggling chainsaws but forget to take off the blades?"

Nick smiled meekly. "Something like that, yeah."

"You're not lifting weights with those hands. Not in my gym. No way that would be safe."

Nick held up his hand and nodded. "Hadn't planned to. Headed to the *VersaClimber*. I need to work out the kinks in my arms and back. Don't worry. I plan on going slow. I'm in too much pain to do anything else."

Ali shook her head in disgust. "So who did you kill this time?"

Nick smiled. "No one... really."

She shook her head. "Uh huh... sure."

Nick climbed on the *VersaClimber* slowly and carefully started moving his arms and legs. About a half an hour later, he was moving more smoothly, but his bandages were slowly changing color from white to crimson red. He stopped and got off the climber and headed toward the door.

Ali shook her head in disgust. "I'll wipe down the machine this time. The shape you're in, cleaning the machine will be a waste of time."

"Sorry, and thanks!"

Meanwhile, Bexx and the team had reached the halfway point in their run. The team usually talked and joked on the morning run in spite of the brisk pace set by Special K. The team talked and joked this morning, but by the halfway point they'd noticed Bexx hadn't said a word. She was in no mood to laugh and joke with anyone. The private conversation she'd had with Nick weighed heavily on her mind. She walked silently with the group. Occasionally, one or another of the team would steal a glance uneasily in her direction, trying to decipher her body language and facial expressions. It was clear she was troubled.

When they started to ask what was bothering her, she spoke loudly to Special K. "Let's go! Set the pace. Too much talking going on!" Special K set the usual pace, and two hundred meters later Bexx said, "Pick it up!" The pace increased. Bexx yelled out, "Again!"

The talking had stopped. Formerly smiling faces were now stern, each focused on not being the first one to drop back. The pace was now sub five-minute mile, and they had three more miles to go.

Special K was gliding effortlessly at the front. Running for her was instinctive. She smiled at Bexx. "Again?"

Bexx spoke in ragged breaths. "Open it up the last mile. Last one in does one hundred pushups."

The team now grew very serious. The challenge had been issued. When they hit the final mile, Special K flew away from the group. Bexx followed, and the rest of the team struggled to stay with them. When they finally hit the farmhouse, Nick was watching. Special K and Bexx were about a hundred yards ahead of the rest of the team. The team was in a tight group, formed in a wedge, like migrating birds. There would be no stragglers. Bexx and Special K sprinted the last hundred yards, each trying to defeat the other. Rank had no meaning. It was all out until the finish. Special K pulled ahead and finished and then spun around and encouraged Bexx. Then together they yelled to the rest of the team to push it. No one did pushups that day.

The team continued to warm down while Nick asked Bexx to have the team medic re-bandage his hands. While the medic cleaned Nick's hands, the team continued their morning routine in a less jovial mood. No one spoke carelessly, and everyone paid attention. The message had been received. Bexx was in no mood to tolerate anything but laser-like focus on their training. Nick grimaced while the medic scrubbed the wounds on his hands. Trying to distract himself from the pain, he started making smart-ass remarks about the morning run.

"Looked like you guys were opening it up a bit that last stretch, or was the whole run wide open?"

The medic said nothing for a moment or two and then said, "Bexx is serious this morning. I assume you're the reason for that."

"Why would you assume that?"

The medic shrugged her shoulders. "It doesn't take a genius to figure out you've said something that has her anxious—something you haven't shared with the rest of us."

Nick smiled. "So you're a mind reader, huh? How about we call you The Mentalist?"

The medic scrubbed his hands a little bit harder. "You won't be assigning me any ridiculous nicknames. Do you understand me?"

Nick cried out, laughing and grimacing at the pain. "Sure, I got it. So what *is* your name? What do they call you?"

"My name is spelled Dzheyn in Russian. It is pronounced Jane."

Nick smirked. "Really? Jane? Like Patrick Jane? He could hardly contain his laughter."

"What's so funny?" Jane asked. "Who is Patrick Jane?"

Nick couldn't hold the laughter in anymore. The coincidence was too funny. "You know there are no coincidences, right?" The medic was lost. Nick laughed harder.

"Just shut up, funny man, and let me finish your bandages." Jane mumbled to herself in Russian. "No wonder Bexx is so irritable today. Ten minutes with him, and I'm ready to let his wounds fester."

Nick laughed harder. "Now you're cursing me in Russian? Tell me, Jane. What am I thinking right now?"

Jane glared at Nick and said nothing. She'd have to ask Special K what *The Mentalist* was.

The Mentalist returned to the team and training after she finished with Nick's hands. Bexx asked how Nick's wounds were.

"The hands will heal. His personality, however, may never be tolerable," The Mentalist replied. "How do you do it?"

Bexx frowned. "What happened?"

"I mentioned that you were more irritable than usual, and I thought he was the reason for it, and he must've said something to you that made you this way. He laughed and called me The Mentalist. I told him I wouldn't be assigned a nickname and told him my real name. He could hardly contain himself. He laughed harder and said there are no coincidences."

Bexx looked to Special K. "The Mentalist?"

Special K smiled. "Television. The main character's name is Jane... Patrick Jane."

Bexx shrugged and smiled at The Mentalist. "Well, you walked into that one. Next time, ignore him. I'm afraid now it's too late. You're marked!"

Red faced, The Mentalist was silent. She wished she had another shot at scrubbing Nick's hands.

The team continued their training while Bexx considered what The Mentalist had said about her being irritable. When they were done, she called them around her in a circle and began to explain that Nick had a theory—more of a hunch, really—about Svetlana's abduction. Until they had more information, he was keeping it to himself. They needed to be more serious about their preparations. They'd be in battle soon. She dismissed them from the morning workout.

While Bexx spoke to the team, Nick had gone downstairs into the Bat Cave to check in with The Driver and Buffy. They were hard at it, setting up fake accounts on high end escort sites, looking for a connection with an escort that fit Svetlana's description. They'd set up both male and female accounts to make sure they covered all the bases.

Nick watched and nodded as The Driver explained their strategy. When he was done, Nick said, "Good job, brother. Keep at it, she'll be there. No other place she can be. If I'm right, we're supposed to find her."

The Driver nodded and then stopped. "What? What do you mean we're supposed to find her? What the hell does that mean?"

Nick said nothing. He just raised his eyebrows and looked at The Driver. "Keep at it. Let me know when you find her." He turned and went back up the stairs to the kitchen.

The Driver turned again to Buffy. They looked at each other silently, brows furrowed. "What did he mean we're supposed to find her?"

Three hours later, they did.

Arthur had been calling the number Nick had given him all morning. There'd been no answer. He'd located the man The Director had hired, the man who'd survived the fight at the missile facility. He explained Nick's offer of his continued survival in exchange for information. Initially, he declined the offer in a barrage of expletives and insults. Arthur waited for the barrage to die down and then suggested it may be wise to reconsider. The Director had mysteriously died since the failed mission at the missile facility, and it'd be very wise to come to some understanding with Nick. He'd gain the information he wanted one way or another. That much was clear from the past. The man thought it over and reconsidered. He would speak to Nick only—no middleman. He didn't trust Arthur to set up his guarantee of survival with Nick. He allowed Arthur to forward his contact information.

Bexx had just finished her shower from the morning workout and was getting dressed in her room when she heard her phone buzz. She checked it and saw several missed calls and two messages. She typed in the security code and unlocked the phone and then pulled up the voicemail. Arthur had called and wanted to speak to Nick immediately. Bexx sighed, finished getting dressed, and went to find Nick.

CHAPTER THIRTEEN

Nick was outside, walking around the area around the barn, pacing, thinking, and trying to figure out what to do next. It felt like the clarity he now had of the events surrounding Svetlana's disappearance were a day late—maybe too late to do anything about. He was frustrated on one hand and relieved on the other. He'd at least finally seen how it was all related. The more he considered the circumstances, the more he thought no way anyone could have predicted them. That didn't lessen his feeling somehow responsible.

He saw Bexx come out of the farmhouse and watched her looking for him. He could see from her demeanor—the way she walked, the purpose in her movements—something had happened. He paused and waited for her to walk up to him.

She looked directly into his eyes and said, "It's Arthur. He's called several times." She then handed him her cell phone.

Nick nodded and pushed the call-back button. Bexx turned to walk back to the farmhouse.

Nick spoke. "No, please stay."

"Are you sure?"

"Yes, stay. I need you to hear this. I already know what he'll say. I need you to understand it, as it comes from him, not from me."

Bexx nodded.

Nick put the phone to his ear and listened to the connection being established and then the distant electronic ring. He closed his eyes and waited.

"Hello, Nick?"

"I'm here Arthur. Did you talk to the other half of the sniper team?"

"Yes, it took some convincing, but he agreed to talk to you only. I asked him to answer the questions you'd asked, but he refused. He wanted to speak to you directly."

"Understood. What about the rest of the information? The documents? The timeline?"

"Yes, I have it. It's a bit concerning."

"I see. How concerning?"

"Very. The most concerning detail is the missile facility cleaning. Just like you thought, it doesn't add up."

Nick closed his eyes. He stopped pacing. "So...?"

"Yes. Exactly."

"Arthur, you know what this means. You have to be very careful." Nick paced more urgently now.

"I am. My eyes are wide open now, Nick. I'm making plans as we speak. I'm a little bit afraid. I won't lie. Who wouldn't be? Nick, you have to realize that without your heads up, I'd be blind. You know that, right? At least now I have a chance."

"Thanks for saying that, man. I appreciate it. Send me the documents. Scan them and send me PDFs to my e-mail."

"Hold on. I need to write it down. Okay, shoot."

"Lostetruscan@gmail.com."

"Got it. If I need to send anything else, how will I reach you?" Nick stopped pacing and looked at Bexx and nodded. She nodded back grimly and then stared at the ground as Nick paced. "Send anything else Care of General Delivery to Dresden, North Dakota. We'll be moving there. With this information, it is the only place we will be safe... in the missile facility."

"Got it. Take care, Nick."

"You too, Arthur." The line went dead.

"So you were right?" she asked.

Nick took a deep breath and let it out. "Shit! I wanted to be wrong, dammit! I need to walk. He handed her the phone. I'll be back in a while."

"I want to come with you."

"Okay, just don't try to make this something it isn't. Don't try to make it better... somehow not my fault. Just let me walk and think."

"I will. I just want to be there, is all."

Nick nodded. "Thanks. I appreciate that."

He turned, and they began to walk out of the barnyard and down the driveway and onto the road.

Meanwhile, The Driver and Buffy finally had made a connection to Svetlana. They double-checked the information to be sure. It was definitely her, and where they found her was even more unexpected. The Driver and Buffy stopped and looked at each other.

"Nick said we were supposed to find her. Do you think this is what he meant?" Buffy asked.

The Driver shrugged his shoulders. "Don't know. But we need to brief Bexx. Let's go find her."

They left the Bat Cave in a hurry and with mixed emotions. They finally had success after many hours spent searching the Web. The search had been tedious and unproductive at first, and they had little to show for their efforts. The Driver had been demoralized at the lack of success initially. After Nick had his painful epiphany, The Driver had thrown himself into the task with renewed hope and determination. He felt he and Buffy had risen to the challenge. He was proud of their accomplishment and the way they worked together and the way they complemented the other's skill set.

Bexx and Nick had walked for several miles before either said a word. Bexx spoke first.

"So, when do you think we should begin the move to North Dakota?"

"As soon as this thing with Svetlana is over." Then he hesitated. "Assuming we survive."

She nodded. "One thing at a time. I agree. Focus on the now. Deal with the future when it comes. We both have lived this way for so long, it's hard to imagine any other way now."

Nick nodded. "I know you like to keep some distance between me and your team. I get it. I can be a disruption. I don't think like a team member. I can't. You see that now, right? I mean, whatever this is that I do, it is... I don't know how to put it. It feels organic... feral. It can't be trained or taught. It just is."

She nodded.

"I need to explain what we now know. I need to do it in my words. They have to know it comes from me. With your permission, of course, but I feel responsible. I need them to hear it from me. When The Driver and Buffy find Svetlana—and they will, I promise you that—it will be crystal clear. Please consider allowing me this."

She nodded, and they were silent again.

Far off, they heard a vehicle approaching. There had been many cars that had passed them in the hour or so they had been walking. This one was different. It was coming at a pretty decent clip—too fast for the dirt road they were on. A large cloud of dust was swirling up behind it as it approached. When it came closer, Nick and Bexx could hear the horn honking repeatedly and urgently. It was Nick's truck.

Nick's face was grim as they watched the vehicle approach. "That would be The Driver. My guess is they found her. They found Svetlana."

Bexx nodded as they both watched and waited for the vehicle to reach them.

The Driver pulled up abruptly and rolled down the truck's driver side window. Buffy was in the passenger seat. They were both boiling over with excitement.

"We found her! We found Svetlana!" The Driver blurted out victoriously.

"That's awesome, brother," Nick said with much less enthusiasm than they expected him to have.

Bexx listened as they spoke. Her face betrayed her lack of enthusiasm as well.

The Driver was perplexed. "Nick, we found her! Don't you get it? We found her! Why the long face? I thought—we thought—you would be happy... both of you."

Nick nodded. "I'm happy you found her, brother. Now the work begins. We have to find a way to get her out safely. Head back to the farmhouse. We'll be there when we're done walking."

"But don't you want to know where she is?"

"I already know, brother. It all fits. She's in the States. Am I right? Somewhere like Vegas or Atlantic City. Somewhere we can get to her. Someplace where there are people who have the money to pay the fee for her sexual services. Either on the east coast or west."

The Driver was speechless. How could Nick know?

"Don't speak, brother. I can see from your face I'm right. You two keep this quiet. We'll meet tonight and discuss it all. Front to back, you'll understand then, okay?"

The Driver and Buffy nodded.

Bexx spoke up. "For now, we need to walk and be alone. We have some things to work out. Go back and tell no one what you've found. It's good news. You're right, and we're happy you've found her. Now we all have to get down to business. Now we all go to work and get her out of there."

The Driver sat for a moment in the truck, thinking about what Bexx had said. He nodded and turned the truck around and headed back to the farmhouse. They had searched the roads around the house for some time, looking for Nick and Bexx. They had no idea which direction they'd walked, and it'd taken them a while to find the couple. When they finally did find them, they expected their announcement to be met with praise. It was, but the reality of locating Svetlana hadn't hit them until Bexx's comment about now the real work begins had settled in. She was right. Knowing where Svetlana was, was half the problem. Now they had to get her safely out.

The truck pulled away slowly. The air had been let out of The Driver's sails, and it showed in how he drove back to the farmhouse.

Bexx and Nick watched as they drove away. "Sorry to be such a downer, brother," Nick said quietly.

They turned and walked the direction they'd been going and began to discuss plans on how to get Svetlana out. This time, they both knew it'd be much different than the assault on the missile facility. They each recognized the other's skill set and understood they would need every talent they individually possessed to solve the problem. What's more, they needed some inside help. Arthur was out. He would be on the run in a matter of days, maybe hours. If Svetlana was in Atlantic City or on the east coast, Nick was unsure of what to do. He suspected she wouldn't be. So far, it had all fit in his head. If his intuition was right, she would be in Vegas. If she was, Nick had an idea of who he could turn to.

CHAPTER FOURTEEN

L ater that night after Bexx and Nick had returned to the farmhouse, they began to prepare a huge meal. Nick insisted on cooking a huge roast, potatoes, and anything and everything anyone requested. The kitchen table was covered with dishes and plates overflowing with food. It was a celebration with a touch of sadness and mourning felt just under the surface. The team knew something was up. Bexx's edgy attitude the past week compounded by Nick's bizarre epiphany was now seasoned with The Driver and Buffy's refusal to answer questions about their progress in the search for Svetlana. They all ate heartily but with a bit of anxiety, waiting for what they all felt was coming. Something had happened. Somewhere a break had come in the search for Svetlana. It was just a matter now of which direction it would go, good or bad. The reality would be neither and both.

When everyone had finished the meal and eaten probably more than they should have, given the expected morning run they all knew was coming in a few hours, Bexx asked Special K to build a fire. The team was quiet as they all sat around the fire. No one said a word. Bexx stared at the fire and gave no hint of what they should expect. After far too much time had passed, the team grew restless.

Finally, Jane, The Mentalist to Nick, spoke up. "Commander... Bexx, why are we here? What has happened?"

Bexx stared at the fire and said nothing. Finally, she looked at Nick and said, "You may begin."

Nick nodded and swallowed several times. The things he had to tell them would be hard to speak out loud. Saying it seemed to make real what he'd hoped would never be. It seemed surreal, but it all fit.

Nick spoke. "Sorry for all the mystery. It isn't something I want to say out loud. First, the good news!" Nick looked at The Driver and said, "Go ahead, brother."

"We found Svetlana today, exactly where Nick said she would be. She's an escort in a very exclusive escort service. It took us a while to get accepted as a potential client. They're very selective and careful. We had to throw up a very convincing smoke screen on the Web to gain access. She's still alive and within reach."

The team cheered out loud, praising The Driver and Buffy for the success of their efforts. Everyone but Special K. She watched Nick, her eyes never leaving his face. His face betrayed the news was not all good.

Someone said, "Where is she?"

Nick smiled grimly and mouthed "Vegas" silently.

The Driver looked at Bexx and then Nick. "She's here, in the States. We expected her to be in Europe or perhaps the Middle East... Dubai maybe. But no, she's here."

The team was confused. Europe made sense. They'd all expected Svetlana to be there. The sex trade in Czech and the surrounding areas made her being found there make sense.

Nick spoke. "It makes sense when you know the details. First, you all know Bexx and I went to visit Arthur. He gave us access to the missile facility. When we arrived, we found it booty trapped." Nick smiled at Bexx. She smiled back. Even now, with all that had happened during the week, he was still Nick. He continued. "Anyway, we disarmed them, but it bothered me. Something about it felt wrong. The facility is now secure. It's ours if we want it. But that's for after we're done with this mission. I couldn't figure out what we were missing until the other night. Then it all came clear. I went to the gym and realized I wasn't doing the things I used to do. When we killed The Director, I let my guard down. I relaxed. It cost us dearly. This is my fault." Bexx shook her head in disagreement but stayed silent. She'd agreed to let Nick speak. "I realized when I started to think it over, we missed someone at the attack on the facility. A spotter— every sniper has a spotter. He escaped. He reported back to The Director the events at the facility. So then we gained access to Arthur, set up The Director, and Special K delivered the poisonous whiskey glasses. Arthur verified The Director's death. Mission successful."

Nick paused. "Then a week or two went by, and I noticed I was the only one who had relaxed. You guys were gearing up. I was out of the loop. I watched, and Special K here seemed to be the most affected—silent, turned inward. So, I started working on her, and she told me what was up. Her sister Svetlana had disappeared. I didn't see the connection. It all seemed so random."

The Driver listened while the dots Nick was mentally connecting came clearly into focus. He turned and whispered to Buffy. She looked back at him in disbelief.

Nick paused again. "It isn't random. I kept having dreams about random things—Nõn, the gym, things people said out of context. I don't believe in a higher power or Nõn's spirit guide. I think deep down I knew something was wrong. I just couldn't put it together. My dreams were my sub-conscious working to wake me up. Bottom line, the dreams told me there are no coincidences, and this thing with Svetlana was a business deal."

The team was lost. Nothing Nick said made sense.

Nick looked around and saw the confused look on everyone's faces.

"Confusing, huh? It should be. It's a complex mess. That's why I didn't see it. It took this to make me see." Nick held out his hands, bandaged. "So, after I gave The Driver a new direction to look, I spoke to Bexx privately and told her the rest of what I'd realized. The Mentalist, Jane there, pegged it. She was upset. You were right. I caused it."

The Mentalist turned red, angry at the new nickname being spoken in the meeting. She would be stuck with it forever.

Nick smiled as he saw her face flushed.

"I called Arthur and asked him to locate the spotter. He has, and I spoke with him today. He wouldn't speak to Arthur, so I had to call him directly. He confirmed my suspicion."

Special K impatiently spoke up. "And what was that? What's your suspicion?"

Nick looked into the fire. It was hard to admit. He felt responsible.

The Driver cleared his throat. "It's The Director, isn't it? We didn't kill him, did we?"

Nick shook his head no.

The Driver continued. "He lost the revenue from the camp when we shut it down and needed a new source, right?"

Nick nodded yes.

"And he went after Special K's sister. He made it personal for the poisonous whiskey glasses. He went after her sister as payback."

Nick nodded, his face grim.

"But we killed him. You saw the video. Arthur sent it. He watched The Director die!" The Mentalist said loudly.

"Exactly!" Nick said. "That's why I didn't put it together until the other night. Svetlana's abduction was a message. Sent to us. Sent to me."

"What message?"

"The Director wants us to know he is still here. I take that back. He wants me to know he is still here. And if you, if any of you stay in this fight, he'll come after all of you like he's come after me. Svetlana was a warning shot."

"How is that possible? You saw him die too! We all did," Buffy said.

"We saw Oelsen Hauer die. That was the mistake. Let me explain. Remember when I told you government workers are structured and semi-neurotic? Okay, paranoid was the word I used, and it's accurate. It would be very tough to find the right person to gain access to The Director."

The Driver nodded. They all did.

"Same applies to the way they organize things. Who we—or I— thought was The Director wasn't. Oelsen Hauer was what's referred to in government programs as a program manager. He handles all the details for his bosses. We killed the program manager. The Director is still out there."

The team was silent.

Nick continued. "Today, the spotter confirmed it. I already knew what he would tell me—or at least I felt I was on the right track. But he confirmed it."

The Driver spoke. "What did he say?"

"I asked him how many interviews he and the sniper had with The Director. He said one. Then I reframed the question—a cop thing. When you aren't getting the answer you need, you have to realize you have a blind spot and change the way you frame the question. I asked how many interviews they had for the job. Not the same question, you see?"

They all nodded.

"He told me they had two interviews. One with Oelsen Hauer and another after they'd been hired. They were told in the second interview to target me and Nõn first if we showed up at the missile facility. So you see, The Director—the real Director—expected us. This has all been about that day. When the real Director lost his income from the camp and then his program manager, Oelsen Hauer, he came after us. He came after Special K's sister to get a message to me and all of you. If you enter this fight—if I enlist any help—all of you are targets. All of your families as well."

Nick spoke directly to Special K. "I'm sorry it took me so long to see the message he had sent. This is my fault. I shouldn't have allowed any of you to join this fight and you to deliver the poison." To the team, he said, "Now you all see why I didn't want any of you involved. The Director is real, and he plays for keeps. After we get Svetlana free, you all need to go... leave. This will not end well. It's not your fight. I asked Bexx to let me speak to you tonight and detail the way it all fits together. I wanted you to hear it from me. I'm done now. Now you all understand what I suspected. Unfortunately, it's been verified."

No one spoke for quite a while. They each processed the information Nick had detailed. Nick looked at Bexx and nodded. Silently, he got up and left the fire. This was their agreement. He would have his time before her team, and when he was done, he would leave.

It was now her turn to speak. "Each of you has your own decision to make. But not tonight. We'll all make our decision after we recover Svetlana. Until then, I want your complete focus to be on the mission. Nothing else. Is that clear?"

The group all nodded yes. It was clear. They had a lot to think about.

Bexx sat and stared at the fire while the team members each departed. Some walked off alone, others in small groups. Finally, she sat with only The Driver and Buffy remaining. She handed them a list.

"Nick gave this to me earlier today. He said that if Svetlana was in Vegas, I was to give you this list of things to do."

The Driver nodded. He and Buffy went to work on the list, leaving Bexx alone to watch the glowing embers and small trails of smoke drifting from the dying fire.

CHAPTER FIFTEEN

Nick woke up later and reached across the bed for Bexx. She was gone. He listened for a moment and heard faint voices coming from the kitchen. Swinging his feet over the edge of the bed, he sat up and listened. It sounded like several people were talking quietly in the kitchen. Nick got up and dressed and started downstairs. He'd woken up with heartburn from the large meal and wanted a glass of almond milk. It always worked on his heartburn without the side effects the usual cures brought with them.

As Nick slowly walked down the stairs, his legs still sore from splitting wood, he heard Bexx and The Driver, then Special K and The Mentalist—a war council if there ever was one. He smiled and managed a small middle finger fuck you salute to The Driver as he walked into the room.

"A war council has been convened, and no one woke me up? Where's the love? Who has the ring of power?"

No one spoke as he opened the fridge, pulled out the carton of almond milk and began to shake it. Once he felt it was shaken up enough, he cracked the carton's twist top and drank directly from the carton.

The Mentalist rolled her eyes. "Last time I drink from an open carton in this house."

Nick shrugged. "If you're smart, as soon as we rescue Svetlana, there won't be an opportunity to drink from a carton in this house."

No one replied to his comment.

The Driver spoke up. "I have a few questions that need answers."

"Shoot... fire away... lower the boom. Hit me, brother."

"You never did explain what it was about finding the booby traps in the facility that bothered you."

"It was the timing. That's all. They smelled fresh. C-4 has a distinct scent—smells like motor oil a bit. I smelled it as soon as we cracked the doors to the place. When I finally put this all together, I asked Arthur to send me the documents he'd found of the facility being cleaned. The cleaning was ordered after Hauer was dead. How does a dead man request a clean-up crew? Subtle, huh? It isn't magic. I just wasn't paying attention."

"So is Arthur safe? I mean, the real Director has to know he's helped us, right?" asked Special K.

"Doubtful that he or any of us are safe. I talked to him and explained what I thought it meant. He's making plans to take off... disappear. He and his wife are planning on leaving D.C. He's doing what he can to steer clear of The Director, just like we all should be."

"Are you saying you're going to steer clear of The Director?" asked The Mentalist.

"Hell no. I'll do no such thing. You're The Mentalist. You should know better than that!" Nick smiled.

Jane's face flushed again.

"Any other questions?"

Bexx spoke. "I have a confession. Your blindness to what was happening is my fault. I'm sorry. I made a decision, and it was the wrong one."

Nick studied her face. Frowning, he asked, "What decision?"

"Arthur sent word that The Director—or who we thought was The Director—had six bottles of wine in his liquor cabinet. One was named Baroota, one Cachibaché, and there were four more. He thought it implied there were at least four more camps. I asked The Driver and Buffy to keep this from you. I'm sorry."

Nick nodded and thought it over. "Don't beat yourself up over it. I figured as much; there would be more camps. It wouldn't have changed much for me. I just assumed with The Director dead, it didn't matter much. So, what's next? Spin the bottle? Truth or dare? Hot tub time machine?"

No one laughed.

"Y'all need to lighten up. We're in a death match with a psychotic killer. What more could you ask for? This is heaven on Earth. We won the lottery! Lighten up, bitches. Tomorrow we go to war. He's had a free ride long enough. Time to get medieval on his ass." Nick raised his voice. "Bring me my armor!"

Bexx looked at him, puzzled. Nick looked at The Driver and saw the same confused look. "Lemme guess. Not one of you one here ever watched *The 13th Warrior?*"

No one said a word.

"Driver, we need a movie day, damn it! No one appreciates me because no one gets my humor. I'd be the most popular guy in the house if only the girls understood how funny I really am."

The entire table spoke at once in disagreement. "Sorry, man," said The Driver, "it isn't that at all." They all laughed while Nick poorly pretended to be hurt and then laughed himself.

The Driver asked, "So what's your plan now?"

"I'd quote *The 13th Warrior* again, but it would be lost on you."

"Have at it, brother. Share the wisdom," The Driver said sarcastically.

"We ride 'til we find them and kill them all. I like simple plans, you know?" said Nick.

"That's it?" said Special K.

"Sure. We ride to Vegas, rescue the girl, kill everyone and anyone who had anything to do with this, burn the buildings to the ground, scorch the earth under The Director's feet. Time to send a message back." Nick mimicked in a different voice, "Western Union for The Director? Oh, oh I'm The Director. I have a singing telegram, sir! Oh please, sing it to me.

Cue the kazoo. 'Ding dong, the witch is dead. Which old witch? The wicked witch!'"

Bexx shook her head and brought her hands up to cover her face in
disbelief.

Nick smiled and put the almond milk back in the fridge. "Night, all.
Time to get some rest. Tomorrow we're off to see the Wizard. This time,
however, it'll be different. We know better than to pay attention to the curtain. The man behind the curtain has our entire focus now."

Nick started back upstairs, still talking. "When I find the six-fingered
man, I'll look into his eyes and say, 'Hello, my name is Inigo Montoya.
You killed my father. Prepare to die.'" The entire table now looked at
Bexx as if silently asking, *How do you put up with this?* She shrugged and
said, "He grows on you!"

The next morning, Nick was up early. He waited for the team's morning workout to be finished and called The Driver and Buffy up from the
Bat Cave. When they'd all gathered around in the kitchen, he began.

"Driver, what was the site you located Svetlana on?"

"It's called Izadi. It's a website that promises educated women interested in entertaining wealthy clients, men and women."

"Okay, so we're going after Svetlana. The account that found Svetlana
was one Buffy set up. It was a female, looking for the companionship of
another female. I think we roll with that. Driver, we need a bulletproof
identity—someone with old money, a decent track record on the Web, and
hints of being a lesbian in the information available as well. She'll have
to be a high-end businesswoman—legit or criminal, it doesn't matter. Can
you make that happen? Backdate the information?"

"So who gets to be the lucky girl?" The Driver asked.

Bexx spoke up. "I do. You can use my real identity. It'll save time."

Nick was puzzled. They'd already discussed this option on their long
walk. She would be the last person The Director would expect to come for

Svetlana. She hadn't mentioned using her real identity, however.

Nick asked, "Driver, can you make her look wealthy and aristocratic on the Web? Some kind of old money from Eastern Europe?"

Bexx spoke up again. "No need. Just use my identity, and that'll suffice. Let's continue on with planning."

Nick wasn't pressing on with any planning. "Listen, I know you're Amazon and playmate rolled into one with a touch of Xena Princess Warrior, but we need you to be filthy wealthy—old money. So wealthy, you can't figure out how to make your own coffee or tie your own shoes without help. Like, Clinton money."

Bexx nodded. "I understand. Use my identity. It'll be more than adequate for our needs."

Nick shook his head. "How much you got in the bank, Bexx? Couple of thousand? I really appreciate the sentiment. You're all in. I get it. Thanks for the show of support. I never thought you'd leave anyway. But..."

Bexx cut him off. "I'm worth four hundred million in American dollars. Is that adequate?"

"Bullshit," Nick replied.

Bexx nodded. "It is, but I am. My father left me everything. When our country failed, he invested wisely. It's all in my name. I just prefer to live my own life and not the life money would bring. May we continue now?"

Nick looked at her sideways, curiously. "Yeah, I guess we can. So our newest gazillionaire, Bexx, will play the part of out-of-towner looking for a good time. The rest of you will need to clean up. You have to fit the part of Vegas girls, working the casinos. It won't be much of an effort. We just need you to dress to fit in. We need to load up all AK-47 pistols and equipment your team thinks it'll need. Driver, we need vans. No air travel on this trip. We need to come in with equipment and under the radar. I'm thinking two vans, eighteen-passenger. Is that doable?"

"Sure is. The Driver will deliver. To stay off the radar, we'll need a place to land. Somewhere out of the way... not on the strip."

"I'm working on that," Nick said. "Any idea where the physical location of Izadi is? Where they're keeping Svetlana?"

"Not yet. It won't be in Vegas proper. Prostitution is illegal in Nevada in any county that has a larger population than seven hundred thousand. Still, it goes on in the bigger counties. They may fly her in on a private jet. Izadi could be anywhere. We'll be lucky if it's physically located somewhere near Vegas."

"We'll deal with that when the times comes. I admit, I'd love to have a building to burn down. But our first priority is getting Svetlana out of The Director's control. Look, I know this isn't much of a plan. There are no bells and whistles to impress. We have to wing it... play it by ear. Once she shows up to meet Miss Money Bags here, the plan is simple. We keep her with us no matter what."

When everyone had dispersed, Nick turned to Bexx. "Remember that picture you mentioned last night? The one Arthur sent with the six wine bottles?"

"Yes," she said regretfully.

"Do you still have it?"

"The Driver downloaded it. I believe he has it in the Bat Cave. Why?"

"Just tying up loose ends. Let's go see it."

Bexx and Nick walked down to the Bat Cave and found the door locked. They had interrupted The Driver and Buffy just as they were about to complete a wired connection and merge their hard drives, so to speak.

"Sorry, kids. Mom and Dad here, walking in at the worst possible moment," Nick said, laughing.

"The Driver is busy at the moment, my friend. Can you come back when the deal has been sealed and the download is complete?"

Nick grimaced, his face making a sneer. "Does everything he says have to be so creepy and sexual? I mean, even when he has sex and talks about it, it's creepy."

Bexx grabbed his shoulder and spun him back toward the stairway. "Come on. Let's go upstairs. This may be a while."

Nick raised his eyebrows. "Really? What have you heard?"

Bexx smiled. "Girls talk. Come on. You can tell me what you're looking for in the photo."

"Do you talk about us?" he asked.

Bexx ignored the question. "Come on upstairs, funny man. Let them have their privacy."

CHAPTER SIXTEEN

A while later, much longer than Nick would have imagined possible, The Driver opened the basement door and called out, "If you're up there, you can come down now."

Bexx said, "Let's go see if what you told me you think will be in the picture, will be."

Nick hesitated. "Don't you want to wait a minute? I mean, doesn't it have to air out or something?"

Bexx rolled her eyes. "Come on!"

Bexx walked down the stairs while Nick followed apprehensively at a distance.

"Nick wants to see the photo Arthur sent. The picture of the wine bottles. Do you have it?"

The Driver pulled the picture up on one of the many computer screens in the Bat Cave.

Nick spoke up, suddenly all business. "Can you blow it up? I want to see the bottles."

The Driver enlarged the picture to one hundred percent. Nick said, "Scan from left to right." As The Driver moved the cursor, pulling the enlarged picture across the screen, Nick watched. "Stop," he said. "Right there!" He pointed at the screen while he turned to look at Bexx. There, enlarged on the screen, was a wine bottle. On the label clearly written was the winemaker's name—Izadi. "As if we needed more proof The Director was behind Svetlana's disappearance, there it is for any doubters," Nick said.

Bexx asked for copies of the picture—both the original and the blow-up. "Two to three of each should do," she said.

Buffy had them printed and handed them to Bexx. She turned to Nick and said, "Well, shall we?"

Nick nodded. "You two, um, return to whatever you were doing. I mean, uh, keep at it... looking for the physical location. Jesus, now everything sounds weird and sexual! Just find a building I can burn down, okay?"

"On it, brother!" The Driver smiled. Buffy waved, smiling.

Nick walked up the stairs, shaking his head. "You knew the entire time?"

Bexx tussled his hair. "You have been focused, haven't you?! How did you put it before? Duh, big red truck?"

Nick looked down, embarrassed.

"I know you expect to see everything happening around you before it happens, but I've some news for you. You do have some blind spots. You may be target locked on The Director, but you aren't all-seeing and all-wise." Bexx smirked.

"Since when?" Nick asked, confused. "I mean, what else have I missed? Anything big?"

Bexx laughed and said, "Come on. Let's go show the team the photos."

Nick said, "Wait, I'm serious. What else have I missed? I mean, besides the fact you're some rich heiress. Is it important? Is it obvious?" He trailed behind Bexx, continuing to ask questions as she went back to the kitchen, ignoring him.

Once they arrived in the kitchen, Bexx spoke to the team members who were there. "In case any of you doubted it's The Director behind Svetlana's abduction, look at these." She laid out the photos of the wine bottles and explained their significance.

Nick's opinion of The Director's involvement carried weight with some of the group. Evidence, however—proof, really—that he was right meant a lot more.

The next day, the vans The Driver had rented were ready for pick up.

Nick and The Driver went to get them from the only car rental company that carried them in the area, Advance Rent-a-Car. When they returned, the team began to load up their equipment. Bexx checked off a list she had made of the items they would need. When the vans were loaded, they were ready to go.

An hour later, they were on the road. The Driver and Buffy were staying behind. They still hadn't located the physical location of Izadi, so they stayed to provide support for the team from the farmhouse.

They traveled US-395 from Moses Lake until it intersected with Interstate 84 Eastbound. They followed that to Interstate 15 and went south all the way to Las Vegas. When they arrived in Pendleton, Oregon, they stopped for food. Special K wanted to get Chinese at The Jade Garden. That was quickly vetoed by the entire team with one loud and simultaneous, "No, girl!" No one wanted to be stuck in a van with her after the Chinese food worked its magic on her digestive system. She pouted while they collectively decided on lunch at Arby's.

When they hit the Idaho border, Bexx's phone rang. It was The Driver calling with information for Nick. Bexx handed Nick the phone.

"Hey, man, did you find that number?"

"I did. The Driver delivers, day or night. No matter the request, The Driver will find a way to satisfy!"

Nick cringed. "Okay, okay, I got it, you're the sex god of the Web. Can I just get the damn number?"

"Sure thing, brother. Ready to write it down?"

"Just tell me. I'll remember it."

The Driver passed the number along to Nick and then hung up. Nick cleared the phone and then typed in the number and added it to the memory on Bexx's phone. Nick held the phone for a few minutes and stared out the window of the van as they drove.

Bexx was puzzled by his behavior and asked, "What's that about?"

Nick replied. "Huh? Oh, a number for a guy I know in Vegas. He might be able to help us out."

"Are you going to call him?"

"Uh, yeah. Well, it's complicated. It isn't just call up and say, 'Hey, man, long time, no see. You may have heard I died. Not so. Wanna help a brother out? Oh, and did I mention I'm bringing five mercenaries from Ukraine?'"

"Why is it complicated?"

Nick sighed. "Hmm, well, the last time we spoke, it wasn't in the friendliest of circumstances. It's a long story."

Bexx looked at him. "Seriously, we have nothing but time. It isn't like this drive is exciting or even mildly interesting."

Nick shrugged. "The last time we met, I was taking him out of a Ford Bronco at gunpoint."

The van that had been previously full of the sound of the team talking back and forth between each other, pointing out sights as they drove, was suddenly silent. Nick looked over his shoulder. Everyone now was looking at him and waiting to hear the rest of the story.

Bexx smiled. "Now you've done it. You have all of our attention. Let's hear it!"

"Well, it was a long time ago. I was a detective. He was a suspect in a case I was investigating. It was an aggravated assault. I found him, after a couple of hours of searching, in the back seat of a Ford Bronco. I pulled it over and stuck a gun in his face and pulled him out of the car. I had heard a lot about him. He was kind of a legend on the darker side of the city. He had a reputation as a scrapper and tactician. Kind of a warrior poet—lethal and wicked smart. When we were in a room alone, and while I was interviewing him, I realized we were very much alike. Looking at him was like looking in the mirror at what I would have been if I hadn't gone into the military and got out of the city. He stayed in the city, and his reputation followed him. No matter where he went or what he did, people challenged him. When we were done talking about the crime he committed, we just talked. Man to man. That was the last time I saw him in person. He went back to prison, and I went back to work. Anyway, he's out of prison now and straightened out his life from what I can tell. He lives in Vegas and runs a gym there. Now he trains MMA fighters."

"How long ago was it when all this happened?"

"It was nineteen ninety-eight, give or take."

The van was silent. Finally, someone in the back said, "Are you serious? This is who you're planning on asking to help us?"

Nick smiled. "Yes, I am. We're going into the lion's den here, ladies. Don't think for a minute The Director isn't expecting us to eventually locate Svetlana and try to rescue her. We have some advantages. He doesn't know when we're coming, and he won't expect Bexx as a customer for her services. I think he'll be looking for me or Special K."

"So why this guy?" the voice asked.

"Lion's den! Did you miss that point? Richard Pratt said, 'If you've just escaped the lion's den, don't go back for your hat.' Make sense?"

The team all looked at each other. Bexx spoke first. "I don't think any of us get that one, Nick."

"We're going into the lion's den. There won't be second chances to go back if we lose anything or anyone. Lose a hat, too bad. Lose one of us? Might as well burn it all to the ground, then, because I'm not leaving anyone behind. We're going to war, and this guy is the kind of guy who will not leave anyone behind. Bring a lion into the lion's den. That's my plan."

Bexx nodded. "Do you think he'll help us?"

"Depends, I guess, on how he remembers our conversations. If all he remembers is my Glock screwed into his ear, this could be ugly. Might be a really bad idea, to be honest. But if he remembers the rest of it, then he may help us. It's a gamble, but hey, we are in Vegas right? When in Rome? Make sense?"

Nick paused for a minute, looking out the window, and then dialed the number.

"JT, what's up, man?"

"Who is this?"

"Nick, from back in the day."

"Don't know any Nicks."

"Nick, one time? Cop... you remember? West Side? Ford Bronco? Hands out where I can see them. One wrong move, and you die right here... sound familiar?"

"All right, I remember. What was the color of the Bronco?"

"Tan"

"Okay. Who was I with?"

"Gilbert."

"Nick! It is you, Loc! Heard you checked out, man. What happened?"

"Long story. I *am* checked out, actually, for the daywalkers. I'm officially dead. Staying that way too. Got myself into a little confrontation with some bad people."

"Sounds serious. One thing I learned, there is a next level in everything."

"There is. Listen, man. This is short notice, I know, but me and a few friends are coming to the strip."

"On business?"

"On business. We need a place to crash for twenty-four, maybe fourty-eight hours, off the grid, out of sight. This is a hit and run operation and could get very real, very fast."

"Understood. How far out are you, bradah?"

"Ten hours, maybe a li'l more."

"Call me when you get in. I'll see what I can do."

"Thanks, brother. How's the gym and training going?"

"Damn, man, you've been keeping tabs on me, huh? It's good. All good. Life is much better now that my mind is unchained."

"Sounds good. Glad to hear it. We'll talk soon."

"Peace."

"You too, man."

Nick pushed end call and disconnected. "He says he'll help. Just the same, when we do arrive, everyone stay in the van until I know for sure he's on board."

"If you're that concerned, do you really think this is a good idea?" Bexx asked.

Nick sighed and raised his eyebrows as he said nothing and continued to look out the window.

CHAPTER SEVENTEEN

This is it. "This is where JT said he would meet us," Nick called out as Bexx pulled the van into a dark parking lot. Nick smiled at her and said, "Wish me luck." He took off his glasses, emptied his pockets, and pulled off his hoodie... and left it all in the van.

Bexx asked, "What are you doing?"

"Stripping anything that can be used against me in a fight."

He smiled and closed the door and then walked out into the dark parking lot toward the grey Hummer H-2 parked about twenty feet away. Nick could hear the loud thumping coming from the Hummer as the stereo's bass beat rattled the windows and sheet metal of the vehicle. No one got out.

Nick stood in front of the vehicle and waited. He expected nothing less. JT was sizing up the scene. He hadn't survived as long as he had by walking into dark parking lots with no plan.

A few minutes passed, and the Hummer turned off. Nick heard the alarm chirp, and then off to his left he heard a voice call his name. Nick smiled. The Hummer had been set up as a diversion.

"Nick?"

"Yeah, it's me. Cautious as ever, I see."

"Not every day a dead man calls me and wants to meet—even less often he wants my help."

"Happens a lot, does it?"

"Never, as a matter of fact."

There was silence for a few more seconds, and then Nick could hear footsteps coming out of the dark toward him. JT began to walk carefully towards Nick, scanning the parking lot and keeping an eye on the van behind him.

"So what's up, man?"

"Like I said on the phone, we need a place to land—somewhere on the down low."

"What's your business here?"

"Coming to rescue a friend from human trafficking. She was abducted in Germany and is working as a high-end escort here, somewhere."

"So, what's your plan, then?"

"Arrange an expensive date and take her back. Her sister is in the van behind me. There's another van down the street with us. I told them to hang back. Didn't want you to get the wrong idea when two vans pulled in. It's not a set-up, man. Really need your help."

JT stepped out of the shadows and walked up to Nick, standing directly in front of him. "What's up, bradah?" he said.

"Good to see you, man. Still fit as hell, I see. How's the gym life? You don't look like you've aged a day, JT."

"Life is good. You look old as hell, man. How long has it been?"

"Nearly twenty years, I think. Listen, man, this could get kind of serious. I just need a place to land. We'll run this mission and be gone out of your hair. Don't want you to be involved. You've been clean for a while. Let's keep it that way."

JT said nothing for a few seconds. "I see it's serious, bradah. You've got armed people flanking us now. Apparently, everyone involved is ready to put in some work."

"What?"

Nick looked around and saw a figure in the shadows to his right. Bexx stepped forward out of the shadows, armed with her Romanian AK-47 loaded with a thirty round clip.

Nick smiled. "Oh, yeah. Well, she *is* a bit protective. Sorry, bro. This is Bexx. She leads the team in the van."

"She leads?" JT's eyebrows raised. "What's your role, then, Nick?"

"Freelance, like always. Riding my own path, man. You know that won't change."

JT nodded and then extended his hand. Nick did the same, and they shook hands and exchanged a bro hug. "Follow me, bradah. My gym is just a few miles away. You'll be crashing there."

JT walked back to the Hummer and got in while Nick walked to Bexx and smiled. "See? He wants to help. You seem a bit edgy, Bexx. Everything okay?"

She ignored him and walked back to the van, taking off the AK and tactical sling. She handed the weapon to someone behind the driver's seat and started the van. The van began to vibrate to the bass of the stereo in the Hummer as it passed and pulled out of the parking lot. Nick watched the Hummer pass and then realized Bexx was suddenly very serious.

"You okay?" he asked.

She said nothing, but Nick could see she was mad.

"Thanks for doing that," Nick finally said. "I know this is hard, but this was the life I lived for so long, I don't know any other way. I was always on my own. I can't think any other way. So trust my judgment, okay?"

Bexx nodded silently.

When the Hummer arrived at the gym, JT opened the doors and waved the team in. Bexx had them unloading the vans rapidly while Nick was on the phone to The Driver.

"Driver, make the appointment with Izadi. You need to set up a room. Make it the Bellagio with a view of the strip and the fountain. Make the reservation for at least two adjoining rooms. I want to be close if things go south. Also, need you to be in the hotel's surveillance. I want your eyes on everything, okay?"

"The Driver is way ahead of you, brother. Been watching your progress on traffic cameras the entire way. Already have the reservations set. Three rooms, room service, and a check-in date. All is ready and waiting for Bexx to arrive. A limo is scheduled to pick her up at the airport. Like we discussed, she'll change clothes there and come out to the limo and then go straight to the hotel. The Driver has the timing down. It's all good to go. How's things there?"

"Things are good. Send the details to Bexx's phone so she has them. Let's plan on setting the plan in motion after we get some rest. I'll call you back when it's time."

"Nick!" JT called out. "The gym will be closed for repairs from a broken water pipe for the next two days, so you have the entire place to yourselves. It's a front, so no one will suspect a thing. Feel free to move around. I stay in an apartment attached to the office, so if you need me, I'll be there. Anything you need?"

"Don't know yet. Lemme get with Bexx, and I'll let you know. Thanks, man."

Nick went looking for Bexx. He found her making sure the team had set up in the basement of the gym. Each had sleeping bags and clothes laid out. She was making sure they all knew where the equipment was and that everything was accounted for.

"Anything you need?" Nick asked. "Food... drinks?"

Bexx thought about it. "We could use food and bottled water. They need to rest to be sharp for the big day. And a shower. I think we could all use a shower after that long drive." Nick nodded and went back to find JT.

"Girls want to know if there is a place they can shower, bro, and do you know any good places for food that deliver?"

"It's a gym, bradah. Of course I have showers. Tell them the locker room is open and it's all ready to go. What kind of food do you want to order?"

"Anything but Chinese."

JT shrugged. "Really? There's a great Chinese just a minute out."

"Not for this crew. Trust me. Pizza, sandwiches... anything, How about Jimmy John's? Is there one close?"

"Sure is. They're everywhere here."

"Can you write down the address, and I'll have our IT guy call it in. Nothing should come back to you—no charges, not the name they deliver to, not even the phone call. We'll buy you dinner. Least we can do."

JT nodded and said, "I'll take a number ten. Here's the gym's address."

Nick went back to the basement and told Bexx about the showers and took everyone's order. Then he called The Driver and relayed the team's food order and the closest Jimmy John's phone number.

An hour later, everyone was showered and fed. Some lay down and tried to sleep. Special K, Bexx, Nick, and JT sat in his apartment off the gym's office and planned the next day's events. If all went well, they'd have Svetlana back at the gym and be on the road in less than 24 hours. Nick impatiently hoped for a little extra time to disrupt The Director's Izadi operations, but Svetlana's successful rescue took priority.

The initial plan had been to get Svetlana into a room in the Bellagio and then clear a path for her to escape out of the basement car garage with the team. They talked through the plan, going detail by detail.

When they were done, Nick asked JT, "What do you think, man? This is your home territory. Thoughts?"

"Sure you want to hear, bradah? I mean, it's your plan. And everything is set, right?"

"I'm asking. Spill it. Can you see a better way?"

JT nodded. "Too complicated, too many parts, too many things to go wrong. Remember when we pulled that armed robbery at the Wendy's on 12th? It went smooth as silk cuz we cut it down to a bare minimum of moving parts. We hit it and cleaned out the cash registers in broad day-light. Disappeared before you cops had a clue. Bellagio is packed with off-duty cops and retired cops on every damn floor. The place has security like Fort Knox. You really think you're gonna slide on out of there un-touched without a firefight? No way."

Nick sighed. He knew JT was right. Truth be told, he wanted a fight. He was hoping to pick one. He'd lost focus. "My bad. You're right. What do you suggest?"

"If it was me, I would put people in the underground lot in cars, close to the elevator. No way they're going to deliver a high-priced call girl to the front door. Bad for business to have hookers in short dresses and no panties coming through the front door next to Mr. and Mrs. White Bread America. You feel me?"

Nick nodded. "So she comes in the basement, and...?"

"And we station people near the elevators, watching. Think of it like an armored car robbery. We watch for the delivery guy and never let them enter the building. Hit them before they get into the place. Whoever gets her into a car first gets the hell out of the parking lot. The rest of the lookouts get into their cars and run interference, locking up the exits so the cops or security can't follow. Ya dig, bradah?"

Nick looked frustrated. "Damn, why didn't I see that? Yeah, man. Makes a lot of sense, man. Quick and clean. Bexx doesn't even have to be in the room. They won't know who she is, and they never have to see her anyway. Damn it! This is a much better plan."

JT smiled. "Can't change a tiger's stripes, bradah. You're still a cop at heart. Can't make you into a criminal... least not entirely. It's a mindset."

Nick stared at the diagram of the Bellagio, nodding. "Thanks, JT. This is much cleaner. Makes a lot more sense. What do you think?" Nick asked Bexx.

Bexx agreed and now had a new understanding of why Nick held JT in such high regard. He was exactly as Nick had described.

She said, "When the team wakes up, we'll brief them of the new plan. Let's run through it one more time. I need to be able to answer any questions they have."

Nick turned to Special K. "Do you see anything? It's your sister we're going after. Speak up if you see anything. We need everyone's eyes on this plan."

"How many elevators does the Bellagio have that access the parking garage?" she asked.

"There are elevators on all four levels of the parking garage. We'll need to post someone close to each elevator and on each floor. We have no way of knowing which level Svetlana will arrive on. Also, we don't know if she'll be dropped off or escorted into the hotel to make sure she doesn't try to escape. Depends on how much they've broken her down, I guess. She may not try to escape at all," Nick explained. "I would guess they'll take her to the top level. That would be the easiest to park and drop off. It usually has the least amount of traffic. We need at least one car per level. We have the two vans, so we need two more."

JT spoke up. "Three! You have three. You can use my Hummer. I'll drive. I am in, bradah. No way I'm sitting on the sidelines for this. I'll be careful. Have no plans to go back in the pen. He motioned to Special K. "You can ride with me. Everyone else will know what she looks like. I'll need your eyes to look for her."

Special K nodded but looked at Bexx. "Is that okay with you, Commander?"

Bexx nodded yes.

CHAPTER EIGHTEEN

Nick called The Driver the next day and let him know the change in arrangements. They'd still rent the rooms and make the plans with Izadi as if their original plan was in place. The façade would still work in their favor. Instead, they would need another vehicle, and the plan was to snatch Svetlana before she ever entered the hotel. When they were sure they had her, they'd return the vehicle and leave for Moses Lake in the vans.

Meanwhile, JT told Nick he had some errands to run. He came back with four sports walkie-talkies.

"Communications, bradah. Gotta be able to communicate between cars. That way, we'll know who has her and when. Just like back in the day. We'll be able to regroup afterward and still be able to let each other know what's going on. Their range is short, but they won't show up on cellular repeaters. No one will be able to track us if your phone number doesn't show up on the repeater. Also, you want to make sure no one has a phone on during the operation. Cops can track the phones through the cell towers and pin us down to a small area. Even if we don't speak on the phones, they still can be tracked. If this Director of yours is as tied into the system as you think, we'll have to take every precaution." He handed the extra sports talkies to Nick, Bexx, and Special K, keeping one for himself. "Whoever is the driver for the fourth car gets that one." He motioned to Special K. "They're all set to channel number six and have new batteries. All set."

Nick smiled. "Excellent idea. Anything else we need to do?"

"License plates. We need to swap the vehicle's license plates out with ones we acquire from a friend of mine."

"These new plates will be stolen, I assume," said Nick.

"They'll be 'borrowed,'" JT said, smiling.

"Just have to make sure they're 'borrowed' right before we go; otherwise, they'll show up as stolen on the cops' databases. Once it's known

Svetlana has been taken, the cops will be out in force, checking the cameras in the parking terrace and the streets nearby. We have to be careful. Is that an option? Can your friend get us fresh plates?"

"Can do. Costs a bit more, but yes, it can be done."

"Best if they all come back to a rental car company as well. Ties them up even more when they do figure it out," Nick said. "Which reminds me, I'm going to call The Driver now and have him plot a way out of the city that avoids traffic cameras as much as possible. We need to disappear once we have her."

JT smiled. "Now you're thinking, bradah. I like it."

Nick called The Driver and made the request. The Driver began the search for a way out of the city without traffic cameras and informed Nick the appointment with Izadi had been made. Svetlana would be scheduled to arrive at the Bellagio at nine PM.

Nick thought more about what JT had said about too many moving parts. He said, "I have a suggestion we cut out even more of the original plan." Bexx nodded. "What is it?"

"I think if we do get Svetlana and no one gets injured, we bolt. Let's have everything packed and ready, so if we're successful, we leave Vegas immediately. The Driver will plot the course, and we roll out caravan style until we're clear. We can stop at a rest area or truck stop and change the license plates back and dump the new rental. Then nothing we do will come back to JT."

"Excellent idea! Let's plan on that and then improvise later if we need to," she said.

It was six PM in Vegas—a couple of hours to go, and they would set the plan in motion. Nick wanted to be in place an hour before the appointment was scheduled.

~

Arthur was set. He'd rented a car, cleaned out their bank accounts, and told his wife to pack enough clothes for a couple of days' vacation in the Cayman Islands. She protested to the no-notice vacation. She was still receiving treatments for her bone cancer and needed to continue treatment to survive. Arthur feared she wouldn't make it through the week if they stayed another day. Nick's phone call requesting documentation on the missile facility clean-up had piqued his curiosity. The more he looked at the timing of the clean-up, the more alarmed he became. It was clear to him the momentary feeling of freedom he'd felt when his boss had died was a façade. The Director, the real Director, was still out there planning, plotting, and scheming. He knew from his years in service to The Director's program manager, the man was ruthless and resourceful. He'd never allow such a betrayal as Arthur had committed without an immediate and ruthless punishment. The fact that he was still alive made him even more afraid. Whatever The Director had planned would be seamless and brutal. They had to get moving before it was too late.

Arthur had rented a black Chevy Tahoe to handle all their luggage and the emergency medical supplies his wife would need. He'd booked two tickets to the Cayman Islands as a diversion and told his wife that was their destination as well. He told no one their real destination was White Fish, Montana. He assumed their phones were tapped and the house as well and that The Director would expect them to try to make it to the Ronald Reagan Washington National Airport in Washington, D.C.

Arthur loaded up the Tahoe with his wife's luggage and medical supplies and then helped her into the vehicle. The sun had just gone down, and they were leaving under the cover of darkness, hoping no one noticed and no one was watching. The terror he felt was hard to hide. His wife knew something was wrong, but he wouldn't answer her questions honestly. They'd been married long enough for her to know he was upset and the trip must be very important to him—obviously much more than the "long needed vacation" he'd claimed it would be.

Arthur pulled out of the driveway of their colonial style, four-bedroom home and headed to Interstate Sixty. He meant for anyone watching to think he was, in fact, headed to the airport. He even planned to pull in the short-term parking lot and then pull right back out and begin their desperate run for the hills of Montana.

Once on the interstate, Arthur couldn't keep the Tahoe under the speed limit. The need to put as much distance between him and the Washington, D.C. area was intense. He was running for his life, and he knew it. Speed limits seemed ridiculous.

In a remote office, The Director was listening to Arthur and his wife through their rental car's OnStar remote vehicle control system. He liked the fear he heard in his future ex-employee's voice as he tried to explain to his wife the urgency of their trip. The Director was waiting for the right time—the precise moment when Arthur's fear would be at its highest. He wanted to hear the final words Arthur and his wife would scream when they realized their trip had been planned much too late and much too poorly. He smiled a wicked smile as Arthur approached the point of no return. The Director had no intention of letting Arthur get anywhere near the airport, much less begin his ill-planned ruse. None of it would matter in a few short, violent moments.

Arthur took the on-ramp, keeping left at the fork and continued on to exit fourty-three A. He followed the signs directing him to Washington, D.C. He merged onto Interstate Sixty-four East and then used the right two lanes to take exit one-hundred seventy-seven for Interstate Two-hundred ninety-five toward the airport. He had moments left to live.

The Director's voice came over the vehicle's OnStar system. "Hello, Arthur," a voice said through the vehicle's speaker system. "Planning a trip?"

Arthur jumped at the unexpected sound of another voice in the vehicle. It took him a moment to realize where the voice had come from.

His wife said, "What was that?"

Arthur asked, "Can I help you?"

"I doubt that, Arthur; although, you have been helpful in the past. Now you have become a very naughty boy... yes, a very naughty boy indeed."

"What do you want?"

"I want to know what you've told The Wild Card. What dirty little secrets have you shared, Arthur?"

"Nothing. I've told him nothing."

Arthur's wife asked, "What is he talking about, Arthur? Who is The Wild Card?"

"Yes, Arthur, why don't you tell her? What am I talking about? I'd like to hear your version of the events of the past few months. Does she know about your private sessions with Mr. Hauer? My, what a naughty boy you have been behind her back. Go ahead tell her how you two share a mutual experience in this life—one few men in your place would admit to. I want to hear you tell her, Arthur. Tell her the dirty little deeds you did to pay for her expensive medical bills."

Arthur tried to shut off the vehicle's stereo system, turning the volume all the way off. It didn't work. The voice was still there, taunting him.

"Come on, Arthur," the voice continued. "You can tell her, or I will."

"Don't listen to him," Arthur said. He was unaware the vehicle had been slowly accelerating since his conversation with the mysterious voice had begun.

"Oh no, *do* listen to me, Mrs. Look," the voice continued. "Arthur, I'm waiting. Let's hear your little confession to the Mrs. I want to hear you explain the nearly daily lunch-hour trysts you had with your former boss. Come on, Arthur. Share with her your secret life."

Arthur's wife now looked at him, horrified. "What's he talking about, Arthur? Tell me now! What's he talking about? What did you do to pay for my medical bills? Tell me!" she screamed.

The voice laughed mischievously over the vehicle's speaker system. "Arthur has been a very bad boy, I'm afraid."

The vehicle was now approaching one hundred miles per hour, and Arthur still was unaware of its gradual acceleration. The Director's ruse was working perfectly.

The vehicle was approaching exit forty-three on Interstate Two-hundred ninety-five. Arthur took the exit. He still hoped somehow, they would escape. The vehicle approached the one hundred and fifteen miles per hour mark, gently increasing speed while The Director kept himself entertained.

"Arthur, do you ever wonder if you would have subordinated yourself in such a manner had your wife not been sick? I mean, do you ever occasionally think back to those moments with Hauer and secretly admit to yourself you enjoyed it?"

Arthur said nothing. His wife looked at him, shaken by the realization of where the conversation was headed with the anonymous voice in the vehicle. She suddenly recalled events she had suppressed, conversations with Arthur that'd made no sense. She had dismissed her suspicions of Arthur and blamed them on her illness. Now she knew he'd been hiding something from her. She could see from the look in his eyes the voice was speaking the truth about Arthur—a truth he'd been trying desperately to hide.

"Arthur, it has been a pleasure to have you as an employee. I must say, I did enjoy watching you pleasuring Hauer. I have each and every session—as you preferred to call them—recorded. My, your oral skills did become quite exemplary, didn't they?"

Arthur screamed in frustration, "Shut up! Shut up! Shut up!"

The voice came back over the speakers. "Oh, Arthur, isn't this your exit? Exit forty-three A is just ahead, and then onto Interstate Ninety-five. Isn't that right, Arthur?"

The Director had planned this moment with exquisite detail. The exit was a sharp loop that required no real skill under normal driving conditions, but the top heavy Tahoe was now traveling one hundred and twenty miles per hour and would never successfully negotiate the curve. The last moments of Arthur's life were spent trying to keep the vehicle on the road. His efforts were valiant but meaningless. The centrifugal force of the vehicle's inertia in the curve was beyond his skill to control. Arthur and his wife hit a cement barrier with no time to slow down. The vehicle's airbags inflated violently. The explosive cartridges worked perfectly. Arthur and his wife survived the initial impact. They were unconscious when the car that'd been following them pulled up behind them and the driver exited his car. He carried two bottles and a fire extinguisher. One bottle was full of rubbing alcohol, which he poured all over the interior of the vehicle. The other was a bottle of Cachibaché Malbec. The driver stepped back from the vehicle and tossed in a lit match. The vehicle was immediately engulfed in blue flames. When the driver was satisfied Arthur, and his wife had died in the fire, he extinguished the flames with the fire extinguisher and put the bottle of wine on Arthur's soot-covered and smoking lap. The not-so-subtle message had been delivered.

CHAPTER NINETEEN

The team was in place, each taking up a position close to the elevators and with a clear path to the parking garage exits. Bexx had supplied each of them with the most recent photo of Svetlana The Driver had been able to locate in the Hessen police files. JT and Special K didn't need the photo, but she gave them one anyway, just in case. Better to be prepared and cover every base. JT had no idea what Svetlana looked like, and Bexx wanted everyone's eyes searching for her.

They waited, silently watching every woman who walked toward the elevators. As the deadline for the appointment drew closer, the team's anxiety also grew. Nick conducted a radio check when there were ten minutes remaining before the scheduled meeting. All of the radios were working well, and everyone sounded loose and focused. Three minutes later, on the third floor of the parking garage, a man exited a Black Mercedes AMG GLS63. He walked to the right rear passenger door and opened it and held out his hand for the woman inside to hold as she exited the vehicle. JT and Special K had the third level of the parking terrace and were watching the pedestrian traffic in the garage when Svetlana stepped out of the Benz. JT noticed her first.

"Hey, is that her? The woman in the silver see-through dress?"

Special K looked hard at her sister. "It could be. If it is, she's lost a lot of weight, and her hair is a different color."

"That's a working girl, no doubt about it—a high end one, as well. Let's get out and get closer. I'm going to put my arm around you. Act like we're together as we get closer. All I want you to say is yes if it's her. Nothing else... understand?"

Special K nodded, and they both exited JT's Hummer. They walked carefree, weaving and joking as any couple would, looking at each other and talking. As they approached the glass enclosure that surrounded the elevators, they stopped and turned toward Svetlana and her male escort. Special K watched her approach while JT held open the door for the approaching couple.

Special K finally recognized her sister, turned to JT, and said, "Yes" as she looked into his eyes.

The transformation from the smiling happy couple to aggressors there to end Svetlana's involuntary servitude was instantaneous. JT's smile disappeared as he dropped into a fighting stance. The male escort was a professional and sensed something had changed in the couple's demeanor. The violence of the throat punch was delivered in a blur of motion that was too fast for his brain to comprehend. The escort dropped to the floor. JT had immediately recovered and was already in position to deliver the next punch as the man dropped to the floor. He bounced on the balls of his feet, ready for a battle that never came.

Special K grabbed Svetlana and said, "Svetlana, it's me, Katerina!"

Svetlana had been drugged heavily for more days than she could recall. She felt like this was another dream—one of many where she'd imagined being rescued.

She shook her head and said, "No, leave me alone."

Katerina started to fight with Svetlana, trying to convince her she was really there. Svetlana became hysterical and screamed, drawing unwanted attention their way. JT recognized they had very little time left to get Svetlana into the Hummer and make their escape. Svetlana had to be subdued and silenced immediately. A swift, simple carotid strike dropped her to the concrete and silenced her. He picked her up in his arms and walked rapidly to the Hummer.

"Open the rear passenger door," he said to Special K.

When it was open, he slid Svetlana carefully inside and pulled out a roll of duct tape and wrapped her hands and legs with it, sticky side out. It would restrain her and not stick to her skin. When her arms and legs were secured, he did the same to her mouth, wrapping the tape around her head and covering her mouth. They had to get going. Security had undoubtedly watched the incident on camera. The window to escape successfully was already closing.

JT yelled to Special K, "Get in now." Once inside, he said, "Buckle up, and then tell the team we have her."

The Hummer roared to life as he pulled out of the parking spot and into the driving lane to exit the parking lot.

Nick was sitting in one of the vans, watching the people enter the elevators on level two when he heard Special K announce over the small, hand-held radios, "We have her, and we're heading out. Time to go."

Nick jumped on the radio and said, "Copy. All teams, exit the parking lot. Let's go!"

Nick was on the phone immediately to The Driver. "Brother, we need that camera-free route out of the city. Are you ready?"

"The Driver has something better in mind, Nick. Take your time. Take the route of your choice. Leave Vegas in style. No need to rush. Leave like you're The Driver—windows down and waving to the ladies as they frantically call your name and throw their panties."

"What the hell do you mean? We need to be out of here with no information on our direction and no descriptions out to the local cops."

"Understood, brother. I've been recording the last thirty minutes on the traffic cameras' live feeds. I set it to loop and fed it back into their system. The cameras are all turned off now, and the loop is playing. The Driver delivers like a case of Spanish Fly spiking the punch at a high school prom. Everyone will be equally satisfied at the end of the night. No worries. You're in The Driver's capable and experienced hands now. Sit back and relax and watch my fingers do their magic."

Nick let the other drivers know to head to the interstate and they would meet up at the first rest stop. They stopped at Exit 64 on Interstate 15 and pulled into a Love's travel stop, heading to the back of the trucker's parking lot, out of the way of prying eyes. JT carefully picked up Svetlana from the back seat of the Hummer and put her in the back of one of the vans. Bexx told The Mentalist to ride with Svetlana and keep an eye on her. She would undoubtedly be drugged and combative. The teams switched out license plates and were ready to go in less than five minutes.

"Thanks, brother. I owe you one," Nick said.

JT reached out, and they shook hands. "Stay safe, bradah. If you're ever back in Vegas, look me up."

They parted ways. The vans were back on the road, headed north on Interstate 15. JT turned the Hummer south and headed back to Vegas.

As the vehicles pulled onto Interstate 15, Bexx turned to Nick and smiled and then looked into the mirror, looking at her team. They'd recovered Svetlana with no loss, no injuries, and so quickly and stealthfully, it almost seemed surreal. She said as much out loud to all of them.

"Can you believe it?" she asked.

The team all responded, laughing and cheering. Everyone except Nick. Bexx was angry at him.

"What is it now? You're mad because you didn't get to burn down a building? No bolt cutter manicures, so you pout? Why can't you ever be happy?" Her words cut him deeply. He just shook his head and looked out the window. She pulled the van over. "No! I want to know right now, what's wrong?" The van was instantly silent. They had never witnessed an argument between Nick and Bexx.

"You really want to do this right here? Now?"

"Yes, answer me."

"It's too damn easy. That's what bothers me. The Director doesn't let anything go. He doesn't lose. Think, damn it! He went halfway around the world just to kidnap Svetlana to send a message. That's the only reason. To send a damn message. Do you really think we just got away because we planned so well? No way. Either he has another plan, or his attention is somewhere else. Think!" He slammed his fist against his head. "If he isn't expecting us, great, but what is he doing? Where is his attention now? We didn't check Svetlana for trackers. She needs to be stripped of all clothing, all jewelry, all body piercings. That needs to be done immediately. We can't dump her clothes on the side of the road either. It needs to be put in a trash can or another vehicle headed away from us. You're happy because we got away from the Bellagio with no injuries and no fight. Did it ever occur to you maybe that was his plan? To let us have her? He thinks on many levels. A success is supposed to look and feel like one. He wants us to think we won. Can't you see that? You don't win with this guy. You survive, and only if you're very lucky."

Bexx said nothing for several moments, processing what he'd said. "Check her immediately," she said.

The team was stunned, and no one moved. "*Now*! Strip her. Remove everything. Put it in a bag. Let's go! Search her for trackers." Then to Nick, she said, "What will they look like?"

"When Nõn and I found them in Baroota, they'd implanted them between our shoulder blades. Someplace we could not get at them without help. They had to be cut out. We searched our clothes and shoes, and finally, we found them on each other. They looked like a small capsule you'd get out of a pill bottle."

The back door of the van was opened, and The Mentalist stripped Svetlana. Everything went into a bag they were using for garbage. Svetlana had nipple and genital piercings, and The Mentalist asked, "Are we sure they have to be removed as well?"

Bexx looked at Nick questioningly.

"Definitely. This is how he thinks. She's his property. He doesn't let her out without some kind of a leash—some kind of a way to locate her if she escapes."

The Mentalist started to remove the piercings. The nipple piercings came off easily. The genital piercing would not come off.

"It isn't coming off," she said. "It's locked on somehow."

Nick said, "Of course it is. The prick would make it painful to remove. We had to cut ours out. You don't get free from The Director easily or pain-free. Do we have any wire cutters? Any tools at all in the vans?" There were none. "What about your medical kit?" he asked The Mentalist.

She shook her head no.

Nick thought for a minute. "We need to go back to the truck stop. Turn around and go back. They always have tools at truck stops. We can cut it off of her and then put all her clothes and jewelry on one of the trucks. We shouldn't go any further until we know she's cleared of any possible trackers." He turned to the Mentalist. "Make sure you check everywhere—hair, skin, under her nails, ears, everywhere. Cavity search her. Make damn sure she has nothing. If we miss it, The Director will be at our front door before we have a chance to escape."

Bexx was less angry now. Nick's logic made sense in a dark, twisted way. They got into the vans. She looked at him for a moment. He smiled.

"Look, don't make me split more cords of wood to stay in this mindset. I know it isn't all rainbows and unicorns. It's what it takes to survive this prick. Remember how we got here in the first place. I know this asshole. I feel how he thinks. To answer your question, of course I wanted to do more damage back there—burn down the whole damn city if that's what it takes to get him—but reality is, it's Vegas. Every block is like Fort Knox. No way we were coming out of there in one piece once a fight erupted. You're right. We're lucky to have escaped. Now let's make our luck last more than a few moments."

The vans crossed the grass median and turned back toward Love's travel stop.

CHAPTER TWENTY

JT was nearly back inside the Las Vegas city limits when his phone started to blow up. Call after call was coming in.

He answered. "What's up?"

"JT, the cops are all over your gym, man. What happened?"

JT pulled over. "Tell me what you see, bradah."

"Four cars... Vegas Metro. They're out with gauges, and it looks like SWAT is about to breach the door. What happened, bro? You okay?"

"Yeah, I'm good. Thanks for the heads up."

"No problem. Stay safe, bro. Cops don't look happy. Don't let them get all Rodney King up in your ass."

"No worries. Thanks."

JT looked in the Hummer's rear-view mirror. Now what? One time was already up his ass. No going back now.

"Gotta find a place to land, and fast." He spoke softly, already calculating what the next best move would be.

When the vans had pulled into the lot, Nick had Bexx stop and let him out. He ran to the store to look for wire cutters to cut the final piercing off Svetlana. Nick was in line, waiting to pay the cashier, when the sports walkie-talkie on his waist started to static. He reached down to turn it off and then stopped.

He heard JT calling faintly. "Nick, you there?"

"Yeah, I'm here. Hold on. Can't talk right now."

"Got it."

Nick paid for the wire cutters and then walked to the door. Once he was outside, he called JT back. "JT, what's up?"

"Cops made me, bradah. Got a call from a friend. They're at my gym now. Ready to make an entrance like only Five-O can. I'm not even back to the city, and they're there at my gym."

Nick stopped and whispered, "Shit! Already?" He thought, *How the hell did they make that connection already?*

Nick stopped and took a deep breath. "Understood. Come back to the truck stop as fast as you can, bro. Haul ass. We'll be there waiting."

Nick walked back to the vans, trying to control his breathing. That bastard was already on them, but how? There were no cameras, they had stolen plates, and they'd been extremely careful. How did The Director make the connection to JT and the gym already?

He walked up to Bexx and smiled. "So much for the celebration. JT is made. Cops are at his gym now. He called me on the sports walkie-talkie when I was in the store. He didn't even get back to the gym, and they were already there."

"What do we do now?" she asked.

"Stay with the plan. Clean up Svetlana. JT is on his way here. We need to break out the AK pistols. We may have to fight after all. Here are the wire cutters. Get that damn thing off her and in a bag. Make sure The Mentalist checks her closely. You watch it—no slip-ups now. We have to leave here with no trace, or we'll die here in the desert. The Director is onto us somehow."

Bexx and The Mentalist searched Svetlana from head to toe and found nothing more suspicious. They gave the bag to Nick. He walked into the row of trucks, climbed under one of the refrigerated trailers, and forced the bag into a crack between the frame and trailer.

He whispered to himself, "Sorry man, we need to get clear, and you're the lucky truck."

He walked back to the vans and paced, waiting for JT to arrive.

Bexx asked him, "What's next?"

"What's next? Hell if I know. Get everyone loaded in the vans. We need to be gone. As soon as JT shows, we'll talk and go from there. I need to think. Get your team ready for anything. Sorry, I hate to have to burst everyone's happy, little bubble. This is what it means to fight The Director. You can't let up, ever! Get Svetlana dressed. We may need to switch vehicles again, and we don't need a naked woman to draw even more attention to us. Find one of the team who's close to her in size and get her dressed."

Bexx gave the order while Nick paced. What had he missed? They cleared the Bellagio with no issues and made it through traffic—again, with no issues. How could they know about JT's gym already?

Nick dialed up The Driver.

"Driver, we're already in it, man. Cops have made JT. They're at his gym right now. We need to know if they've made us. I need to know how they made him, fast. Was it The Director that clued them in? Get on it, and call me back when you know."

Nick hung up. Moments later, JT drove into the parking lot and pulled up. He got out of the vehicle. "Sorry, bradah. Seems like we always meet under a dark cloud."

"Screw that shit. They made you somehow, but not us... not yet. How, is what bothers me. What did we miss?"

"Don't know, man. Sometimes shit just happens."

"Not this time. Nothing with this guy is a coincidence. He doesn't make these kinds of mistakes."

"What mistakes?"

"Letting the cops do his work. He doesn't want you. He wants me. The girl we saved—that was a message, bro... a message to me. No way he would bring in the cops unless he had to. Nope, either he's desperate, or we missed something. Let's walk around your truck. Maybe we missed something."

They walked around the truck two times before Nick saw it—a small sticker on the left rear corner of the back window. "JT's Gym MMA and Fitness."

"There it is, bro. That's how they were on you so fast. Clean out the Hummer of everything you want. Drive it up to the front lot where the most foot traffic is. Leave your phone, and keep the keys in the ignition, windows down. Then come back. We're out of here. You're with us now if you want to be."

"Hell, yeah. Other choice is a cement cell, counting time, floating kites. I'll pass let's go!"

JT was back in moments while the team loaded into the second van. Bexx had just finished dressing Svetlana and closed up the back door of the first van.

Nick briefed her on what they'd found on the Hummer and what he thought it meant. Then he asked her, "Think we have room for a world-class trainer and tactician on the team?"

She nodded to JT standing in front of the van, his jet black ponytail braided and hanging to his waist. She shrugged. "You mean JT?"

Nick nodded.

She nodded silently.

Nick yelled to JT, "Load up, brother. This van. We gotta get on the road."

Moments later, The Driver called back.

"I got it. It isn't The Director, as far as I can tell. I guess someone at the Bellagio took a cell phone picture of the Hummer as it left the parking lot, and there..."

"There's a sticker on the back window that led them to JT, right?" Nick interrupted.

The Driver was cursing on the other end of the phone. Nick smiled happily while he listened. "Damn it, how do you do that? How did you find that out? I hate the sloppy seconds you serve when I'm least expecting it." The Driver cursed.

"Sorry, bro. Sometimes there's no substitute for being on the ground, eyes on the target. Any word about the vans? Are we made?"

"No. From what I can see, the picture of the Hummer was a lucky break. The only lead they had was the sticker in the back window," The Driver said.

"That's good news. We're back on the road, brother. Keep an ear to the ground, and let me know if things change. While you're at it, wipe any memory of the appointment we made with Izadi from their database. We need to disappear completely. No record of any appointment, background check, nothing. We don't want to give him a hint of what happened. The Director will know it was us. I just don't want to give him a clue of where to look."

"On it, brother. The Driver will make the appointment information disappear like a back-door man in the night after the deed has been done, the package delivered, and another woman is calling my name. 'Driver where are you? I need you,'" he moaned in a feminine voice.

Nick hung up. Shaking his head, he looked out the window.

Bexx said, "What is it?"

"We're clear. Nothing about us is out there. The sticker on the Hummer was their only lead. Someone took a picture of the Hummer and gave it to the cops. Sorry, I missed it."

Bexx asked, "Why did you shake your head?"

"The Driver," Nick said. "You know how everything for him is a sexual conquest."

Bexx laughed and spoke in Russian to the team. They all laughed, and several of the girls patted him on the head and shoulders with apologetic tones in their voices.

"What did you say?" he asked Bexx.

She smiled coyly and said nothing.

A half an hour later, Svetlana woke up, panicked, and began fighting. She opened the back door of the van in an attempt to escape. They were traveling freeway speeds, eighty-five miles per hour. If she'd succeeded, the rescue would have all been a waste. She would have died right there. JT, acting quickly, hopped over the back seat of the van and grabbed her before she could jump out. For a few brief moments, they both teetered on the edge of the door threshold, barely staying inside the van. Bexx tapped the brakes lightly, bringing them abruptly back against the back seat and closing the door at the same time. Once the door was closed, she accelerated. Svetlana fought briefly but soon fell back to sleep.

"You got her, bro?" Nick called out.

"It's all good, bradah. She's sleeping like a baby. I'll stay with her to make sure that doesn't happen again."

About an hour later, The Mentalist looked in the back seat of the van, checking on Svetlana. She turned and spoke to Bexx again in Russian. Bexx smiled. The rest of the girls looked over the back of the rear seat.

"What?" Nick said.

"Your friend is asleep with Svetlana," she said, smiling.

CHAPTER TWENTY-ONE

The rest of the trip back to Moses Lake passed without incident. Svetlana needed constant attention from The Mentalist as the withdrawals from whatever drugs she was on set in. It was a painful trip for her. Nick had his own demons to struggle with. The more he processed the scene at the Bellagio, the more confident he was that something was definitely wrong. They'd missed something. He was sure of it. He talked through it with Bexx as they took turns driving through the night. The more they talked, Nick felt like a dark, ominous cloud was over them. He couldn't shake the feeling.

Bexx tried to console him at first and then realized this was how he processed things. He juggled them — examined them from every angle. Threw them back up into the air and tested out how they felt in context with what had happened. It was maddening for him. He didn't do it because he wanted to. He did it because he was built this way. It did her no good to console him. The best she could do was listen and try to see things from his point of view. It was difficult. He made leaps in connecting the dots that seemed obscure at best and ridiculous if she were honest. But then she reminded herself his connections had found Svetlana — a needle in a stack of needles. What was more, he made the connection to The Director and Izadi. He did all that with nothing more than seeing the connections from seemingly unconnected facts.

When he finally stopped the verbal processing and mental examination, he was silent for a long time. She waited for him to speak, and finally, he did.

"When we get back to the farmhouse, I think we need to get packed and move to the missile facility as fast as we can make it happen. The place is a fortress and in the middle of nowhere. No drone strike will destroy it. The Director won't be able to get to us there. It's our best chance at survival while we plan our next move. When Svetlana is healthy, we need to question her. She may have information that'll help us. Also, I think we need to check in with Arthur if that's possible and see what he knows about any of the remaining projects The Director has in his twisted portfolio."

Bexx agreed it made sense to move to the missile facility and they needed to gather all the information they could on The Director. She didn't mention it to Nick, but she felt their success in liberating Svetlana had been a result of several different things: timing, the element of surprise, a lot of luck, and excellent planning. This was how she processed the events that'd occurred. She couldn't change it any more than Nick could change what he saw. She'd learned, however, to respect his insight even when she couldn't understand it.

They arrived at the farmhouse and settled in. It would be several days before Svetlana would be anything resembling healthy. Meanwhile, after the team took a day to rest up from the trip, Bexx called a meeting to discuss the team's future. They'd agreed to take stock of where they were headed and decide individually if they wanted to continue.

When they were all gathered around the fire — The Driver and Buffy, Nick and JT, and the rest of the team — she began.

"Well, here we are back at the farmhouse. Before we left, we agreed to meet and take a long look at where we were headed as a group after we located and freed Svetlana. Honestly, I didn't expect the mission to go so smoothly." She looked at JT. "No disrespect meant to your own losses, but I expected to return here with much more damage."

JT nodded. "None taken. I made my choice to help out. I knew the consequences could be severe."

Bexx nodded in return. "So now we know. The Director is still out there, and he took Svetlana. I told you each to individually consider what you wanted to do when we returned. The time has come to do just that. I'll go first. I'm staying. I already told Nick I wasn't leaving. I think our work here matters. You've all learned of my true identity and the monetary wealth I've inherited. I chose to live this way. I could live another less difficult and dangerous way, but I want every day of my life to be spent making a difference. Nick and I will remain on this path. Whoever wants to speak next may do so."

JT spoke. "None of you knows me, but I'm in if you will have me. My path is set now. If I go back, I go to prison. This is a much better option than prison."

Special K spoke next. "I'm in. I'll stay."

Bexx said, "Just like that?"

Special K nodded. "Yes, just like that. Svetlana will need me, and I owe you all for the risks we took to get her here safely."

Bexx nodded and then looked at the rest of the team.

One by one, they all restated their commitment to the team. Bexx was proud of them. Nick, on the other hand, shook his head and silently looked into the fire. Bexx knew not to assume she understood what that head shake meant. They all sat quietly around the fire.

Nick broke the silence. "Driver, how soon can you be ready to go? You'd be the hardest to move and set up in the missile facility."

"All ready to go. The Driver is way ahead of you. My entire system here will shut down. Site 'A' will be the missile facility. Servers are on order, upgrades actually. I needed to upgrade. Now it will happen in the facility. Thought about keeping a site 'B' here, but that seems risky, much too risky. So, The Driver is gonna break down the original Bat Cave and close up shop on the farm."

Nick nodded. "Then it's decided. We move to the facility. Personally, I want to move as fast as we can. I feel we're very vulnerable here now. So for me, the sooner, the better."

The next day, Nick got up early and went to the gym. To be back in his routine felt good, he thought to himself as he walked in for what was probably one of the last times. *Gonna miss this place.*

Ali saw him as he approached the door. As soon as he walked in, she said, "How serious were you about buying some of my used equipment?"

"Very serious, why?"

"Just to be clear... you aren't going to be setting up a new gym in the area and becoming a competitor, agreed?"

"Definitely won't be in the area and won't be a competitor."

"What does that mean?"

"Gonna be moving. Thought I told you it was a possibility."

Ali rolled her eyes. "Like I pay attention to everything everyone says in here."

"Apparently, you paid attention to the fact that I wanted your used equipment."

"Apparently I did, so you're interested?"

"Yes, I am. Already said that. You really don't pay attention, do you?"

She rolled her eyes. "I'm going to do some replacement of inventory. What would you want to buy from me?"

"No point in me telling you what I want. Make a list of what you'll replace, add your price for each piece, and I'll tell you what I'll buy," Nick responded. "It's a business, right? See, I was listening."

He smiled and walked to his favorite, now slightly-used bench. When he was finished with his workout and had wiped down the equipment, he walked back to the counter. Ali had the list waiting.

"I need to know as soon as possible what you want on the list. I have another buyer waiting for what you don't want."

Nick looked at the list. "Do you have a pen?" he asked.

Ali handed him a pen.

Nick went down the list and marked off what he wanted with check marks. "How soon will it be available?" he asked as he checked off more items.

"Tomorrow, if you're serious."

"I'll take those items and maybe a few more. I'll be back in an hour with a friend. He may suggest I buy other pieces. Sound like a plan to you?"

She looked at the list. "Did I mention this is a cash only deal? I don't take checks, and credit cards leave a paper trail."

Nick smiled. "I assumed so, yes. I did hear you the first time. This is a business... got it."

"There is seven thousand dollars' worth of equipment here. No offense, but the truck you drive, the clothes you wear... I never would have thought you had an extra dime to spare."

"I buy the pharmaceuticals with cash, don't I?"

She nodded, thinking, *Damn it. I missed that. I should have added a little more to the prices.*

Nick walked to the door. "Be back in an hour. Don't sell anything until I get back."

An hour later, Nick returned with JT.

"This is my friend, JT. I told him about the fire sale you're having. Can we see the list again?"

They looked over the list for a moment. JT pointed at an additional couple of pieces he thought they needed, and Nick handed the list back to Ali with the new items added. "We'll take all of that. When do you need to be paid, and when can we take them off your hands?"

"I need payment by the end of the day. I'll close the gym tomorrow. After we close, you can load them. The new equipment arrives this weekend. Can you have it out by then?"

Nick looked at JT, and they both nodded. He said, "Yes, we'll have it out by then. I'll get you the money and be right back."

They left and went to the nearest bank to withdraw the money from Nick's account. "I know you just lost your gym in Vegas, brother, but now you'll have a new one in North Dakota with us. Bexx and I agree the team could use your expertise. Hope you're up for a new group of warriors to train."

JT smiled a broad smile. "Definitely, bradah!"

Nick smiled. "This will all happen in one shot. The timing is perfect! We're moving at the end of the week anyway. We can just add the weight equipment to the list."

They returned to the gym and paid Ali. "We'll be back to load it all tomorrow night. What time is good for you?"

Ali was counting the stack of hundred dollar bills, making sure Nick hadn't shorted her a single bill. "Closing time! Same as always. You don't get special treatment. I have a business to run!"

CHAPTER TWENTY-TWO

By the end of that week, they were ready to go. They had rented and loaded two large rental trucks with all the household items and the equipment from the Bat Cave. In the end, The Driver thought it would be very careless to leave any of his equipment if The Director did somehow make the connection between Svetlana's disappearance and the farmhouse. When he explained that to Nick, Nick nodded in agreement and smiled. Finally, they were all grasping the seriousness of their adversary.

They pulled out of the farmhouse the next morning early with three trucks total — two from the farmhouse and one loaded with the gym equipment. Nick felt some small amount of relief they were on their way. The sooner they were behind the three-foot concrete walls of the facility, the better.

The trip to North Dakota passed without incident. They made a point to avoid Mosby, Montana. No point in pushing their luck and chance a random encounter with any more of the locals there. The town was too small for the gas station incident to have died down.

Nick smiled at Bexx when he suggested they find another route. "Yes, that might be wise," she replied.

JT listened and asked, "Why? What's so special about Mosby, Montana? Something bad happen there?" He guessed from the team's reaction to his question something had definitely happened. No one would answer him, but they all communicated non-verbally it was an incident that made the small-town worth avoiding. JT smiled. "I see. Don't ask. Don't tell. I've got it." The nervous laughter in the group confirmed his intuition was correct.

Once they arrived at the missile facility, Nick and Bexx entered one of the vehicle entrance tunnels and told the rest of the team to wait outside. They wanted to make sure no one had come in and set more trip wires or booty traps, Nick explained with a disturbing giggle. A couple of hours later, they emerged from the three garage doors above ground, and the unloading of the trucks began. The move was fairly uneventful. There were some changes in the plan they had roughed out for who went where. JT and The Driver were in competition for the best space for their specialties and equipment, but in the end a compromise was found both could live with.

In a week, the entire move was completed, and the team was operational. Nick threw himself into the physical labor of the move, dripping with sweat, carrying boxes and equipment. He enjoyed the brief break from the paranoid fear that they'd missed something. The hard work cleared his mind and allowed him to focus on something other than the nagging feeling that whatever it was they'd missed was right in front of their faces and incredibly important.

Nick became so preoccupied with the move and the success of how it all came together, he demanded that when it was completed they have a movie night as a team so finally everyone would understand the obscure references he constantly made. The Driver and Buffy had set up their latest procurement, a Samsung 8K ultra HD seventy-eight-inch black, curved-screen television. It was an early test version of the next level of 8k technology that had been secretly headed to a wealthy executive's mistress's home when suddenly (and mysteriously) it was rerouted and disappeared somewhere in North Dakota. It was set up and ready to go within hours of arrival at the facility. Nick made a list of movies for the team to watch. He probably should have known it would never go as he'd hoped.

First off, he played *Willow* to explain the Queen Bavmorda reference to Dr. Warsaw. Then *Dune*, again for the Bene Gesserit references to Dr. Warsaw. The girls got it but were less than entertained. Next was *The Princess Bride*. The team was polite but obviously now very bored. Nick decided to pull out *John Wick* and *John Wick 2* - some of each of the Wick movies were spoken in Russian, and he assumed since it was an action flick and Russian dialogue, the team would finally be into one of his movies. He was about to get a rude awakening.

As John Wick pulled into the gas station and Viggo's son walked up and began to speak in Russian, threatening John Wick and asking how much for his car, the team burst into hysterical laughter. Nick was stunned. Bexx explained, wiping tears from her eyes and in-between uncontrolled bursts of loud and raucous laughter, that the Russian spoken by the actors was ridiculous and poorly pronounced. It wasn't threatening at all. It was like listening to 'Yoda speak Russian on Sesame Street while huffing helium. It was that bad. So much for movie night.

The image in Nick's head of the team finally understanding his quotes and style of humor was gone. John Wick would never be the same. Even Svetlana laughed and JT shook his head as he watched the girl's laughter. Finally, he left the room and went back to the sanity of his gym. Nick sat brooding while the team replayed the Russian quotes over and over, laughing hysterically. From then on, when he least expected it, they would repeat the line "Everything has a price, bitch" and answer, "Not this bitch" and then burst out in laughter. Later that night, Bexx tried to apologize to Nick while they lay in bed, still trying desperately to stifle her laughter. Nick rolled over and pretended to fall asleep while she tried to muffle her childlike giggles.

An hour later, Nick rolled over and saw Bexx was asleep, a slight smile still on her lips. He traced the line of her profile with his eyes and watched her breathe. She turned over away from him, and the spell was broken. What had they missed? Nick thought over in his head every tactic The Director had used. First, at Baroota, he'd been lured in with the idea of an off-the-books black ops mission to rescue victims of human trafficking. That hadn't been enough to get him signed on, he realized. It was the promise of carnage—brutal, bloody payback that enticed him. It wasn't the justice the daywalkers spoke of when they faced into reporter's cameras, begging the powers that be to find whoever had wronged them. It was street justice—eye for an eviscerated eye, tooth for a bloody and shattered tooth.

That's what drew him into Baroota's web. He realized as he played back the conversations he had with the extraction team and Nõn that each had been lured to Baroota with a different promise. The team wanted compensation for their efforts in wealth. Nõn wanted to write the story and bring to light for the world the plight of those bought and sold as human slaves. Nick wanted carnage. That was their weakness. That was how The Director exploited them. He somehow understood what each of them desperately desired and promised them exactly that.

The Director not only did it, he did it in a way that they had no desire to question his motives. Nick remembered he knew in his gut it sounded like a ruse. It was way too good to be true, but he didn't care. The idea of finally being able to extract a pound (or more) of flesh from these human trafficking shitbags was too enticing to pass up. He guessed Nõn felt the same about her role, as did the team. That was their weakness, and The Director exploited it exceedingly well.

So what was his plan now? What were Nick's weaknesses now as The Director would see them? It was maddening to try to see himself through someone else's eyes. Nick fell asleep trying to imagine what he would respond to that The Director could use against him.

The next morning, Nick slowly rose into consciousness from a dark, toxic sleep. His head ached, and he had trouble opening his eyes. Eventually, the cobwebs cleared, and he was able to focus. Reality had returned when Bexx shifted in her sleep and rolled over, away from him. What had changed and why, he didn't know. He felt it though. He got up slowly and rolled his feet off the bed. The missile facility was incredibly quiet. He liked the way it felt and sounded. Three feet of concrete in all the exterior walls had a way of making you feel safe, and the depth of quiet reinforced that empirically to his more tactile senses. At last, the ground beneath his feet felt solid... safe. Bexx woke up as well.

Nick dressed and walked up the metal stairs to the above-ground facility. Opening the heavy metal door, he was immediately assaulted with sounds of life and laughter. The team was eating breakfast in the facility's only kitchen. JT was sitting on a countertop, dressed in Under Armor workout gear. He nodded to Nick silently as they made eye contact. Nick nodded back. Nick's mood had changed. That was obvious. The entire team sensed it immediately and assumed he was still brooding from the movie night disaster. Bexx, however, had learned to never assume when it came to Nick. Nõn had told her that, and experience had driven the point home. She could see the change was more than the disappointment he may have felt in the movies' reception. This was darkness. Darkness was back.

Nick grabbed a couple of boiled eggs and a drink and headed to the exterior doors. The noise of the team's laughter and individual conversations was overwhelming. He needed quiet. Bexx watched as he left the building and got up to follow him out. The team became silent, each member looking at the other. What now? Silently passed from one team member to another in an infectious gaze.

The Mentalist rolled her eyes and quietly whispered, "Glad it's her and not me. That's one moody individual."

JT nodded. "If you came from where we came from, saw what we saw, you might understand."

The Mentalist said, "Really? How do you know Nick? He started to briefly explain that you met under some tense conditions."

JT looked down for a minute, deep in thought, recalling the memories. "Well, we were both very different then. You know Nick was a cop?" He looked around the room as everyone nodded. "I wasn't. I was the opposite, and somehow Nick realized as different as we appeared to be, we were the same. I didn't know who he was, but he knew me. He was actually sent to hunt me down and put me back in prison. Ordered to do so, I believe. We lived in the darkness every large city has. The dirt, the grime, the hopeless-ness—and we belonged there... thrived there. Each of us in our different, and from an outsider's point of view, very opposite way. Turned out not to be so opposite, but only Nick saw that."

The team listened silently as JT told them his memories of Nick and how they met. Out of all of them, Svetlana especially listened to what he said. She had a lot to catch up on.

Nick sat down on a concrete retaining wall that separated the three-car garage from the pedestrian entrance for the military personnel that had never used the facility. He looked at the metal turnstile that controlled the entrance into the above-ground building. Memories flooded back from his time in a restricted area, controlling access into a nuclear facility that no longer existed.

Bexx sat down next to him and smiled as she put a hand on his thigh. "What's up?" she asked.

Nick closed his eyes and was silent. Finally, he said, "It is so weird to me how that feels when you put your hand on my leg. It is so different with you than it has ever felt." He stared at her hand, expecting to see something that would explain it—mystified.

Bexx smiled. "You aren't answering me. What's going on?"

"Sorry, I'm not avoiding answering you. Just let me be in this moment for a few moments more," he said, staring at her hand.

CHAPTER TWENTY-THREE

Bexx asked "So what do you want to do, then?" After Nick finished explaining why he had been so gloomy.

"I don't know. All I know is, somehow The Director always seems to know how to exploit the people he uses. He does it in plain sight, hiding in their blind spot. Sounds contradictory, I know, but it makes sense when you look back. In Baroota, he used what each of us wanted against us to get us to where he wanted us. Nõn and I escaped... barely.

At Cachibaché, he brought in those people to be Dr. Warsaw's patients, using their desire to be free from their phobias against them and then providing just the opposite. He employed the Bene Gesserit bitch to kill them with their fears. None of them would have survived if we hadn't intervened. Now he has sent me a message with the kidnapping of Svetlana.

What bothers me is, somehow we've won the day again. We found her, rescued her, and returned to Moses Lake unscathed. How's that possible? And now we're here at the missile facility he bought, moved in and comfortable, just like we'd hoped. This cannot be an accident. It feels like we're exactly where he wants us to be, feeling like he wants us to feel. Safe."

"So what should we do then? I see what you're saying. I understand how it looks to you, not saying I agree with you. I can't make the connections you seem to make. To me, we escaped Las Vegas barely and only because we changed the plan at the last minute. We wouldn't have fared so well had we stayed with the original plan. Don't you agree?"

Nick was silent for some time, mulling over what she said. "The last minute," he muttered, staring off into the fields that surrounded the missile facility. He cleared his throat and began. "I don't need you to understand what I'm saying. I need you to realize it's there. You don't have to see it or feel it. Roll your eyes when I leave the room, fine. Shrug your shoulders when the rest of the team wonders why you tolerate me. But remember, you have said many times you don't understand what I see or how, but it's there. We found Svetlana. We took this missile facility. And before you bounced halfway around the world with Nõn, I survived Baroota.

I know when I have defeated The Director, and I know what it feels like to be set up by him. I just hope I can figure this out before someone else gets killed. He told the sniper team to target us, me and Nõn first. Think about that. How did he know to do that? He knew we were headed here before we were actually here. Think about what that implies."

Bexx thought silently about what Nick had said. It was a little bit frightening if he was right, and the more he detailed what felt wrong, the more she agreed. It felt very wrong. Then they were very much in great danger still. She felt suddenly very vulnerable, sitting outside in the open, unprotected.

Nick watched her as the realization hit her of what he had said, what it meant on many levels. "We, you and I, need to plan very carefully and in secrecy. We can only trust each other. No one else. Do you agree?"

Bexx nodded. "I do agree, but our strength is in the different points of view we each bring to the table. We all have a unique skill set, and the more narrow we focus and exclude the others, the more we risk not being able to utilize their skills to the benefit of the team."

"I agree," Nick said. "How about a compromise? We start with you and me for now. As needed, we can add others."

Bexx nodded grimly. Nick began. "So let's talk through it. What could The Director be using against us now? And then when we figure that out, we need to determine how could he see it as a trait to be exploited. How does he know us better than we do? Once we figure that out, we need to figure out a way to take advantage of his knowledge of us. It will be exhausting."

Bexx laughed. "I'm tired already just trying to wrap my head around what you just said. What's our first step?"

"We need to talk through everything that happened at Baroota and Cachibaché and now Vegas. We need to examine it from every angle and try to see what he saw." Nick continued. "So, Baroota. Now that I look back on it, it started way before I realized I was being targeted. I suspected something was up, but I didn't see it clearly. The Director hid right in front of me."

Bexx asked, "How?"

Nick began to describe the details of the dinner at the Mash House. When he finished, Bexx asked, "So what you are saying, if I understand you correctly, is The Director used a proxy within a proxy?"

Nick nodded. "Yes, a feint within a feint, with probably a few more layers added to that I'm still not even aware of. A ruse, within a ruse, within a ruse. That's what makes it so hard to identify what's really going on versus what you find. Each layer you peel back is just that, another layer. And they all seem legit."

"How will we know when we get to the end of the feints?" Bexx asked a bit mystified.

"Simple. The Director is dead," answered Nick. "As long as he's alive, the threat will exist."

"Okay, now what?" Bexx asked.

"Now we need to see what Svetlana can tell us about her time in The Director's grasp, and then when we're done, we need her to contribute."

"Contribute how?"

"She was a student at a German university when she was abducted, and her specialty was finance. We need to use her skills along with The Driver and Buffy to locate and track The Director." Nick smiled a mischievous smile and then stood up and stretched. "Auughh, I'm stiff. Who knew moving would be such a workout?"

He reached out a hand to Bexx and helped her up.

"When do you want to talk to Svetlana?"

"Now. Let's do it now. The Driver will need some time to set up shop, so until then, let's make the most of our time," Nick said.

They turned and walked back into the facility. Just as Nick was about to open the door, he stopped and turned to Bexx. "I think we should compartmentalize this from now on. Until we get a handle on what's going on, let's be very selective about what we share with who. That way when we shake the tree, we'll know where whatever falls out came from. Does that make sense?"

Bexx paused for a minute, thinking over what he had said. Finally, she nodded, yes. Nick opened the door.

Inside the facility, they could hear JT talking to Svetlana. The rest of the team had fallen silent, listening.

"So you were in prison? And Nick put you there?" asked Svetlana.

"I was in prison, Nick did not put me there. I put myself there. It took me a while to understand that. For a long period of time, I felt persecuted — wronged — and then one day that all changed. I realized I'd made choices, knowing the consequences would be severe. I made those decisions. I was a leader. People looked to me for leadership. When I realized what that meant, what it really meant, I saw I had to change. I couldn't complain about how I'd been wronged by the system as a leader when I knowingly made the choices that put me in prison. How was that leadership? Taking credit for the success but not the consequences. That's not being a leader."

Svetlana nodded. "What was prison like?"

JT shrugged. "Prison was like prison. There's nothing in your life I can compare it to... to help you gain an understanding. Make sense?"

Svetlana shrugged and shook her head no.

JT said, "For example, I could ask you what was it like to be abducted? And be forced into sexual slavery. What could you compare that to, to help me understand it?"

Svetlana nodded, she understood. There are some experiences that just are what they are. There are no comparisons.

Nick and Bexx walked into the room. Everyone was silent, acting as if they'd been caught doing something wrong.

Nick spoke up. "What JT isn't telling you is that he's the exception. He was and is a gifted leader. I realized that immediately when I started to interview him. He holds himself accountable because he knows who he is. To be anything less would be a lie. JT is a lot of things, but a liar isn't one of them."

No one commented. Everyone was uncomfortable with the relationship the two men shared. To see Nick through JT's eyes and memories was difficult. They all thought of Nick as unhinged and a bit alarming. To see him as a cop, a protector, obeying the rules of society, was a huge stretch. On the other hand, to see JT as Nick described him versus how he had been was also a stretch. They instantly trusted JT more than Nick.

Nick turned to Svetlana. "Do you have a minute? There are a few things I'd like to clear up about your abduction and time spent with The Director's people. Bexx will listen in to make sure I don't miss anything." Svetlana nodded. Nick said, "Let's go somewhere a little more private."

Several hours later, Nick had finished. Svetlana was exhausted and went to her room. Bexx waited for her to leave and then looked at Nick, questioning. "Was that what you expected?"

Nick shook his head. "No, that wasn't what I expected. I have more questions, not less. I'm going to take Svetlana with me tomorrow when I go to set up our post office box. Maybe JT too. The drive will be good for me to think."

CHAPTER TWENTY-FOUR

Getting Svetlana to go for a drive with Nick and JT was a lot harder than Nick had planned on. She flat out refused to go. Finally, it took a few quiet words from JT, and she agreed, but on the condition, she sat by the door. They eventually all crammed into the ancient Yota and began the trip to the small post office. No one spoke for some time. The silence was uncomfortable, and finally, JT asked, "Where did you pick up this fine piece of machinery?"

"Cost me a couple hundred bucks. Wasn't running when I bought it. Just needed a new coil, and it was good to go. Missing your Hummer?"

"Yeah, I miss it, especially now, crammed into this POS driving in the middle of nowhere with an ex-cop at the wheel. Who knew?"

Nick laughed. Svetlana looked out the window at the bleak North Dakota landscape and said nothing while Nick and JT continued to playfully exchange comments about the ancient Yota and its rusted and worried appearance.

When they finally arrived at the tiny post office and general store, JT raised his eyebrows but said nothing. Nick laughed. "Welcome to civilization, my friend. You're a long way from Las Vegas!"

JT nodded grimly. "Could be a lot worse. I could've been in the gym when the SWAT teams hit the door."

Nick nodded. They went to the small store first and loaded up on supplies. When the food was loaded into the bed of the truck, Nick went into the post office. Svetlana and JT had already gone in just ahead of him. The single employee sat behind the desk and asked if she could help them.

"I need to open a post office box. We just moved into a place on the outskirts of town," Nick said.

The postmaster replied, "I'll need a form of picture ID and the address where you are staying. There are some additional forms you'll need to fill out."

When Nick was done, and his new identification was accepted, the postmaster said, "Oh, I think I may have an item here for you already. It came general delivery a week or so ago, care of your name. No address was listed. Just the name, sent general delivery, which is very odd."

Nick stared at JT and then Svetlana. "No one knows we're here."

JT went to the door and looked outside. A few moments later, he said, "Looks clear."

Svetlana said nothing as Nick stared at her. She showed no emotion, nothing. For a moment, Nick wondered about their conversation the night before. Was she lying? Could she be part of The Director's plan? His mind raced, running through the police reports Special K had read, the entire process of Svetlana's abduction, and then the search for her and her eventual rescue.

Nick came to two conclusions immediately. Neither was good.

The postmaster brought a medium-sized box to the counter and placed it between her and Nick. "There you are. Glad to have that off my shelves."

The comment seemed threatening to Nick as if somehow the postmaster was in on some scheme. He looked at Svetlana and saw she was looking at the postmaster, smiling. The look they exchanged seemed to have more significance than a casual glance. Nick looked at the return address on the box and saw it was mailed for Arthur Look and sent by a legal office in Washington, D.C.

Thinking quickly, Nick said, "Ahh, my good friend, Arthur, of course." Then, turning to Svetlana, he said, "Svetlana, would you carry the package to the truck for me?"

He watched her reaction. She seemed more guarded than before. JT was still at the door and had immediately picked up on the change in both of their demeanors.

Svetlana said nothing. Looking away from Nick, she didn't move a muscle. Finally, he picked up the box and handed it to her. "Ready?" he said, smiling.

Svetlana could see he was smiling; however, the look in his eyes frightened her. It reminded her of the men who abducted her. They smiled too, but their eyes were cold and evil.

She finally reached out for the box, and when she had a firm grip on it, Nick turned away and walked to the door. "Let's go," he said as he walked past JT.

The drive back to the facility was even more ominous. The silence in the small cab of the truck was oppressive as no one spoke. The package had its effect on each of them for different reasons.

When they arrived at the facility, Nick walked in first, followed by Svetlana and JT walking side by side. Bexx was sitting at the table. Nick momentarily flashed back to placing the body parts he removed from Sgt. Schidel right in front of where Bexx was seated.

Nick closed his eyes for a moment and then spoke. "Commander, our trip to the post office was very interesting. Seems we have a package from Arthur that was sent several days ago."

The tone of Nick's voice, along with the use of her title and not her name, made it clear. Things were suddenly very serious. Bexx nodded to the rest of the team and then looked to the door. They all left immediately. Nick asked Svetlana to sit down and went to the stack of kitchen drawers that contained the cutlery they all used to eat and prepare food.

He removed a small knife and handed it to Svetlana. "Would you open the box, please?" Nick asked politely, his tone measured and careful. He watched her every move and gesture.

Svetlana began to cry but nodded she would. In Nick's mind, she was already guilty. He didn't know how, but her behavior spoke volumes. Somehow, she was in with The Director, and she was caught. He watched as she sliced through the brown paper that covered the box and removed it, placing it to the side as tears rolled down her cheeks. When she was done opening the package and had removed the contents and placed them on the table, she sat quietly weeping.

Finally, she managed to speak quietly. "What have I done?"

An hour had passed; the roller coaster of emotions they each had felt had taken its toll on the crew that had gone to the post office. JT was in his gym, working the speed bag with a fury that spoke volumes. Bexx and Svetlana were outside talking quietly while Nick sat at the table reading the volumes of paperwork that had been inside the mysterious box. The top sheet of several hundred pieces of paper was a short letter from Arthur.

Nick, hoping for my sake you never read this. But you have impressed on me to never let my fate be in someone else's hands again. If you do read this, it means we didn't make it. My wife and I tried to escape, but it didn't work out. I left this box of documents with my attorney with instructions to send it to the missile facility in North Dakota if for any reason I died or disappeared. Apparently, I've died, or you would not be reading this. Enclosed is everything from Hauer's office I found relating to Baroota and Cachibaché. As you can see, there are several other code names mentioned. Since I'm dead, I can only assume The Director has been watching you as well... and our meetings. I think you know what this most likely indicates. Since you are at the facility, you're safe for the moment, but The Director now knows where you are and who is with you. The question is, how? How did he accomplish this? It wasn't until Hauer was dead I realized the camps weren't his idea. The Director is still out there, and he is coming. Good luck to you and yours. Hope these documents provide some intel. Since I'm gone, I guess that is as good a place to start as any. Look into my death. Know that it wasn't an accident; although, I'd assume it will look that way. Hope you get the bastard. Arthur

Nick put everything back in the box and went to the basement of the facility to speak with JT. When they were done talking, they both came back upstairs and went outside, looking for Bexx and Svetlana. They found them walking slowly and speaking in their native language on the far end of the chain-link fence that surrounded the facility.

Bexx spoke to Nick as he walked up rapidly. "Can't it wait?"

"No, it can't wait. This has to be now, and they need to know what we're up against," Nick said, nodding to JT and Svetlana. He tried to explain the situation as best he could.

When he was done, they were all silent, even Bexx. Somehow his description of the situation made it sound like he was really losing it and quite insane. Hearing it from him was different. It sounded delusional. Bexx began to wonder if it was all paranoia as Nick searched each of their eyes desperately for some sign they believed him. Maybe even Arthur was infected by Nick. What if he'd just died and it had nothing to do with The Director? Bexx kept those thoughts to herself. She had to remind herself she had completely bought into the danger they felt the previous day, and nothing had really changed except Nick's desperate description of the events at the post office.

Later that night, Nick lay in bed staring at the ceiling of their new home. Metal conduit ran from room to room, secured with bolts to the monstrously thick concrete. He thought about the construction of the site and wondered if any of the construction crews were still alive.

His mind wandered, and finally, he spoke quietly. "Are you awake?"

Bexx immediately answered, "Yes."

"Was my performance convincing?"

Bexx rolled over and looked at him curiously. "What performance?"

"In front of Svetlana and JT. Did I sound insane... desperate?"

"That was an act?" Bexx whispered, astonished.

Nick said nothing for some time. "I don't know who we can trust anymore. Svetlana's account of her abduction doesn't fit. What if she is part of this? What if we were meant to locate her and bring her here? Think about that. The Director made her a victim, knowing we would buy into that, come to her rescue, and come with all hands, ready for a war. He planned it to draw us out, and it worked. What I don't know... is Svetlana just a part of his plan to draw us out or..." He paused.

"Or?" Bexx asked.

"Or is she working with him? Is she a hired hand?" Nick whispered as he turned and faced Bexx.

Bexx held her breath. Neither option had occurred to her. She looked at Nick intensely, searching his eyes. "So that was an act?"

"Yes, if she is a mole sent here to be a spy for The Director, she can report back to him that I'm losing it, cracking under the pressure. If she isn't, and someone else is a spy, word will get around, and they'll report back to The Director I am cracking up. Either way, it's a ruse."

Bexx took a deep breath. "Well, to answer your question, yes, it was very convincing. I was completely convinced. Did you have to push her so hard?"

"Yes, I had to see if she would fight back or submit. A woman who has been truly forced into the sex trade would most likely crumble. She fell apart, but is it an act? A plan? Part of The Directors plan? I can't honestly say. He's a clever bastard, and she may be an academy award winning actress for all I know. I had no idea my wife, my dead wife, was in on Camp Baroota until I saw it with my own eyes. So yes, stay convinced I'm crazy and watch her, watch everyone, until we figure this out." Nick smiled. "For now, Nick is cracking up. Run with that. It shouldn't be too hard to sell." He smirked and then giggled. "Gotcha big time, Scully."

"What?" Bexx asked.

"Nothing. More movie humor, that's all."

Bexx rolled her eyes and lay her head on his shoulder as he put his arm around her. Tracing the outline of the wolf head tattoo with her fingers on his chest, she said, "So what now, crazy man?"

They stayed up for several hours afterward, talking.

CHAPTER TWENTY-FIVE

The next few days were pretty quiet in the facility. The team settled into a routine of training that now included a couple of hours in the gym under JT's guidance. Bexx pulled him aside one day and asked if he had any ideas on a routine for Svetlana. She was incredibly emotionally fragile, and they needed her to be able to step up and contribute to the hunt for The Director. Bexx explained that Svetlana had no previous experience with the tactical kind of training they did, both physically and mentally. Her limited time in any gym had been spent in spin and step classes.

JT nodded. "I know the type, both men and women, who work out only for appearances, not realizing the martial side. The reality that they're training for combat. No matter what, it all comes down to survival. Whether it's for health or combat, it all comes back to surviving."

Bexx nodded, relieved he understood this intuitively. "Do you think you could help?"

"Definitely. First thing I need to do is reach her mind. The body follows the mind. If I can't get her mind to buy in first, then I'll be wasting her time and mine. Give me a few days to listen to her and understand her mentality, and I'll get back to you."

Bexx nodded and then said quietly, "Also, keep this between us."

JT nodded. "Lots of secrets around here, huh?"

Bexx was walking away and stopped. Turning, she said, "What do you mean?"

JT shrugged. "Nick asked me to do the same thing. 'Keep it on the down low,' he said after we talked about Svetlana and the post office thing."

"What did he say?"

JT met her gaze calmly. "You'll have to ask him. Like I said, he asked me to keep on the down low. That's where it stays if you get my meaning."

"I do. Thanks." Bexx smiled as she turned again and walked away.

Nick had spent the days isolated in a small room, reading and re-reading the documents Arthur had sent. He made notes and cross-referenced items that stood out in the pile of paperwork. As he'd had hoped, the rumor that he was losing it, cracking up even, had spread around the facility quickly. He didn't care who said what. What he cared about were the results it produced. Bexx did little to stop the spread of the rumor. She denied it, of course, just enough to give it some validity. The bait was out, so they waited to see who bit.

When Nick finally did leave the room, he went straight to The Driver.

"How's the new Bat Cave, and brother, how long until you have secure Internet access established?" Nick asked.

"I can get you secure now. Ask The Driver for secure, and you get a locked down STD safe internet connection. The Driver knows no other way to be, my friend. Protection is a must when you live and love in the fast lane."

"No, I mean secure. NSA secure. No prying eyes secure. Not hotspot on my iPhone secure. I need a couple of searches done as soon as you're up and running."

"Sure thing. I'll let you know. I still have to set up a couple of VSAT links and establish some back door, my-husband-is-out-of-town, satellite comms. Please, Driver, come share your gifts with me and get the switches warmed up. Give me a day or two, and I'll have the Web up and willing, aching, writhing, and beggin' you to explore her with your nasty li'l queries."

Nick rolled his eyes, "Okay, man, just let me know."

The Driver nodded and then asked, "How you been, by the way? Haven't seen you much since the package arrived. Anything I can do, let me know. Word is, you were pretty upset by its contents."

Nick shrugged. "I'm fine. The sooner you're able to get up and running, the better." He turned and walked out.

The Driver looked at Buffy and rolled his eyes and mouthed the word "psycho!" She nodded in agreement.

A couple of days later, The Driver had his equipment up and running. He explained to Buffy they were going to piggyback on several satellite Internet providers. Each had a different bandwidth. Some were Ku band, and some were Ka, so they each needed equipment specifically designed for their unique wavelengths. Buffy smiled and pretended to be in awe of his skills. She already had a very in-depth knowledge of the satellite Internet systems used worldwide by both the civilian and military sectors. Funny thing that most people had no idea of, the military piggybacked the civilian satellite providers for their unclassified traffic. They made real-time communications between military families possible. That traffic made piggy-backing companies like DirectTV and Dish Network a walk in the park. They had so much of their satellite Internet capability contracted out to various agencies, they had no idea when someone piggybacked their signal. The sheer volume made it impossible to track.

Once The Driver had his system up and tested reliable, he went to find Nick.

"Brother, the time has arrived! My servers are aching to be used, and the Internet hasn't experienced the capable hands of The Driver in far too long. Time for some backdoor action. Mama is lonely, and The Driver is willing!"

Nick nodded. "Let's go to the Bat Cave. I have a list of things I need to know."

"Sure thing, brother. Let's hit it hard and pull her hair. The Driver is back in action!"

Once they were back in the new, improved Bat Cave, Nick began. "Okay, man, pay attention. Arthur is down-dead. I want the report: all the details, first photos, interviews, then the rest. Everything. Got that?"

"Sure, sure, I got it."

"Next, when you're done with that, I want you to go back... way back. Search every place I've been... everyone I've had contact with; Jay at the burn unit, and the nurse there too. Anyone I bumped into in the mall, lemme know their status, dead or alive. Got it?"

"Yeah, yeah, I got it. What do you expect to find?"

"Hopefully nothing. What do I expect? You don't wanna know. Just do the damn search. And while you're at it, check the *Hessen Polizei* for any updates on Svetlana's case. Shake the damn tree hard. Let's see what falls out. You got that?"

"Yeah, shit, I got it. Ease up, man. You're in The Driver's capable hands. I'm on it."

"When you're done, come find me. No matter what time, come get me."

"Understood."

A few hours later, The Driver had a stack of police reports printed out along with newspaper articles and some medical records. The message being sent was apparently what Nick expected to find, or he wouldn't have asked for the search in the first place. The Driver's face was ashen when he finished the searches. He looked at Buffy and leaned back in his chair.

"Damn, this shit is getting ugly! These two will not quit until one or both of them is dead. I only hope we don't get caught in the crossfire again."

Buffy nodded as The Driver stood up. "Well, time to deliver the news to Nick. I'll be back in a few." He got up and grabbed the stack of papers and walked out of the Bat Cave. Buffy nodded again, saying nothing. She was troubled by the comment The Driver had made.

"Hey, brother, here are the results of the searches you asked me to do. Guessing, but from what I found, you've had another significant leap in understanding what The Director is planning?"

"Yeah, I guess."

"Care to share what you think is going on?"

"Not yet, no. I need the reports." Nick reached out as The Driver handed him the stack of papers.

Nick began to sift through the reports one by one, line by line. The picture was clear, very clear. When he was done, he started again, reading more slowly while pacing the floor after each report was complete. Juggling the details. Examining them in his mind from every angle. Finally, The Director had made a mistake.

Bexx was in the gym when Nick finally found her. She was watching JT run the team through another workout. His rapport with them was instant and mutual. He had a knack for teaching martial arts that was clearly near genius. She hoped he could reach Svetlana soon. She watched as he listened to her at meals, and from the seemingly insignificant questions he asked about her schooling and plans for her financial degree, she hoped he'd found a way in.

Nick walked up to her directly, purposefully, and stopped. His face was dark and serious. "We need to talk, now, outside. I need to walk, please."

She nodded and jumped up. "Let's go." She called back to JT. "I'm done for the day. Going for a walk."

The team snickered when they'd left the room. JT asked what they were laughing at. The Mentalist sneered. "Bexx coddles him like a child. Mr. Moody calls, and she comes running. She's our leader, but she jumps when he calls. It makes me sick."

JT stopped the workout and stared at her. "You've heard nothing I've said. That's obvious. Perhaps I'm not speaking clearly. Let me try again." JT cleared his throat. "Bitch, I ran the city. I owned it, understand? One day, this motherfucker starts talking shit about how I'm a punk, and he's gonna kick my ass. That I went soft in prison. He put that out on the streets... like I wouldn't get word of it. I came at him straight, put a gauge to his family's heads, asking his punk ass what the fuck you got to say now? When it was over, I left. His family was alive, but my point was made. I'm back. Don't doubt that shit. The next day, I was feeling pretty good. Hooked up with some friends. Went to see some people and get shit rolling again. Then, bam, this car pulls in front of us. Damn near runs our asses off the fucking road, and this crazy ass white boy gets out, sticks a gun in our faces, and says to me, 'Get the fuck out, JT. Move one fucking inch wrong, and I'll kill every fucking one of you.'"

JT paused. "You listening now?"

The Mentalist nodded, yes. "I got out carefully. I've faced down a lot of cops with their guns drawn. Most are soft and shake like hell when they pull out their damn guns. This crazy fucker was like ice cold. He wasn't afraid. He was on fire but solid, thinking, calculating. Angry as hell. He wanted to kill us all. I could see that. This motherfucker wasn't playing. I got out and did exactly what he said. I tried to calm him down, understand? Me, trying to calm him down! I'm trying to calm this motherfucker down because he might still kill us all anyway. I can see that. He's really pissed off! Then he takes me to the police station, puts me in this room, and starts talking to me like a person. Like I'm a human being. Got that? No one ever did that. Especially just a few minutes after scaring the shit out of me and my set."

The room was silent. JT looked around, making sure everyone was listening. "Make no mistake, Nick is a killer. You feel me? A motherfucking killer. Somehow, he keeps it under wraps, but you don't want to question that. I had no idea who he was when he pulled me out of that truck. He knew everything there was to know about me. That's how he rolls. He does his homework, learns all he can about you, and then bam! He drops the fucking hammer. He strikes, hard and relentless, and it's up to you if you survive the moment. He comes prepared to kill, but the choice is still yours. Do you want to die today?"

Silence filled the room.

"Whoever this motherfucker is now, that's his target? Jesus, you don't want to doubt he will find him. He's more focused now than I've ever seen him. I'm just glad to be on this side of his rage and not the other end. Been there. Didn't like it. Moody? Don't be stupid. That ain't moody. That's some shit you don't wanna know about. Trust me. That's death! That's the fucking Grim Reaper barely contained. This motherfucker is a straight-up demon when he's unleashed. Don't forget that. Understand this. Where we come from, there's no one you can trust. No one! Especially not some bitch. 'Trust no bitch' is written in stone on the gravestones of many of my homies. So if he trusts Bexx, it's for a damn good reason. God help whoever crosses this motherfucker."

JT looked around at each of them. "Any questions, ladies?"

There was none. No one moved. No one spoke. On some level, they already knew. JT's words, however, hit home. "Good. Then let's get back to work. Too much talking going on in my gym. Mentalist! You owe me twenty minutes on the heavy bag. Let's go, Asgarda!"

Special K was standing next to JT and said, "By the way, that whole Nick trusts Bexx thing. Yeah, not so much. You're misreading that."

"What do you mean?"

"It's a funny story, actually. Remind me to tell you sometime, or better yet, ask Bexx."

"Okay, I will. Back to work! Let's go!"

Listening to JT, Buffy heard what she hoped was an opening, Nick's questionable humanity.

CHAPTER TWENTY-SIX

Bexx and Nick walked for several miles. He asked about the training with JT and how the team was responding. Bexx replied they were very open to what he had to teach them and JT was a natural mentor. They were lucky to have him.

Nick smirked. "Lucky? As if luck had anything to do with it."

"What do you mean?" she asked.

Nick was quiet. His angry eyes gave every indication of the insanity that was coming to the surface one more time. "Nothing that's happened has been by chance. Well, almost nothing."

Nick began to describe for her the information Arthur had sent and after pouring over it several times, the insights he had finally pulled from the minor details. "First, The Director was closing the loops he had with anyone remotely associated with the camps they'd compromised. I had The Driver check into anyone—I mean literally anyone— I had any contact with or who had anything to do with Baroota or Cachibaché. I suspected there would be a pattern there."

"So what did he find?" Bexx asked.

"He found that one by one, The Director was removing anyone I've had any contact with. For example, Jay, the guy who recruited me for Baroota, was sitting in a burn unit in Colorado, miserable, living a life no one would want. I think he was kept alive only to amuse The Director and as punishment for his incompetence in Baroota. He's dead now. Taken off life support. That was a gift, really. His life was nothing I'd ever want. That's a good thing, I guess, but then there was his nurse. She gave me the contact information that led to Cachibaché. Somehow, The Director figured out what she'd done, and now, she too is dead. She died in a car fire. Her car suddenly caught on fire one day on her way to work. The door locks malfunctioned, and she couldn't get out. Crazy coincidence, huh?"

Bexx nodded. "Crazy."

Nick continued. "Then there's Arthur. He too dies in a car fire. But the fire investigators' report is a confused mess. Nothing fits. The vehicle he and his wife were in crashed. But the airbags deployed. They survived, and then for some mysterious reason, a fire erupts. But get this. Inside the car. Not in the engine compartment. Not from the gas tank. The inside of the car is where the fire started, and then it was put out. And if you think I'm being paranoid, listen to this. When the first responders arrived, they found Arthur and his wife dead, burned to death in the fire, but sitting on Arthur's lap is a bottle of Cachibaché. Fire investigators are unsure how it got there. It was completely free of soot. When a human body burns, it produces a significant amount of greasy soot. The bottle was pristine. Nothing to indicate it had been present when the fire was burning."

Bexx's eyebrows raised at the implications of this. "So, someone planted it after they put out the fire? How do you know Arthur was still alive when the fire started?"

"The coroner's report mentioned both Arthur and his wife had soot in their lungs. And the heat of the flames had damaged their lungs and tracheas as well. That means they were breathing when the fire started, and they breathed in the smoke and flames. And one other interesting side note. Arthur died at almost the exact moment we were arriving at the Bellagio in Las Vegas. Coincidence? I seriously doubt it."

Bexx was quiet. "This is a lot to take in."

"Yes, it is. Everyone we've met, everyone involved in any aspect of the camps is dead. One by one, The Director is closing the loops to anything that could possibly come back to him. I had The Driver check in with the *Hessen Polizei* to see if anything weird had happened there. Sondra, the woman Svetlana said hired her for a modeling job, has died. Apparently, she just decided to commit suicide. No warning. No suicide note. One day she took an overdose of random prescription meds, and then to make double sure she completed the job, she decided to eat the barrel of her department-issued firearm. See the pattern?"

Bexx said nothing and then finally shook her head no.

"He closes the loop after he knows we know about them, not before. These people are assets. They serve a purpose until we compromise them.

Then he kills them. Svetlana is the exception. Here is where it gets weird. He killed Arthur, Jay, and the nurse after I had contact with them, not immediately after, however. But Sondra he killed immediately after we rescued Svetlana. Why? The pattern breaks there. And only there. How does he know we know about Sondra?"

"Do you know why the pattern changes?"

Nick shook his head. "No, but I have a suspicion. We need to get Svetlana a laptop and get her working on the financial side of this yesterday. We're behind the curve. She needs to start earning her keep here. I don't care how fragile she is. Get her working on this now."

"Are you sure she isn't in on it with The Director? The last time we talked, you said she could be a part of his plan."

"She's a part of his plan. I have no doubt about that! Get her the laptop, but before you do, put a keylogger on the laptop. Make sure she has no idea. Ask The Driver or Buffy to install it. Make sure you tell them what she'll be using the laptop for and emphasize that we want to know what she's doing, what she's seeing, and who she's talking to. While you're doing that, I have a couple of phone calls to make."

"Phone calls?"

"Yes, we're about to gain another member of the team. If I'm right, The Director has no idea we know about this loop. If that's true, we can start to turn the tables on the bastard today."

"Who is the loop?"

"I'm going to call the survivor of the sniper team that killed Nõn. I have his number. Arthur gave it to me. When I detail what's happened to everyone else involved with The Director, I think he'll see he has no choice but to work with us."

"What? You're not going to invite the guy who was part of the team that killed Nõn to join us?" Bexx asked, stunned at the idea and that Nick would even consider it.

"Yes, I am. It's exactly what The Director would hope I would do. Just not the way I'm going to do it. He left him alive either as a mistake or as bait. Either way, we're going to make the most of that option."

"How do I explain this to the team? They're not going to like this at all."

Nick shrugged. "Oh, you know. Nick has lost it... crazy man, etc. Shouldn't be too hard to sell."

Bexx stared at him, searching his face for some sign this was a bad joke. Maybe some weird movie reference she had missed again. There was no sign he was joking.

"You're serious?"

"I'm deadly serious. If this works, we turn the tables on The Director now, today."

"And if it doesn't, and this sniper is part of The Director's plan?"

Nick smiled an evil grin. "Well, then payback is a bitch, I have a wicked scar that requires some pain-filled retribution, and oh, then there's the small matter of Nõn's death. Mr. Sniper had better be on our team, or he'll be spending the rest of his miserable life in one of the silos, starving, covered in his own shit, dying a slow, miserable death. That's after I have my alone time with him, of course." Nick smiled again. "Gotta love that me time!"

"Uh huh. Me time. Got it," Bexx said. "So can we go back now? I've had about enough of Nick's world for one day. I need to process this myself. We're going to open the gate and let this guy in, actually hoping he's part of The Director's plan. The only safe place we have is about to be compromised. Do I understand you correctly?" Bexx asked as they turned and began to walk back to the facility.

Nick nodded yes. "If I'm right, we're already compromised, but this will put us out in front of The Director. He won't see us coming with this move because just like you're realizing, it makes no sense. But that's exactly why it'll work. Up until now, The Director has moved us around like pieces on a chessboard. Time has come to start playing the game and stop being played by the game. Think of it like this. We've been playing chess with The Director for some time, and he's handing us our asses. Occasionally, we get lucky and take a piece here and there, but for the most part, he's winning. I tried to figure out why, and then one day it hit me, *Star Trek!*"

"What?" Bexx asked, confused.

"Star Trek! Star Trek chess. You never watched Star Trek?"

Bexx's eyes glazed over. "No," she said coldly, "I haven't spent a lot of time in front of a television set."

"Yeah, I get that, okay? Well, when you look at a chessboard, it's flat, one dimensional right?"

Bexx nodded, eyes still flat, and she was beginning to become impatient.

"In Star Trek, they play chess on three levels. Multidimensional chess. It makes sense, really, since in space you have to be able to navigate thinking about using three points to determine your path instead of like here, where we just go from point A to point B. So their thinking on the show would be more complex. Don't you see how that makes sense?"

Bexx said nothing and just glared at Nick. A few minutes before, he was talking about retribution and torture. Now he was talking about space travel on some random, fictional television show. She was getting perturbed. "Can you get to the point?"

"The Director is playing chess on multiple levels. That's why we never see him coming. We have to play that way as well, outplay him, actually. That's what bringing the sniper will do. We'll be playing on a level he hasn't realized we know exists."

"You're sure about this? Absolutely sure?" Bexx asked.

Nick nodded. "Of course. Remember the insane plan I had to take Cachibaché? It worked, didn't it? I mean, there were some hiccups, but for the most part, it worked. I just needed your help. You're the one who said we're stronger together, so we use Svetlana, JT, the sniper, The Driver, etc., and we all go at The Director."

Bexx shook her head in disbelief. "Anything else?"

"There is one thing I want you to do. It occurred to me we need to go back and look at the Vegas operation one more time. Ask The Driver or Buffy to check into it, but let's divide their tasks. Tell The Driver to handle the laptop for Svetlana and Buffy to check into Vegas."

"What should I tell her to look for?"

"Ask her to see who else had reservations for the floor you were supposed to be on at the Bellagio. Add to that the floor below as well. Just to be safe."

"What? Never mind. Let me guess. You expect to find something there, but you want to wait to tell me."

"No, I'll tell you, but don't tell them. Remember, this has to be compartmentalized."

"Okay, so what do you expect to find?"

"Absolutely nothing. Nada. Zip." Nick laughed.

"More movie humor?" Bexx asked.

Nick burst out into insane, childish laughter. "Nooo. I mean exactly that. If I'm right, they won't find a damn thing. You'll see."

They walked for some time, Nick still laughing about the movie humor comment and Bexx silent and mulling over what they'd discussed. Finally, she spoke up. "I spoke to JT, and he mentioned you asked him to keep a secret."

Nick asked, "So he didn't tell you what I asked?"

"No, he said you asked him to keep it on the down low, whatever that means. He wouldn't tell me."

Nick nodded, smiling. "JT... solid as ever."

"Well?" Bexx said. "Are you going to tell me?"

Nick nodded and then began to explain what he'd said to JT.

CHAPTER TWENTY-SEVEN

Bexx and Nick arrived back at the facility, and immediately Bexx reached out to Svetlana and told her they were going to task her with looking into The Director's financial assets and transfers. Given her training, she would be a natural fit for the task. Svetlana agreed. She wanted to have something to sink her teeth into. Meanwhile, JT was listening to the entire conversation.

Bexx told Svetlana she would task The Driver to procure a laptop, and in maybe two or three days she'd be up and running. Then Bexx went to the Bat Cave and instructed The Driver to set up a laptop and install a keylogger when it was ready. Svetlana was to be given access to the Web as needed and allowed to work on her own, looking into possible links to The Director in the banking industry. Someone had purchased the missile facility. It was most likely done in Hauer's name, but there would be a money trail that should lead to someone. While The Driver went to work ordering a laptop, Bexx spoke quietly to Buffy and explained her task, hacking the Bellagio's reservation software and locating every reservation on the floor the day they'd planned to capture Svetlana and the floor below.

"Collect any and all information on any of the reservations." And then Bexx gave her a silent, meaningful look. "I want to know from now on if anything looks out of place, out of the ordinary in anything you do or search. We're missing way too much. We have to up our game. Do you understand? Anything, no matter how minuscule or ridiculous."

Buffy nodded. She said nothing but felt the weight of Bexx's gaze. It was not a comfortable feeling. Perhaps they already suspected something was wrong. Buffy decided to wait and see.

Later that night, they are all gathered in the area around the facility's kitchen. JT was making dinner that night. They all took turns, and he had something different planned, Tonkatsu or Chicken Katsu. The transformation from martial arts instructor and master of the gym to chef was striking. JT was just at home in the kitchen. He moved around the large commercial ovens and cutlery as smoothly as he did the boxing ring and weight room. Gone were the sweats. He wore an apron with a "hang loose" hand sign across the chest. At first, the team laughed and made jokes in Russian as Nick watched silently. After a few minutes, the team was silent as well, watching their coach transform into a master chef.

When JT was done, he served them each a portion of the meal on plates and lined them up on the counter. "A large part of training is changing your mindset—never accepting less than your absolute best every day. Agreed?" JT scanned the eyes of the team, making sure each one of them was listening. "What you eat is part of that. What you put in your body matters. Put in good, healthy food, and you get good, healthy results."

The Mentalist snickered. "What I'd like is a nice, greasy double-decker hamburger and some cheese fries."

Everything stopped. JT was suddenly deadly serious. "Bad food is like an abusive relationship. It poisons everything you do."

The room was quiet. JT was making a point. Training was his life. He took this seriously. He meant it. The girls said nothing for a while, and then The Mentalist whispered in Russian, "No wonder he and Nick get along so well. They're both a little off center." Some of the team smiled. Others giggled. But the message was sent. Nothing JT did or said was to be taken lightly, in or out of the gym.

While the team ate, JT slowly went from member to member, checking on the food, making sure they ate the meat first and then the rice. He explained that controlled the insulin spike their bodies would produce and kept the carbs from turning to fat as quickly. Everything had a reason and a purpose.

When he came to where Svetlana was sitting, he stopped. "How's your food?"

She replied, "It's excellent!"

"Good... that's good. Listen, I've been thinking of setting up some investments. Do you think you could advise me on what would be the best way to establish an investment portfolio?"

Svetlana said nothing for a second and then said, "Yes, I could do that."

JT replied, "Could you write it down for me? I understand things better when I read them. Just telling me what to do won't be as helpful."

"I can do that, yes. It's simple really. A balanced portfolio is the most productive. I assume you want to invest for a long-term return, not a fast hit-and-run type of investment?"

"Exactly. I like the idea of long-term investment."

"I'll write some rough ideas up tonight and get them to you in maybe an hour. Would that be okay?"

JT smiled and nodded and gave Svetlana the hang loose sign. "Thanks."

Nick watched from the corner of the room and nodded to Bexx and then toward Svetlana. Bexx watched and then looked back curiously. Nick raised his eyebrows and smiled.

JT moved on to another team member, checking on the food. No one was allowed a second helping. The calorie count of each meal was specific. It was a balanced meal of clean protein, healthy carbs, and fruit.

When dinner was finished and the dishes cleaned up, JT took a pen and legal-sized pad of paper to Svetlana. "If you could rough out for me what we talked about?"

Svetlana was a little surprised, "Sure... now? I mean, it will be a basic outline. Then as you learn more, we could delve deeper. How much do you have to invest?"

"How much do I need to start?" JT asked.

Svetlana thought for a minute. "Let's worry about that later." She started to rough out what a balanced financial portfolio would look like and why.

Nick smiled, watching the exchange.

JT was listening intently a half-hour later as Svetlana explained the basics of a balanced investment portfolio. He scratched his head and said, "Wow, this is going to take some time to get the ins and outs of. I don't do free, and all I can offer in return is some training time in the gym. Would that be okay as payment?"

Svetlana thought about it. His curiosity in her educational specialty had been a welcome change. Since coming in contact with the team, she had felt like an outsider. But Bexx had tasked her with financial investigations, and JT was curious about investments. It felt like she may be able to contribute something meaningful.

"Sure, I can do that. One hour of my time in exchange for a half-hour in your gym. Sound fair?"

JT thought about it briefly. "Yes, that would be fair. We'll make your time count on both sides. Tomorrow at two PM, I have half an hour available. Sound good to you?"

Svetlana nodded. "Yes, two PM tomorrow."

JT picked up the paper Svetlana had been writing on and said, "Thank you."

The next day at two pm, Svetlana arrived at the gym. She had started in on the laptop The Driver had shipped overnight express. There was a lot of work there to do. She felt a little bit stressed and regretted committing to the workout time with JT. When she arrived, JT was waiting.

"I took a look at the paper you outlined a balanced investment portfolio on. It was hard for me to grasp, I admit, but when I came to the gym this morning, it suddenly made sense. Can I show you?"

Svetlana agreed to look at it. JT took her around the gym, stopping at one type of exercise or another. He began. "This one seems like bonds to me, stretching. This one like stocks, weights. Then over here, four types of cardio. I think that's most similar to the cash liquidity aspect of the portfolio. They apply to everything you do. Am I understanding you correctly?"

When he finished, he let what he had done sink in. "Seems our specialties as very similar," Svetlana remarked. "I've never seen a gym in this manner."

JT nodded. "I noticed that as well. As a coach, I try to provide each person I train with a balanced portfolio of skills they can draw upon in any circumstance. Sports, combat, or general fitness. The goals are theirs, and I try to tailor the workout for them to reach those goals. Perhaps if you'd be willing, we could help each other reach our goals. Apparently, we both already have the mindset required. We just need to apply the skills we've learned in our own arena to this new field of battle."

Svetlana was quiet. "I do have a goal."

"And that is?" JT asked.

"I never want to feel like I do now again. I never want to fear that someone can take my freedom from me without a bitter and costly fight."

JT folded his arms and looked at her long and hard. "I can help you reach that goal, but you have to be committed. You already have the mental discipline. That's obvious. Can you transfer that to the martial side? Do you have a warrior's mentality and heart?"

Svetlana said nothing for several moments, meeting his stern gaze. "I want to find out."

JT smiled. "Good! Two pm every day, I'm here to take you on that journey. We'll find out together."

CHAPTER TWENTY-EIGHT

While JT was making his gym a financial bridge for Svetlana to cross, Nick was on his way outside with Bexx's phone. It had taken him a while to remember if he had used the burner to call the sniper or if it had been Bexx's phone. Then he remembered and smiled.

Bexx watched him and asked, "Why the smile?"

"I just realized even back when I called the sniper, we'd already started to compartmentalize. Funny how that is when you look back and realize your subconscious is already doing what you needed to do before your conscious mind realized it. There are no coincidences, only awareness of the patterns."

Bexx said nothing. If she didn't know better, she would think Nick truly was losing it. His random comments became more and more disconnected.

Nick looked at Bexx and said, "Well, wish me luck. If this works, The Director is toast."

"Good luck," Bexx said with very little enthusiasm, but she did at least try to smile.

Nick walked out of the facility and onto the surrounding fenced in area and searched the phone for the number he'd called. There in the phone's memory, he saw Arthur's number, the last call he'd made, and then the next number called was the sniper.

"Here's hoping you've kept the same number, my friend." Nick cued up the number and pushed send.

The phone rang and rang. No answer. "Shit!" Nick muttered as he hung up and pushed send again. It took a moment for the phone to connect, but the ringing sound began again. Still nothing, No answer. "Come on, you dumb bastard. Answer the phone."

Nick was getting frustrated. He began to pace, thinking. *Now what?*

The phone had no voicemail set up. After a few minutes, he decided to take a risk and sent a text to the number.

Feeling hunted yet? If you're still alive, I have an opportunity you might be interested in. If interested and alive, text or call me back.

Nick pushed send and waited.

On the other end of this one-sided conversation, the sniper sat hidden in an abandoned building. He had searched the city for a building that had been empty and yet still had electricity. He finally found one, inhabited by transients and homeless people, a well-kept secret in the darker side of the city where the people who were throwaways and lost ended up. The building had power and some amenities like windows that weren't broken and a metal stairway in the back the cops wouldn't climb to check the top floor emergency exit door someone had pried open years before. The sniper was lying low. He knew how to escape and evade any hunter sent to find and or kill him in almost any environment. Urban environments were actually easier than the wild. Too many places to hide in plain sight, dress poorly, walk with a hitch, forget to shave for a few days, and you were just another nameless face no one wanted to acknowledge. No one would remember you. They didn't want to. You simply vanished.

The sniper's phone buzzed quietly. He checked the Caller ID. The number meant nothing to him, probably some robocaller trying to sell some life insurance or congratulating him on winning two tickets to an all-inclusive resort in Maui. The sniper ignored the call. A few minutes later, the phone buzzed again. Same number. Jesus, please! *Hello, thanks, but I don't want to go to Maui. I want to disappear. Could you provide me with a new identity and a passport to, say, anywhere but where I am? No? Okay, then leave me the fuck alone.* The sniper smiled at the imaginary conversation. The caller hung up. "Finally," the sniper whispered.

A few minutes passed, and the sniper had nearly forgotten about the calls. He was focused on the foot traffic on the sidewalks below, watching, scanning everyone. The people who were hunting him were still out there. He thought he had an idea of who they worked for, but he wasn't sure. Until he was absolutely sure, he had to lay low. Reaching out to the wrong person would be fatal.

The phone buzzed softly once. "Persistent bastards," the sniper whispered and looked at the screen again to see who had called. It wasn't a call. It was a text. He opened the message and read it. The sniper whispered, "What the hell?" He reread the message. Finally, he responded, typing *Who is this?* The sniper pushed send.

A few minutes later, the phone buzzed again. Nick had sent *R U the sniper from North Dakota?*

The sniper sent again, *Who is this?*

Nick responded. *The one you thought you hit... but missed. We need to talk before it's too late.*

The sniper felt a shiver roll through his body like lightning crossing the sky before a dark summer storm. *Motherfucker that can't be killed wants to talk? Wonderful!* The sniper thought for a minute, looking out the window. Finally, he muttered, "Why not? What do I have to lose? Can't get much worse than smelling transients' shit in this fucking hellhole."

Nick waited for several minutes, and then the phone rang.

"You have two minutes. What do you want?"

Nick smiled. "What's up, man? Working in the Arctic, smashing baby seals' heads in for the fun of it?"

"What do you want?"

"Got a simple question for you," Nick said.

"Go ahead... ask. One minute, thirty seconds left. Then I hang up."

"Pretty impatient for the last man left alive. Feeling any pressure yet? Notice someone following you? Hiding in a cardboard box under a bridge? Eating rats yet?"

"One minute, fifteen seconds."

Nick sighed. "Okay, asshole. The Director, the guy who hired you to kill me, is closing all of his loops. Anyone who had anything to do with any of the camps I've shut down is dead. Anyone who has had anything to do with anything is dead. You feel me? You're the last one left alive. I know this because I've checked. So you wanna live the rest of your life like Robinson Crusoe, avoiding the cannibals and lusting after the female monkeys, then hang the fuck up on me, man. I don't give a shit. I can do this without your sharp-shooting ass. Obviously, you weren't that good because my ass is still here, and now I'm all you got. You interested, or do you wanna quote me how much more time is left on the clock before you start banging the female chimps in heat? Your call, Romeo."

Silence for several seconds and then, "I'm listening."

Nick detailed all that had happened since they had last spoken. Arthur was dead. The Director was killing everyone associated with the camps. And Nick had an idea that might give the sniper an out. If it worked, they'd both be free from The Director forever. The sniper listened while Nick outlined the plan. Finally, Nick was silent.

"Ballsy plan. How do you know I'm not going to call The Director and ask to be brought back on for old time's sake."

Nick laughed. "I don't, to be honest. Reality is, you need me, and I need you. You in or out?"

"I'm in."

"Come to the missile facility in North Dakota. If you can make it here, you'll find we own it now. Can you make it here?"

"I can. May take me a couple of days, but yes, I remember how to get there."

"Good. Call me back when you're close. Keep your head down. The Director is out there, and he's hunting you. Believe that."

Nick hung up. The sniper looked at his phone. "Crazy bastard." He pulled up another number and pushed send. A moment later, a voice on the other end answered.

"Yes, sir. You hired me to protect a facility in North Dakota a few months back. The current occupants just called and offered me a position in their twisted little group. Sir, I'd like to finish the job you hired me for. Would you be interested?"

The Director was stunned. This was a gift he hadn't expected. The Wild Card was predictable as ever, trying to save the world, and every stray dog and cat along the way. The Director smiled. This would tie up all the loose ends nicely. He could use the sniper to take out The Wild Card and then kill him as well. "Yes, I'm very interested. Consider yourself back in my employment! Let me know when you're in. I assume you'll require your standard compensation?"

"Yes, sir. Usual contract. I look forward to finishing this task, and hopefully, we can continue to work together in the future."

"Well done! Call me to let me know you've arrived at the facility. I'll look forward to hearing from you."

The Director hung up. Smiling, he turned in his chair and looked out as the sun began to set. The Washington, D.C., skyline was most beautiful in the mornings and at night, just as the sun was setting. Today, it looked better than usual.

Nick walked back into the facility and handed Bexx her phone. "Homeboy is on his way. Let's hope he makes it before The Director kills him."

Bexx said nothing.

Four days later, Bexx's phone rang. It was the sniper. Nick answered. "Yeah?"

"I'm outside the gate in an old Ford truck. I had to steal it in Grand Forks to get here. Can we hide it inside?"

"Sure, man. I'll be right with you. Are you alone?"

"Of course. Just as we agreed."

"Cool, I'm on my way."

Nick looked at Bexx. "He's here. I am going out to meet him. Wish me luck, huh?"

Bexx handed him the Romanian AK-47. "Take this just in case?"

Nick paused, thinking. "Nah, I'm good. If this goes south, then it doesn't matter. I'll gut him. This is an all-in play, Bexx. The Director has finally made a mistake. It's time to go all in, cards on the table. Trust me. I know it feels reckless. It has to be."

Meanwhile, the sniper called The Director. "Sir, I'm at the gate."

"Good luck, son. Keep your eyes open. You'll be well-compensated for this mission. You can count on that."

"Thank you, sir. I'll contact you when I can."

Walking through the kitchen of the facility, Nick went to the front door and opened it and began to walk to the gate. When Nick arrived at the gate, the sniper got out of the stolen truck.

"Long trip?"

"Not too bad."

"Couldn't steal a better truck? This is a piece of shit!"

"Beggars can't be choosers."

Nick opened the gate. "Drive it around back to the tunnels."

"You're not going to search me?"

"Nah, I've seen you shoot. You're no threat."

"Okay, cocksucker, just so we're clear, you'd be dead if I was on the long gun. Every team is made up of a sniper and a spotter. They trade-off. You just happened to face the spotter, my friend. I'm the best sniper you'll ever meet. Bar none. If I were on the rifle instead of spotting, we wouldn't be having this conversation. You got that?"

Nick began to laugh. "Okay! Okay! Mr. Sensitive! Jesus Christ, look what the cat dragged in. Need some Midol, brother? Is it that time of the month? Not feeling feminine fresh after your long trip?"

The sniper glared at Nick.

Nick smiled back his most irritating smile. "Just so we're clear, if you'd killed me, you would have no place to hide. The Director would've buried you and your sharpshooting buddy as soon as the job was complete. So, before you go getting all your pretty feathers ruffled, consider that. Now, you want to drive the truck inside, or should we have a wicked match of bloody knuckles to see who the real man is?"

The sniper relaxed a bit. "Sorry. Been up for four days, watching my ass. My bad. Apologies."

"Relax, man. We pull this off, all is forgiven," Nick said.

"And if we don't?"

Nick smiled, his eyes were suddenly cold. "Not sure. Haven't planned that far in advance. Come on in, and let's get started."

CHAPTER TWENTY-NINE

Once the truck was inside the tunnel, Nick brought the sniper to the kitchen. As they were walking up the metal stairway, Nick asked, "Welcome to 'The Hive.' Are you hungry?"

"Yeah, I could use some food. What's on the menu?"

"Let's see what's in the fridge." Nick opened the door. The room was instantly silent as the entire Asgarda team met the new arrival in the room with icy stares.

Nick smiled. "Ladies, meet... what's your name? I've always referred to you as the sniper."

The sniper waved a weak wave to the group. "Umm, my name is Dave... Dave Elliot."

"Dave, these are the Asgarda. That's The Mentalist, Buffy, Special K, the Powerpuff girls, and their leader, Bexx." Bexx stood up, glaring at Dave, and walked directly to him until she stood inches away, towering over him. She said nothing.

"Dave here was explaining to me that he was the better shooter of the team we all faced here the last time we met. Actually, he said he's the best sniper we'll ever meet, bar none," Nick explained.

Dave said nothing, realizing suddenly maybe joining the team inside a fenced and hardened facility may not have been the best choice. Dave refused to meet Bexx's gaze, and finally, she huffed and spoke to the team in Russian. They got up as one and left the room. Nick smiled. So far, perfect.

Nick waited until the Asgarda left the room and then opened the fridge. "Roast beef sound okay? Or are you one of those New Age snipers that doesn't eat meat?"

"Roast beef sounds great," Dave said. "Any beer?"

"One beer coming up." Nick smiled. He noticed the Asgarda had left the room, but he hadn't heard the loud clank of the metal door opening and closing that allowed access to the underground facility.

While Dave ate, Nick asked him a few questions. "So, Dave, when you were here last, how did you escape? I mean, you were here with the other half of your team, inside the fence, am I right?"

"After you...after you tore my friend to pieces, I saw teams were advancing on my position in a bounding overwatch. I understood I was outnumbered and outgunned. I egressed."

"You were armed though. Am I right? I mean, you could've engaged the teams. They were moving, advancing on you. That's a position that can be exploited by a field-trained combat soldier. Movement is a weakness when your target is unknown."

"I was armed, yes. I made a tactical decision to egress rather than engage the teams."

"Interesting choice." Nick laughed. "You think the girls are surly now, you don't even want to be in the area when all their menstrual cycles are synced. I have to remove all the knives from the kitchen, or it turns into a bloodbath. Imagine how it would have been if you'd actually engaged them in the field. Ugly, my friend! Ugly!"

"By the way, there are a couple of others on the site. JT is our martial arts trainer, The Driver is our hacker, and then our most recent member, Svetlana. We just rescued her from your former boss. He'd kidnapped her and forced her into sexual slavery."

"That's fucked up," commented Dave.

"Remember what I told you about your boss closing his loops?"

Dave cleared his throat. "Yeah, I remember," he said as he lifted the bottle of beer to his mouth and started to drink.

"He killed the German Polizei officer who arranged Svetlana's abduction. From what I can tell, she worked for him for several years."

Dave stopped drinking the beer mid-swallow. He looked at Nick and said, "You have proof?"

Nick smiled. "Of course I have proof, but finish the beer, man. No need to get all mission-critical now. We're just talking. Anyway, when you're done eating, I'll take you to your room. Give the girls a few days, and they may warm up to you... and they may not. Still better than being hunted on the outside though, right?"

Dave nodded. "How did you know I was being hunted?"

"Because you're the only one left from any of the camps who's alive. The Director has killed anyone involved. Actually, everyone involved! Every single one, except you. That's why I called and made the offer. I'm hoping we can help each other."

"So you're saying The Director is the one who was hunting me?"

"Who else could it be, Dave? Really, think about it! Ready to go get some sleep?" Nick made sure to give the Asgarda the time to exit the hallway, where he assumed they were listening to every word. He heard the loud clang of the door, and a few seconds later the team reentered the room.

Dave finished his beer as quickly as he could and waited uncomfortably as the tension in the room noticeably cranked up several notches.

Nick, smiling, said, "Okay then, let's go find your room."

Bexx cleared her throat. "Nick, when you're done with... Dave, I'd like to speak to you in private."

"Sure thing, Bexx. I'll be right with you."

After Nick had taken Dave to his room and showed him where the showers were, he returned to the kitchen to talk to Bexx.

"So what's up?" Nick asked.

Bexx asked the team to leave the room and then waited for the sound of the door leading to the basement closing. She turned to Nick.

"I don't like this. Have you searched him?" she asked.

"No, I didn't search him. Why would I?"

"He could be armed," she said.

"He's most definitely armed. But so what?"

"So what? Have you completely lost your mind? He could have a cell phone and be calling The Director right now, and you'd have no idea."

"I'm counting on it."

"What? Why?" Bexx snarled even more angrily at Nick's careless attitude.

"Listen. Calm down for a minute and think about where he is and what you heard him say while you all eavesdropped in the hallway." Bexx denied nothing. "He said he egressed when he saw your teams advancing on him. He was armed and could've done serious damage to the team before anyone actually stopped him or killed him, but he didn't. Why?"

"I don't care why."

Nick grimaced and then rolled his eyes. "Okay, I'll tell you why. He's a sniper. He has no skill set in small unit tactics. He can't fight his way out of a paper bag. His only skill is shooting with a long gun, a sniper rifle, engaging a target from a safe distance, not fighting! Not close quarters fighting. He's harmless, and now he's here. Inside the compound. Do you realize what that means?"

Bexx was a bit calmer now that she thought about what Dave had said and then what Nick had explained it meant. "No, what does it mean?"

"He knows he's being hunted, and he came here... made it here through four days of travel. Think about what that means."

"It means he's lucky? I don't know. What does it mean?" Bexx asked, irritated she didn't understand what Nick saw.

"It means either like you said, he has the most amazing luck ever, or he's here with The Director's blessing. I'm guessing it's with his blessing. In fact, I'm counting on it."

"What?" Bexx said, raising her voice. "You want him to spy on us for The Director?"

"Exactly. We'll feed him information carefully. And meanwhile, we have the only remaining loop to The Director in our grasp, safe and now working for us."

"What do you mean working for us? You just said you think he's a spy, working for The Director."

"Yes, a paid spy, who left his friend to die, and as he put it 'egressed... made a tactical decision.' Bullshit! He's no warrior. He's no mercenary. He's a wet nurse, paid to do a job. He isn't committed to any cause but his own survival. Now he's caught between a rock and a hard place. What do you think he'll choose, The Director? Hell no. The Director wants him dead."

Bexx was silent for a moment, processing what Nick had said. It made sense but felt risky, too risky. "He's caught between a rock and a hard place? How so?"

"Between working for The Director, who will eventually kill him anyway, and working for us. He was foolish enough to come here and enter the lion's den, thinking he was a lion. He isn't. The dude is milquetoast without his beloved sniper rifle. Dude thinks he's Jason Bourne. Reality is, he isn't. We might as well fear The Driver. He has a more lethal skill set."

Bexx nodded. It made sense, at least the comment about The Driver did.

"Listen, we did this all the time back when I was a cop. Turn an informant but make him realize the enemies he just made by being an informant were now leverage against him. If he didn't do everything you asked, you just let it slip that he worked for the cops, and then he had to turn to us for protection from his former friends. Rock and a hard place... get it? Dave has no place to turn except to us. In the end, he's dead meat if he doesn't work for us. He's smart. He puts his survival above all else. He'll come around. Trust that."

"So that's why you didn't search him? You want him to communicate with The Director?"

"Exactly."

"But why?"

"Do you have the results from the search on the Vegas operation yet?"

"No, Buffy is working on it, but what does that have to do with Dave and him communicating with The Director?"

Nick smiled. "It'll make sense when you see the results from Vegas."

CHAPTER THIRTY

The next day, Buffy did have the results from the Bellagio. She checked them twice to be sure and then stared at her computer screen. What the hell did this mean? She knew Bexx had asked for the results for a reason. What that reason was concerned her.

Meanwhile, The Driver had been tracking Svetlana's financial investigations using the keylogger he'd installed on the laptop. He had to admit, she had skills. He had no idea what she was doing or how. He was a hacker, not a banker. He understood how to steal people's credit card numbers and personal information. Svetlana was running financial inquiries so far down in the weeds, he was baffled by what he found. He wished he had her skill set when he was back at the farmhouse in Moses Lake. Things might have turned out differently.

Buffy was headed out of the Bat Cave to go talk to Bexx when The Driver asked her to help him install some new VSAT equipment that had arrived the day before. She was glad to have a moment to think before she had to go talk to Bexx. The direction all these latest inquiries were heading only left one conclusion in her mind, and she didn't want to have to deal with that just yet.

"Sure, I'd be glad to help." She smiled and then lied, "I always learn something new from you anyway. What are we working on today?"

"Wait 'til you see what I have!" The Driver boasted. "Let's head up to the roof."

Buffy pretended to be excited. She knew all about the VSAT systems and actually understood them better than The Driver, but she kept that from him. It made him happy to believe he was always ahead of her. She was always amazed at how the man's ego made him so blind to everyone else.

The Driver began to open and unpack a large military-grade VSAT. Buffy felt a chill. "What's that?" she asked.

The Driver smiled. "It's a military grade VSAT. It'll allow us to hack secured military communications, and in a pinch, if we need super fast and secure Internet access, we can jump on this system for a minute or two and gain access. It runs on the Ka-band like the others but is encrypted."

The Driver droned on and on about the machinery and how it worked. Buffy listened and pretended to be interested, but she wasn't. She'd seen enough. Finally, she said, "I just don't understand all of this as well as you. It's giving me a headache. I'm gonna go lie down."

"Sure thing. Go lie down. I'll be done in a jiffy and then head back to the Bat Cave to set up hardwire links. Get some rest. I just wanted you to see the new toys we have."

Buffy nodded uneasily and turned away, heading back down into the facility. She had a lot to think about before The Driver showed her his new toys. Now she felt overwhelmed and confused.

It was two pm when Buffy curled up in her bed, holding her pillow and rocking back and forth, a stark contrast to Svetlana and JT just starting her workout for the day and Dave and Nick walking around the outside of the facility talking about their military days, each of them from a different era. Nick from the cold war, Dave from Desert Storm and Operation Iraqi Freedom. Dave had gone private contractor afterward, while Nick had gone the civilian police route.

Svetlana had worked up a nice sweat in the five-minute warmup JT had devised, and she was ready for the real deal—twenty minutes of commitment-challenging, high-intensity training and then five minutes of warm down. JT was pleased with her progress. She was committed to the program and listened carefully. While she cooled down, they talked.

"So how goes the financial search on Nick's enemy?"

"It's intense. Whoever this guy is, he hides his money well and transfers it carefully. The electronic trails are very intricate. I've never seen anything like them in my training at school. And he isn't just Nick's enemy. He's mine as well. You do understand he's the one who kidnapped me? Or at least made it happen?"

"I do. I was there, remember?"

Svetlana nodded. "I never did tell you thank you."

"No need. I would've done it for anyone. It wasn't personal. I know what it means to have your mind imprisoned and not be able to find a way out."

Svetlana nodded but said nothing.

JT changed the subject. "I think it's time to start working on more combat-oriented training. Next time you come, we'll step into the ring. I want you to take it slow, but we'll begin to work on your strikes and kicks along with defense. Mentally prepare for that."

Svetlana nodded and said quietly, "Thank you for doing this. When do you want to start learning about investing?"

JT was quiet for a minute. He hadn't really had any money to invest. Everything he owned was tied up in the gym, and that was now gone. "I have a confession. I don't have a dime to my name. Everything I owned is gone."

"Gone because you agreed to my rescue?"

"Gone because I had no other choice. I couldn't sit back and watch."

"Well, we made a deal. I expect you'll set up a time once a week to come to my office and be tutored in the finer details of investing."

JT smiled. "Okay, deal." He noticed already Svetlana was more assertive. The physical training was changing the way she felt, and more importantly, the way she thought. She was more confident.

At three pm, the team arrived for their afternoon workout. Bexx had been thinking about the things Nick had said about Dave, the sniper. She turned to the team and JT. "How do you all feel about some time in the ring today?" The team nodded in agreement. Bexx turned to Special K and said, "Go find Nick and our guest. Tell them they're invited to participate."

Special K smiled. "Right away."

While the team waited for their guest to arrive, Bexx pulled JT aside and briefed him on the history they had with Dave. He agreed to let Bexx set the tempo for the training and sat back, watching. Five minutes later, Nick and Dave walked into the gym.

Bexx called the team together and began explaining the routine. "Today we'll include our newest member of the team in our training. We'll be in the ring. Gloves and headgear are mandatory. Special K is up first. Dave, you too. We'll start you out sparing with the smallest of our team and see where you'll fit in."

The team was silent as they watched Dave's reaction. He turned to Nick and said, "Is she serious? I mean, I must outweigh that little girl by fifty pounds or more. I'm not going to fight a woman."

"Brother, she's deadly serious. If you want to stay here in the compound, you have to train. There are no free rides here. The woman you're gonna spar with can handle herself... trust me. You had no problem shooting Nõn. She was a woman, remember?" Nick smiled a dark smile. "Just think of her as one of your targets. You'll be fine."

Dave was cocky. "Okay, man. Just remember I didn't set this up. She did." Dave nodded at Bexx.

JT smiled as he watched the match begin. Dave was about to get an education. Bexx explained the rules of the match and that the rounds would be three minutes. She asked Dave if he was ready.

Dave nodded, breathing through his nose as the mouthpiece made it more difficult to breathe.

JT rang the bell, and they began. Special K danced a bit, staying just outside of Dave's reach, and then after she'd checked out his defense and footing, she attacked. The barrage of punches and kicks came so fast, Dave had no time to react. The last thing he felt was the left uppercut he never saw coming. Dave dropped to the floor, snot spraying out of his now bloody nose. He was out cold. Special K had barely broken her normal breathing pattern, and the match was already over.

Nick and Bexx exchanged glances and smiled at each other. She nodded to him. He was right. This guy was no lion. Not even close. The Mentalist grabbed her medical kit and entered the ring to check out Dave. Bexx also entered the ring and helped with the smelling salts and bringing Dave back from his Special K instigated nap. As they helped Dave get up and carefully walked with him to the boundaries of the ring, the door opened, and Buffy stepped into the gym. Bexx looked up and could see immediately she was disturbed. She nodded to Nick and then to Buffy. He looked at her as well and then made eye contact with Bexx, nodding his head to one side and shrugging. Nick focused on helping Dave walk to the stairway while Bexx went to meet with Buffy.

"You're late for training," Bexx said.

Buffy nodded. "We need to talk."

"Do you have the results from the Bellagio?"

"I do," Buffy said uneasily.

"And?"

"There's nothing there. I mean nothing. Zero. It's weird."

Bexx was stunned and looked at Nick walking up the stairs, his back turned to her.

"What do you mean nothing? Explain that. Why is nothing weird?"

"There's more than that, Commander. We need to talk. I feel sick with what I've seen. I need you to listen and tell me if I'm crazy."

Bexx could see Buffy was genuinely disturbed and said, "Come with me." She turned and motioned to JT to take over the training and walked up the stairs with Buffy. "Let's go somewhere private, so we can talk."

CHAPTER THIRTY-ONE

Bexx walked with Buffy to the kitchen of the facility and grabbed two cold drinks from the fridge. "Let's go outside." Buffy nodded in agreement.

Once they were outside, Bexx handed Buffy a drink and then opened her own. "So first tell me what you found at the Bellagio."

Buffy nodded. "I checked the reservation software, and at first I thought I'd made a mistake, so I checked twice. It made no sense at first."

"And?"

"And there were no other rooms rented on the floor we'd reserved except the one we reserved and then the room on either side. Remember, Nick wanted rooms next to your room as well... just in case?" Bexx nodded that she did remember. "Then I checked the floor below. It was empty as well. I cross-referenced this with their maintenance schedule, thinking maybe they had routine carpet replacement or maybe water damage or something similar going on. There was nothing. So, I went back into the reservation software and got into the back notes left by the hotel manager." Buffy paused and took a swallow of her drink.

Bexx was impatient. "So, what did you find?"

"I found a note from the manager saying the remaining rooms had been paid for by an outside party. They were not to be rented on either floor until further notice."

Bexx nodded, silent, thinking about the implications of this discovery.

"Okay, what else is bothering you?"

"Well, it's technical IT stuff. Back in Ukraine, you remember we used satellite communications to communicate with the other teams?"

"Yes, I do. That was your field of expertise."

"Exactly. So you know I know what I'm doing."

"Of course. You were the best in the field. That's why I wanted you on the team."

"Well, when we moved here, I helped The Driver set up our satellite communications. Of course, I never mentioned to him I'm an expert in this. His ego is... well, you know. He is 'The Driver.'" Buffy held up her hands and made the quotation signs. "So, I pretended to be unaware and let him have his moment in the limelight again. So he has VSAT terminals set up for two different systems. First, you know VSAT means 'very small aperture terminals.' There are about a million terminals working at any one time worldwide. The Sat Comm systems used by NATO and the UK are broken down into three different groups. One is the older of the three and is called WGS or Wideband Global Satellite. It is a constellation of five satellites in geosynchronous orbits," (Bexx was trying to be patient with Buffy, but all of that technical jargon didn't really matter). "The second system is newer and deployed by NATO and is called DISN, which stands for Defense Information System Network and is the major backbone for all American DoD internet communications. It's a comprised of a system of six geosynchronous satellites, and the last system is military grade crypto. It's called Skynet and is supposed to be nuclear resistant and able to survive EMP in the event of a nuclear strike. All of these VSAT systems use antennae ranging in size twelve to eighteen inches." Buffy continued rambling on for several more minutes, unaware she had lost Bexx several acronyms back.

Bexx's eyes had glazed over as she listened. Finally, she spoke. "Yes, yes, this is all very interesting. I do appreciate your passion for the subject; however, I don't share it. So please, can you get to the point of all the VSAT background?"

Buffy paused, a bit embarrassed. "Sorry. Well, each one of these systems uses a specific bandwidth. WGS uses Ka and Ku bands. Skynet uses UHF and X bandwidths, while DISN uses Ka and Ku bandwidths."

Bexx rolled her eyes. "This is you getting to the point, right? Please! What the hell does this have to do with anything?"

Buffy stopped talking, realizing she had done it again. "Sorry... um... okay. Well, while The Driver was installing the first Batch of VSATs, nothing was unusual. But then yesterday, he installed a Skynet VSAT terminal."

"And that means what exactly?" Bexx growled.

"I've no idea what it means. He shouldn't have it. We have no need for it. It can only communicate with similarly encrypted systems. Meaning, he can only access military communication, and they can, in kind, 'see' him."

Bexx was frustrated as ever. "What exactly are you telling me?"

Buffy was quiet. "I don't want to say this, but I think The Driver may be working against us."

Bexx was stunned. She looked at Buffy for several minutes. "Why do you think that?"

"That system, Skynet, is trackable. The others are not. The military can see his terminal. He can only communicate with other military terminals. The entire system is encrypted. Get it? There is no reason to have it for our purposes. The only scenario I can see that it would be of value to him or us would be to communicate with someone in the government or the military. You have to ask yourself, why would he want to do that? The only reason I can see is that he's communicating with someone on the sly he hasn't told you, me or Nick about, and that reality leads to one conclusion."

Bexx nodded. It was clear. "The Driver is working for The Director."

Buffy said, "Yes." Tears started to well up in her eyes.

Bexx nodded. "Okay, let me think. Let's walk for a while. I need to think."

A moment later, Bexx turned to Buffy. "Could it be anything else? I mean, he is The Driver! He hacks everything. He pillages and violates the Internet at will and all that other bullshit he spews."

"I don't think so," Buffy replied.

"Okay, keep this between us. Can you keep it from him?"

"I can. I have for a while. I've had some suspicions for some time, comments he made, things he has said, and then this military-grade VSAT. It's extremely guarded and controlled. You cannot just pick one up on eBay."

"Okay, do it. Maybe there's another reason we aren't aware of. Until we know for sure, keep this quiet, but keep your eyes and ears open for anything else suspicious."

Buffy nodded. "I'm a little worried."

"Worried? About what?" Bexx asked.

"Nick. If Nick gets wind of this, he will destroy The Driver. This kind of betrayal is going to push him over the edge. I don't want to watch The Driver be tortured by whatever Nick becomes when he gets really angry."

Bexx stopped and realized Buffy was right. She said nothing for a minute and then smiled. "The Driver is caught between a rock and a hard place. Let's keep him there. Don't worry about Nick. I'll handle him."

"Are you sure? I mean, Nick is..." Buffy stopped and swallowed deeply.

"I'm sure. You take care of The Driver. Eyes and ears open. I'll take care of Nick."

"Thank you, Commander," Buffy said and then fiercely hugged Bexx. "Sorry, I just..."

"Thank you for telling me. Now get back to work."

"Yes, ma'am."

Bexx stared off into the field surrounding the fenced-in area of the facility for several minutes. Then she turned and walked back to the facility. Once in the gym, she made eye contact with Nick. He had a mischievous smile on his face. She nodded back.

Somehow, he already knew.

Bexx walked up to Nick and said, "How's the training going?"

"Good, I think. JT has them working on all kinds of new techniques. Dave had a nice reality check with Special K. He'll learn a little bit of humility before your team is done beating him to a bloody pulp, I think."

Bexx nodded and said nothing for several minutes. Finally, she said, "Buffy has the results from the Bellagio. Just like you said, she found nothing."

Nick nodded. His face showed no sign of emotion. "Imagine that."

"I think you owe me an explanation," Bexx replied.

"Not here. Later tonight. There's an envelope in your top drawer. Open it, and then we can talk."

Bexx nodded. "Rock and a hard place, huh?"

Nick nodded. "A very hard place."

"Buffy is worried," Bexx continued.

Nick said nothing for several moments. "She doesn't need to be worried. Tell her not to worry."

Later that day, as they all gathered in the kitchen for the evening meal, Bexx whispered into Buffy's ear. Buffy nodded and then looked across the room at Nick. He returned her gaze and nodded.

"Let's eat!" Nick announced loudly. "Chef Nick has the meal tonight. Pork roast, golden potatoes, and garlic asparagus in olive oil washed down nicely with an excellent Pinot Noir."

JT rolled his eyes and went to the fridge to retrieve a healthier meal he had prepared in advance. The team, however, greeted the roast pork and golden potatoes with a cheer. Nick noticed The Driver wasn't present, and when Buffy walked past, he mentioned it.

"Perhaps The Driver needs a special invitation to dinner? Would you like to get him, or shall I?"

Buffy set her plate down. "I'll speak to him. Thanks!"

"Appreciate that, Buffy. I've been slaving away in the kitchen for hours. It's the least his twisted ass can do to show up and eat when the meal is hot."

As they ate, Bexx whispered to Nick. "So what's in this envelope? Another fingernail gift like you gave Nõn? An ear? Or a lock of hair?" Bexx smiled.

"No, a list of all the questions that needed to be answered. I know you've had your doubts about me and my sanity, so this is proof that what Buffy found wasn't a guess. I'd have been floored if I was wrong. The letter is to show you this isn't some random *Twin Peaks* like series of conclusions that don't fit the circumstances. There are no backward talking dancing midgets telling me what's really going on. This is legit."

Bexx nodded. "But I haven't told you what she found."

"Yeah, I know, but you don't need to. There can be only one answer to that list of questions."

CHAPTER THIRTY-TWO

L ater that night, Bexx retrieved the envelope from her drawer and opened it while Nick lay in bed, staring up at the ceiling, tracing the metal conduit that contained the electrical wires for the facility's power for the hundredth time. It was a calming mental exercise, and he did it nightly, over and over.

Bexx looked at the letter and then put it back in the envelope. She got into bed and looked at Nick.

"I know you're onto something here. How'd you know we would find nothing at the Bellagio?"

"It made sense. I wanted a fight, believe me. I really did. Then JT made his observation that I was thinking like a cop, and it hit me. The Director planned on us coming. He expected it. Just like Cachibaché, he already knew and was planning for it. The only way to win is to do the unexpected. So we went with JT's plan and came out without a scratch. We should've been slaughtered. For that kind of fight to occur, they would have to clear the floor and maybe the one below."

"What do you mean just like Cachibaché? How do you know he knew we were coming?"

"I called Diamond Dave, the sniper, and asked him how many interviews he had for the job. He said two, and then he had specific orders to shoot me and Nõn first. They expected us the first day. But then we changed the plan, you and I came and took the camp. They had orders to wait until we all arrived. Then they began shooting. Only one of us happened to be inside when the shooting started. At first, I thought an odd coincidence. Later, I realized no, it wasn't. It was part of the plan."

"When did you realize this?"

"On the way back from Vegas. Remember you were mad at me because I couldn't accept that the plan had worked and we'd escaped without any injuries, not a shot fired. I didn't want that, stupid as that sounds. Later I realized what that meant. I'm predictable. I have to see the bigger picture. The Director keeps throwing these disposable bodies at me to slaughter and make me feel like I'm winning. Just like in chess, you sacrifice a pawn or a bishop for the bigger play. The king is your goal. Capture the king, and it's game over... checkmate."

"So, this is why you haven't taken down The Driver? Peeled off a few more fingernails? Clipped off a toe or two? This is why Buffy doesn't have to worry?"

"Yes, and exactly why I brought on Diamond Dave, the sniper. The Director wouldn't expect me to do that. He'd expect me to slaughter them both when I knew what they were doing. Now we turn the tables. He thinks he has two spies when we actually control them. Rock and a hard place." Nick rolled over and sighed. "Now you see why we have to compartmentalize everything. We have to control the flow of information out to The Director."

Bexx nodded.

"And one more thing. I am going to ask that the decision of what to do with The Driver and Diamond Dave be yours. I'm taking myself out of that loop. We need to keep up the ruse for this to work. Our feint one-ups theirs. Does that make sense?" Nick asked.

Bexx nodded again. "I do have a question. How are you able to do this day in and day out? Not slaughter The Driver, knowing what you know?"

"It isn't easy."

The rest of the week was rough for Diamond Dave. First, his nickname stuck instantly, and The Mentalist more than anyone made the most out of it, talking mad trash to him, especially after it was her turn to meet him in the ring. The entire week was filled with one Asgarda member after another handing Diamond Dave his ass. JT watched and said nothing. Sometimes he closed his eyes and shook his head and walked away. The beatings were that brutal. Give Diamond Dave some credit. He hung in there like a good punching bag should, swinging back and forth, clueless what his next move would be.

By Friday, his face was swollen and bruised. His lips were twice their normal size and split. After lunch, The Mentalist asked Bexx if she could take Diamond Dave out to shoot. In a sarcastic tone Diamond Dave completely missed as he listened to the conversation, she recalled to Bexx that Dave had told them he was the best sniper they would ever meet... bar none. Bexx hesitated, realizing Dave had world-class skill, or at least that was what he'd told them.

She asked The Mentalist, "Are you sure about this?"

"Of course I'm sure," she replied, cocky as ever. "I want to learn from the master!" She said as she rolled her eyes.

The Mentalist checked out a bolt-action sniper rifle from the armory, a few extra rounds to sight it in, and a couple of targets. Then she and Diamond Dave went for a walk outside the facility. She kept a knife in her right boot just in case Diamond Dave forgot the beating he'd received as a gift from her a few days before.

Diamond Dave started out talking his usual trash about his sniper skills and his classified all-time best shot. It was classified according to Diamond Dave because the government didn't want their enemies to know someone could reach out and touch them (as Dave put it) from so far away.

The Mentalist listened quietly, saying nothing, inserting an occasional "um hmm" or "really?"

Dave sighted in the rifle and then got down to business. He shot a tight group maybe quarter-sized with 4 rounds at a 500-meter target. He was pretty proud of himself. Finally, he was in his comfort zone, not getting his face kicked in by a bunch of angry, hormonal women. Diamond Dave brought his target back to The Mentalist and proudly displayed it. She acted impressed and then asked if she could try. She explained, she had been watching carefully and wanted to see what she could do, she was a quick study.

Diamond Dave agreed, and he set up her target for her. She wasn't about to walk downrange in front of him, especially after the beating she'd given him a couple of days earlier. She wasn't that cocky.

When Dave returned, he gave her pointers on breathing and trigger pull, timing the shot with her breath, and adjusting for the wind. In Dave's mid-sentence, The Mentalist took her first shot. Then her next and three more followed as she quickly pulled back the bolt and reloaded the rifle.

Dave yelled out, "Slow down, slow down! You're a sniper in combat, not some cowboy in a field, picking off glass bottles on the fence for fun."

Dave jogged downrange to retrieve the target. He sat there for several minutes and then turned around, looking at The Mentalist. He returned, head down with the target in hand.

The Mentalist was smirking as he returned. She had unloaded the rifle and put the equipment they had brought with them away. She was ready to go when he finally finished the 500-meter trek back to her position.

"I guess you've done this before, or I'm the most amazing teacher ever."

The Mentalist smiled. "Told you I'm a quick study. Can I see how I did?"

Diamond Dave handed her the target as he said, "So maybe you could teach me a thing or two, huh?"

The Mentalist looked at the target. A small hole the size of a dime was at the center of the target. "Hmm, I need a li'l bit of practice. Maybe we could come out again, Dave? Would you like that?"

Dave nodded, his head down. His week was ending on an epic lesson in humility.

The Mentalist placed her hand under his chin and pulled his face up. "Chin up, Diamond Dave. You're still alive. Trust me. If you knew Nick like we do, you'd realize that is indeed a gift."

Dave and The Mentalist began to share sniper stories on the way back to the facility. As they walked in the door, Diamond Dave made the mistake of bragging and joking to The Mentalist about a Taliban member he'd taken off a ridge with a .50 caliber sniper rifle. The words Nick heard as they walked in the kitchen were, "And the head just vaporized in a mist of brain and blood." Diamond Dave said this as he laughed.

Nick crossed the room in a blur and drove Diamond Dave against the wall, his left hand closing tightly around Dave's throat while the right brought out his favorite razor sharp Gerber lock blade knife and slid it surgically into the flesh under his swollen left eye. Nick whispered, "Do you think that's funny? You really think you can come into my fucking house and brag about killing my friend and live? Do you? Is it funny now, motherfucker? Laugh. Go ahead. Laugh!"

The Mentalist tried to talk to Nick, but he wouldn't listen. She called out loudly to Bexx. "Bexx, kitchen, please. Now!"

Bexx arrived moments later. Nick was explaining to Diamond Dave the finer points of how his life would end, and that would be happening now! Much sooner than he expected when he woke up that morning.

Bexx waved The Mentalist away and walked up to Nick's right side. She whispered in his ear, "Rock and a hard place. Remember? Rock and a hard place."

She reached up to his right hand and gently pulled the knife out of the flesh under Diamond Dave's left eye. Dave would have a nice scar, but his eyes were still very swollen from the week's beatings, and his eye was not damaged.

Bexx took the knife from Nick and kept whispering softly, "Rock and a hard place, remember?"

Nick slowly came back down from the rage that had instantly erupted. Bexx realized then the tremendous effort he was making in letting The Driver and Diamond Dave live. It was almost impossible for him to do. He could barely contain it, whatever it was.

Bexx motioned to The Mentalist to get Diamond Dave out of the room immediately.

When they were in the hallway walking toward the stairs, The Mental-ist put her arm around Diamond Dave's shoulder. "See what I mean? Chin up! You're still alive! Now let's look at that eye. Fortunately for you, I'm the team medic as well as the sniper."

Diamond Dave's first week in the Lion's Den or "The Hive," as Nick called it was a rough one.

CHAPTER THIRTY-THREE

The next week passed with Nick lying low. He and Bexx went for walks and made the most of the rumors floating around the facility. Bexx confirmed Nick had gone off the rails a bit and for no apparent reason. Diamond Dave healed up and started to fit in a little bit more with the team. JT took him under his wing and began working with him to build a better foundation for his sparring matches with the team. He had a lot to learn, physically and mentally. JT had his work cut out for him with his pupil, but he made the most of it. When The Mentalist asked him how it was going with Diamond Dave, he replied, "All students are there to humble their teachers. Some do it by mastery, some by challenging you to be better."

The Mentalist asked which Dave was.

JT replied, "That isn't important. What is important is that we all learn from each other and get better as a team. We'll succeed or fail as a team."

The Mentalist rolled her eyes. "Okay, *Sun Tzu.*"

"Who is that?"

"*Sun Tzu? The Art of War?* Nick made it required reading for the team long before you were in the picture. Figured you had an autographed copy somewhere."

JT didn't bite. He wasn't going to let The Mentalist get in his head. "Good to know," he replied, and he gave her the hang loose hand sign as he turned and walked away.

Meanwhile, on their walks, Nick and Bexx planned and plotted, running through possible scenarios to maximize using The Driver and Diamond Dave without their knowledge.

One day on their walk, Nick asked Bexx, "Do you know what 'inattentional blindness' is?"

Bexx thought for a minute. "No, I haven't heard of it before."

"It's a situation where a person is blind to some type of stimulus, a situation or event. It isn't real blindness. I mean, the person can physically see, but they don't assign meaning to what they see. The trick is to open your eyes and see what's really going on, see what small, insignificant events mean or lead up to. Like The Driver conveniently being in the facility when the shooting started. For example, what do you think would have happened had Nõn and I both been killed? What would've happened to the team? Fast forward now. We're at The Bellagio and say we don't rescue Svetlana, we're ambushed like The Director planned, with The Driver's help, of course. What do you think would've happened to the survivors of the team if there were any?"

Bexx grew angry at the thought of what nearly had occurred but couldn't really imagine what would've happened. She said, "I don't know. What do you think would've happened?"

"Something ugly, I assume. I can't see The Director suddenly changing his stripes. Maybe you all would've ended up like Svetlana, high-end escorts, drugged and beaten down. I don't know. But you can bet he had plans for any survivors."

"What does this have to do with inattentional blindness?" Bexx asked.

"We need to be aware to the nth degree. We have to discuss everything, every angle and be open to any possibility. We have to change the way we see what we see. When we think we understand something, we need to reexamine it from another angle, no matter how ridiculous it seems. It's the only way we'll ever beat The Director."

Bexx nodded. "Isn't that what we're doing?"

"Yes, but I wanted to verbalize it... put a name on it, so you understood this isn't some Nick voodoo doll bullshit like everyone thinks. It's real. Your brain filters out things that you see every day. We have to retrain ourselves to be aware of everything. It'll be difficult."

"Okay, I get it. You just want me to know this is a real thing, something that does exist. Not just made up in your head?"

"Yes. Using this concept is how Nõn and I escaped Baroota and being unaware of it has nearly got us all killed several times now. We've been extremely lucky, but we can't rely on luck to survive. We have to understand this and use it daily."

Bexx nodded.

At the end of the week, Nick slowly reintegrated back into the team's daily routine. The team was quiet around him, and even Diamond Dave tried to be in the room with him and not flinch every time Nick moved.

The following Monday, Nick decided to go to the post office and asked if anyone else wanted to get out of the facility. The usual answer was silence. No one wanted to be in the ancient, weathered Yota with unpredictable Nick. Who knew what would happen? This time was no different. Silence.

Nick shrugged and then heard a voice say, "I would like to go."

Nick turned, eyebrows raised, looking for the person who belonged to the voice he didn't recognize.

Svetlana stood up and nodded once. "I would like to go," she repeated.

Nick nodded in return. "Okay, let's go. The Yota awaits." He turned and walked to the door and then went out through the turnstile. Svetlana followed.

Nick got into the rusted Yota and unlocked the passenger side door from the inside. Even there inside a military-grade fenced-in area in a town of ninety people (more or less), he locked the doors to the Yota. Old habits die hard.

Svetlana got in and closed the door. Nick mumbled, "Seatbelt," and started the truck's motor.

No one said anything for several minutes. Neither knew what to say, really. They'd never spoken except during one of Nick's several-al-hours-long question-and-answer sessions on her time spent in The Director's captivity.

Finally, Svetlana broke the silence. "Why does my computer have a keylogger program on it?"

Nick was stunned. He didn't expect her to have found the program so quickly. The Driver was slipping, or was he? Maybe not. Maybe he wanted her to find it, let her know she was being watched.

Juggling it in his head, Nick decided it was best to be straight with her. "I asked that it be installed."

"Why?" Svetlana asked unemotionally as she looked out the window.

"So we would know who you talked to and what you did. Your story about being abducted didn't add up at first, and then I felt it was much too easy to rescue you. I wondered if you were a plant at first, given to us as a rescued victim when you were really a spy. Make sense?"

"Do you still think I'm a spy?" she asked, looking at him directly.

"No. I know you aren't."

"Good," she replied, "because I have some things to tell you. Things I made sure didn't show on my keylogger. I'm afraid they won't be easy to hear."

"Shoot. Spill it, girl. Show me the money!"

Svetlana looked puzzled for a moment and then nodded. "Okay. Well, when I found the keylogger, I put another similar but better program on my computer and discovered The Driver had been checking my activity. So I did the same to him."

Nick laughed. "Nice! Quid pro quo! Go, Svetlana!" He reached across the truck and shook her and then tussled her hair. "I love it! The arrogant bastard has no idea, right?"

Svetlana was confused. "You aren't angry?"

"No, no. Hell, no! Anytime anyone hands the amazing Driver some humble pie, I'm all for it. The bigger the piece, the better! I've done it a few times myself. So what've you learned about our beloved perverted hacker?"

Svetlana nodded. "He's a pervert, first of all, no doubt about that. Second, he's been working for the NSA for several years."

Nick was quiet and suddenly stoic. "How do you know that?"

"I checked his financials just on a hunch after finding some very weird traffic on his computer. He receives a substantial paycheck monthly. Tracing the electronic trail left by the bank, it came back to a government account. It was coded to look like a payment from a dummy corporation, but well, I know what a real corporation looks like in the banking world. It took very little research to uncover it."

"Can you determine how long he's been working for them?"

"For several years, it appears. It's a well-known secret in the hacking world, if that makes any sense at all, that the NSA employs hackers to work for them, probing other government agencies, countries, and corporations. Anything can be a target. The hacker world is a very sketchy place. You can trust no one. Hackers are allowed to do their deeds, and the government knows what they do. It allows it because it further entraps them and makes them more susceptible to manipulation by agencies like the NSA or CIA. Make sense? The more they're allowed to do, the more entangled they are in their own web of hacks."

Nick nodded. "So before we came along, The Driver was already caught in his own web."

"It appears that way, yes."

"Can you continue to monitor his activities and stay in the shadows, undetected?"

"Of course. He may be a world-class hacker, but his own computer security is directed outward, not inward. He has a tremendous blind spot in his computer security once you're inside the walls. I don't mean the physical walls. I'm speaking in an analogy, you understand?"

Nick laughed and laughed. "A blind spot? That's perfect! Yes, I understand. I understand perfectly! You've made my day, Svetlana. Hell, maybe the entire week!" Nick was genuinely happy.

Svetlana was quiet and then asked, "The other day, I heard you attacked Dave. May I ask why?"

Nick was suddenly dark. "I made a mistake. I thought he was laughing and joking about killing a friend of mine. I snapped. I can do that from time to time, unfortunately. My brain is rewired now, too many years of crisis, I guess. I go from zero to homicidal in the blink of an eye."

Svetlana nodded. "I think I understand. I too feel different now after this experience I've had."

Nick nodded and said, "To others, it looks like I'm crazy. To me, I realize I'd be dead by now if I couldn't react the way I do. In normal situations, it doesn't serve me very well, but in the situations, I've been in, it's made the difference between survival and death."

They were both quiet for some time, and then Svetlana again broke the silence. "Why haven't you done something about The Driver yet?"

Nick pulled over and turned off the car. "I like the way you think. It isn't what are you going to do about The Driver; it's why haven't you yet. That's a subtle but important difference." He looked at her long and hard. "I need him where he is, feeding information to The Director. Feeding The Director what I want The Director fed."

Svetlana nodded. "That makes sense. Disinformation, yes? So allowing him to continue and allowing Dave within our walls, that's part of a plan?"

"Yes."

"I'd very much like to also be a part of this plan. I want to hurt those who hurt me."

"You mean The Director," Nick said.

"I mean The Director and The Driver. I've found a communication from The Driver that lists my sister's name as the one who delivered glasses that were poisoned with some kind of neurotoxin to a man named Hauer and then lists me as her only family member. It was sent out to an encoded e-mail address. I assume it was meant for The Director."

Nick took a big breath and nodded. "Okay, I have to talk to Bexx. We've compartmentalized this, what we're doing, I mean so that we know who leaks what and to who. Besides, I guess it's not like we can keep you out. You've discovered in a couple of days what's taken me weeks to realize." Nick smiled. "Now I'm really glad you're here. We have an eye on The Driver, and he has no clue."

He started the truck and pulled back onto the road. He smiled and mumbled, "Sloppy seconds, my ass. Get ready, brother! Judgment Day is coming!"

CHAPTER THIRTY-FOUR

When they arrived at the small store and got out of the truck, Nick realized what Svetlana had said. She'd found a communication between The Driver and The Director.

He stopped. "How many communications have you found between The Double Ds?"

Svetlana looked at him, confused. "Double Ds?" Her face flushed, a bit embarrassed.

"Double Ds. The Director and The Driver. Double Ds, get it?" he replied.

"Oh, I thought... never mind. I've found several. Why?"

"Can you make copies of them, so we can see what The Director knows? And then we'll know what information to feed The Driver and how."

"Of course. The program I inserted on his computer makes copies of all communications and sends them to me via Bluetooth. It's automated. It turns on, sends the information, and turns off. He's completely blind to what I know and what I'm sent. Additionally, I partitioned my hard drive and installed a new operating system so he can only see what's on one side of the hard drive and not the other. I basically put up a wall he doesn't even know exists. And if he tries to find it, I'll know because it'll show me."

"Awesome!" Nick was gleeful. "What else?"

"What else, what?" Svetlana asked, confused again.

"What else have you found out?"

Svetlana thought for a moment. "Well, I notice you refer to The Driver and The Director by title only. I thought maybe you did that by choice, as a way to put some distance between you and them. Now I realize you don't know who The Director is. I know who The Director is. I know his name if you wish to know."

Nick smiled. "It can wait. I want Bexx to hear this. Let's get some food, do the shopping, and then hit the post office."

They gathered the food for the week's meals and paid the clerk. After they ate, they went to the post office side of the small building. Once inside, Nick went to the post office box and opened it. There was a pink slip inside that said there was a package at the front desk that required a signature.

Svetlana watched Nick's face and saw it had instantly changed. He'd been smiling before and happy. Suddenly, he was motionless. Darkness crossed over his face.

"What is it?" she asked.

"A package or letter. I have to sign for it. If I pick it up, whoever sent it will know it's been picked up and that we're here. The last package we received was from a friend The Director had killed. It was part of his will to have that package sent. Other than him, no one knows we're here. But it's more than that."

"What is it?"

"It's addressed to me, Nick Hudson not the name I use now, but my real name. Only the team knows my real name. Oh, and The Driver, so it only makes sense it's probably from The Director."

Svetlana nodded. "What are you going to do?"

Nick shrugged. "Pick up the package."

Nick walked to the desk and rang the bell at the countertop. The middle-aged postmaster waddled up. "Yes? May I help you?"

"I guess I have a package," Nick replied as both a question and a statement.

The postmaster took the pink slip and disappeared into the depths of the building's aisles and walkways. It again struck Nick the building looked so much smaller on the outside. Inside, the walkways in-between the shelves and boxes seemed to go on forever. He frowned thinking *What the hell?*

Finally, the postmaster returned. "Here you go. Do you need anything else?"

Nick looked at the package. "Could you tell me who it was sent from? There's an address on the package, but I'm curious if there's a way to know who sent it?"

"No, I'm afraid we just track the package and when it's delivered. Our system updates automatically. Unless the sender specifically asks and provides us with an e-mail address, we don't send them a specific message."

"Can you check and see if the sender did ask to be notified?"

"Yes, one moment." The postmaster returned. "No, no specific request was made."

Nick nodded. "Thanks."

"You're welcome. Will there be anything else?"

"No, thanks again."

Nick and Svetlana returned to the truck. After talking it over, they decided to open the package just in case it was a bomb or something toxic. That way, no one else would be exposed. Inside was a single DVD, no note, and there was nothing written on the DVD.

Nick looked at Svetlana. "That can't be good. Someone wants me to see something."

He backed out of the gravel parking lot and turned the Yota toward home.

Svetlana turned to Nick a mile later and reached toward the Yota's in-dash stereo. "May I? I haven't heard any music for a very long time. I miss it."

Nick nodded. "Sure, but up here in the middle of nowhere, you won't get much selection other than country."

Svetlana nodded. "I don't care. I just want to hear some music." She started the auto-search function of the FM receiver and waited to see what came through.

Back at the facility, Bexx, and the team were walking outside, cooling down after the afternoon run. Diamond Dave had gone out on the run with the team and fallen far behind. They waited as he finally caught up and encouraged him to push it the last two-hundred meters. Dave wasn't very impressive as a warrior, even less as a runner, but he'd won over a few of them with his "will not quit" attitude. Dave pushed it as best he could and finally came to a less than dramatic finish at the gate. They walked as a group, cooling down and making small talk.

Off in the distance, they saw Nick's Yota approaching. The Mentalist spoke up. "I'll bet anyone's turn at doing the dishes for a week that Svetlana is crying when Nick pulls up. Who wants to bet?" No one said anything at first, but The Mentalist wouldn't let it go. "Come on! I'll take your turn for a week if I lose. You take mine if I win. Who's in?"

Bexx said, "I'll take that bet."

The Mentalist nodded. "Anyone else? Come on, you chicken shits."

Special K thought about it for a minute and remembered the Chinese takeout Nick had quietly sent to her in Washington, D.C. She said, "I'm in. I'll take the bet."

The Mentalist clapped her hands. "There's one born every minute. Come on, Diamond Dave. You're going to have to do dishes eventually. If you win, it'll be later rather than sooner. What do you say?"

Dave rubbed his still wounded left eye. He wasn't sure he wanted to bet a thing on anything Nick would do, ever. He seemed frighteningly unpredictable. "I'll pass," he finally managed squeak out in-between phlegm-filled gasps for air.

Buffy raised her hand. I'll take the bet. The Mentalist was ecstatic.

"Anyone else?" No one else took the bet.

Bexx walked past The Mentalist, smiling and said, "Double or nothing, smart ass?"

"You're on, Commander!" The Asgarda all started to talk animatedly amongst themselves.

The Mentalist started to verbally paint the picture of Nick coming up all red-faced and psychotic, screaming at poor Svetlana, who would be crying intensely, snot running down her shirt in a river of goop and slime. When the car stopped, she'd run into the facility, sobbing, and go straight to her room to hide.

Bexx began to wonder. The scenario The Mentalist described did start to sound more plausible. Maybe she'd made a mistake. It was too late now.

The Mentalist began to goad Bexx. "Triple or nothing, Commander? Feeling brave?"

Bexx said nothing, but The Mentalist kept at her. Finally, annoyed as hell, she said, "Sure, triple or nothing."

In the distance, they could see the Yota approach. They could see rapid-arm movements inside the cab of the truck. It looked like Nick and Svetlana were in a fight.

The Mentalist was beside herself, laughing and pointing at Bexx. "Triple or nothing. You made the bet! Good hell, she's beating the shit out of him. I can see it!"

As the truck got closer, they heard some music playing, and the entire group stopped to watch. The Yota pulled up with the windows down. Inside, Nick and Svetlana were belting out the final lyrics of *"Ghost Riders In the Sky"* by *The Outlaws*. Nick was playing air drums as he drove, while Svetlana played the air guitar finale. The both sang loudly the final "Ghost riders in the sky!" Bexx cringed. Nick still sang as awful as she remembered, but Svetlana was no better, and if Bexx was honest, she was worse. They sang horribly.

Special K walked up to The Mentalist and nodded. "There's something you don't see every day, huh? Hope you like doing dishes! The next time you won't be doing dishes is so far out, I can't even fathom it. Every night! Every single damn night! From now until... whoa, I need a calendar to see how far out this will go!"

The entire team was feeling a bit uneasy, watching Nick and Svetlana continue their air instrumental rendition of the song's final few notes. Nick smiled, and Svetlana laughed. The team was freaked out. This was the last thing they expected. Bexx smiled, watching their reactions. She nodded to Special K and then looked toward The Mentalist. The Mentalist was sulking, head down, defeated as they walked up to the truck.

Nick got out and spoke to Bexx. "We have a package. I'm not sure what it is, but it's a DVD. That can't be good."

She nodded. "Okay, let's go in and see what it is."

Nick looked at The Mentalist and asked, "What's wrong?"

She didn't reply. There was no way she was going to open herself up to more ridicule.

Nick continued to whistle the melody of the song for the next few minutes as they made their way inside the facility.

CHAPTER THIRTY-FIVE

The team was silent. The only sound that could be heard in the facility was Dave throwing up in the upstairs bathroom.

Bexx stopped the DVD and looked at every one of her team's faces. "This is what we face. Make no mistake, the video is real, and this is our enemy." There was silence for a moment, and then Dave wretched again, this time harder. No one was prepared for the contents of the DVD. Nick stared at the now-blank screen and said nothing. His face showed nothing. No emotion... nothing... not even a twitch. Bexx motioned for the team to leave, and most were happy to oblige her. Svetlana stayed.

Finally, Bexx verbally said, "Svetlana, would you excuse us for a moment?"

Svetlana said, "No. I will not leave. We spoke during the trip to the post office, Nick and I, and I want to be a part of the planning from now on. I will not leave."

Nick finally moved. He stood up and walked to the Blue-ray player and pushed play. "We need to make the most of this. Let's watch it again, pay attention to every detail. Deconstruct it. You focus on the background... every detail, the walls, the paint, the doors. Look for anything we can use."

Nick paused the video and turned to Bexx. "Svetlana can stay if that's okay with you. She's lived inside this monster. Maybe she can help us. We talked, and when we're done here, she'll bring you up to speed on what we talked about. However, that'll have to be in private." Nick motioned to the bathroom, where Dave still enthusiastically tried to void the contents of his already empty stomach.

Bexx was surprised by Nick's sudden change of heart about Svetlana but decided it was best to trust his judgment. She replied, "Okay, let's get started. What do you want to do?"

"I want to take this video frame by frame and analyze everything, every shadow, every movement. Then when we're done, watch it again in real speed." Nick turned to Svetlana. "When we watch it in real time, I want you to listen to the voices. Close your eyes and listen and tell me if you recognize them or anything in their patterns of speech. Try not to get drawn into the emotion of the moment. This video is meant to inflict terror and divide us. No doubt, it's real and horrific. But we must make the most of it."

When they were about ten minutes into the frame-by-frame of the video, Dave finally left the bathroom. The wound Nick had inflicted on his left eye had reopened, and blood slowly trickled down his cheek.

"Last time I saw some shit like that was Iraq. Some dude was a Shiite and got caught in a Sunni neighborhood right after the Sunni Musab bin Omair mosque was attacked in the Diyala Province. They beat him sense-less and then tied him to four cars and pulled him apart. We had orders not to interfere." Nick listened and then said, "This is your boss at work." He waited for the denial from Dave that he still worked for The Director... or at least maybe a reaction to the comment. He made a point of not saying this was your boss. Instead, he said, "is your boss."

Dave was too stunned to notice what had been said. Instead, he replied, "Who is that? Who are they torturing?"

Nick replied, "It's no one, really. She has nothing to do with us, or me. She just ran the gym I worked out in at Moses Lake. This isn't operational, Dave. This is psychological for him and us. First, it shows he hasn't even begun to get nasty yet, and second, it's meant to inflict terror on the team. A reality check. We rescued Svetlana, and now you. He wants us to know the outcome if we fail, make us question our commitment to fighting him. Eventually, you'll have to decide where you stand."

The comment was again directed at Dave. His time was running out. Dave, still too stunned to notice the subtlety, nodded and quickly turned to get out of the room. He had no desire to watch the video again.

He stopped at the door and asked, "What was her name?"

"Ali. Ali was her name," Nick replied, focusing on the video without looking back over his shoulder.

He pushed the video forward frame by frame once Dave had in fact left the room. Nick had Svetlana update Bexx on what they'd shared in the truck. They went through the video step by step until they were satisfied they understood every aspect of it.

Nick stopped the video after the third time through and said, "I count three men. Does anyone disagree?"

Svetlana said she thought she heard four distinct voices just as Ali began to scream and right as the hydraulic system was engaged and her arms and legs slowly, mercilessly were torn from her torso.

"Are you sure?" Nick asked. "Four voices?"

"I am. I recognize them. I remember hearing their voices at the place where they kept me when I wasn't at an appointment. An appointment is what they called my clients."

"So, it's the same people we would have faced, maybe at the Bellagio, maybe not, but definitely The Director's men. And definitely associated with Izadi."

Svetlana shuddered when she heard the name Izadi. "Yes, Izadi. That's what they called it, the virtual escort service. They called the actual physical building 'the meat locker.' But online, it was Izadi."

"Do you remember anything new about the meat locker?" Nick asked.

She shook her head no. "I was always heavily sedated, more compliant that way. You know these are men who don't want any kind of real interaction. They want you subdued and unable to resist in any way."

"Understood," Nick said.

He turned to Bexx. "I'd love to locate these bastards and return the favor, cut them to pieces and have someone video it and send it back to The Director, but that would be playing into The Director's game. We have to find another way. Meanwhile, Svetlana has found communications between our beloved Driver and The Director she needs to brief you on."

They sat for several more hours and talked over the information Svetlana had retrieved from The Driver's computer and then what they planned to do next. There were several options on the table. Finally, Nick said, "Let's break for now and process all of this." He handed the DVD to Svetlana. "Look on the back end. Make sure there's nothing hidden in the formatting. Discs like this can't just play without some command language in the background. I remember a few years back, China had loaded spyware on all their exported DVDs. It was a big deal in the DoD. They couldn't use any DVDs from China in their computers. Keep that in mind. There could be anything. We need to make the most of all of it."

Svetlana agreed.

Nick left the room. Bexx turned to Svetlana. "I need every communication The Driver has made with The Director as far back as you can get them. Everything organized in a timeline. I want to know what he was responsible for and what his intentions were for all of us. We have to assume as well that he had a part in this video and the identification of Ali as the next person to torture. Be careful but be thorough. I want it as soon as you can." Bexx continued. "You wanted in on the planning. That's fine with me. You've already shown your value. However, keep it quiet. We've made too many mistakes. We can't get away with making many more without paying a severe cost. Understand?"

Svetlana replied, "Yes, I do. I'll have you the documents immediately."

Bexx and Nick sat talking in their room for about an hour, and finally, Bexx came out. She had a question for Svetlana. When she reached the kitchen, Svetlana was there, waiting with several large folders full of messages to and from The Director and The Driver.

"That was quick!" Bexx said. "All this in the last hour?"

"No. I had it all prepared to give you. I wanted you to understand why I did what I was going to do."

"And that was?" Bexx asked, confused.

"Kill The Driver," Svetlana said.

Bexx stopped and looked at Svetlana. She saw that perhaps there was much more to Svetlana than she'd imagined. After all, she was Special K's sister and had lived in one of the worst areas in Germany.

Bexx nodded. "I see. What made you change your mind?"

"I realized when I analyzed all the information that was available, there was a plan in place. I didn't know what that plan was, but there was the keylogger on my computer, Nick's obvious discomfort with having Dave in the building near any of us, and the seemingly random event of my being kidnapped immediately after my sister had delivered poison-laden glasses to Mr. Hauer, causing his death. It all added up to a covert plan my rash action may damage, so I waited to speak to Nick alone. Today was my chance to ask him directly. He answered honestly, and here we are."

Bexx nodded. "Makes sense, and from what you've read in the messages, you think The Driver needs to be removed from the team."

Svetlana paused for a moment. "From what Nick has told me, your plan is to make the most of his communications with The Director. Is that accurate?"

Bexx nodded, listening.

"I can take his place in this communication process, seamlessly. My sister isn't the only one who studied languages. I can keep the written communication between them congruent, and I've studied each of their patterns of speech as they write back and forth to each other. It would be a seamless transition if I were to be put into his place. The issue I see would be Buffy. They're obviously close. However, if she sees the communications about her in the documents I've provided, I think she may change her mind."

Bexx nodded. "Nick and I have been speaking the last hour or so about you, and that was exactly what we had in mind, asking you if you felt comfortable taking The Driver's place."

"I do, but I do have a request if I'm to fulfill that role on the team."

"What exactly is that request?" Bexx asked.

After Svetlana had explained what she wanted, Bexx nodded. "Let me think on that one for a minute. I can't see a reason why not, but I want to run it past Nick and JT before I say yes."

Svetlana nodded. "As long as we're clear, Commander, this is non-negotiable if I'm to fulfill this role."

Bexx smiled. She was really starting to like Svetlana. "Understood," she replied.

CHAPTER THIRTY-SIX

Bexx ran Svetlana's request past JT, and he agreed it was a possibility. He'd spent many hours training her, and she'd been a very quick study. Her understanding of mathematics had easily transferred to her training, given the bridge he had created. The training made sense to her, and it was intuitive. JT said she was a natural.

Nick, however, had another point of view. After he'd listened to what Bexx had to say, he said, "We need a trial run of this communications takeover of The Driver. We need her to show us she can pull this off with someone who knows The Driver very well."

Bexx thought it over. Nick was right, a demonstration of the skill set was much more tangible than a mere claim of it. "What do you have in mind?"

Nick smiled. "It's kind of obvious, isn't it?"

Bexx shook her head. "No, it isn't."

"We have her communicate with Buffy. If she can pull that off, then I'd agree to her terms. Talk is cheap. Prove it with someone who knows The Driver better than any of us," Nick replied.

Bexx nodded. It would be a cruel trick, given the direction they were headed with The Driver's fate, but it would be an excellent litmus test of Svetlana's skill.

Bexx returned to Svetlana with the counter condition to fulfill her request. She'd have to convince Buffy she was The Driver. If she could pull that off in the next 24 hours, she was on the team, and her conditions would be met. Meanwhile, Bexx contacted The Driver and asked him to have wood delivered to the facility. They were going to have a meeting, and it had been a long time since they sat around the fire and discussed anything. Given the DVD they'd received, she felt it was time to re-evaluate their direction as a team.

The Driver agreed. "Kind of makes you wonder, doesn't it? Like, is all this worth it? I mean, life is short, and this grudge match between Nick and The Director... is it really worth it? I don't want to end up in some camp or even worse, being pulled apart like a fly having its wings ripped off by some demented kid."

Bexx nodded but said nothing. "Order two cords of wood, and have it delivered." Funny how now she heard what The Driver said differently.

The wood arrived later that night. Meanwhile, Svetlana had gone to work on her task of convincing Buffy she was The Driver. It wasn't long, and she had her proof. She found Bexx and motioned for her to follow her to the new Bat Cave. The door was locked, and they stood outside listening. Svetlana handed Bexx copies of the messages she had sent to Buffy. She read them while they listened to The Driver and Buffy inside. Svetlana had convinced Buffy to meet The Driver for a "nooner." In addition, she'd convinced her to assume a dominatrix role—something specific enough to be proof she had, in fact, convinced Buffy she was The Driver. Bexx laughed as she could hear The Driver being disciplined by Buffy inside the Bat Cave. Soon enough, he would be disciplined for real. She was now convinced Svetlana could pull off the switch.

She nodded. "Okay, you've convinced me. You'll have your conditions met. Are you absolutely sure you want to do this?"

"Yes, absolutely," Svetlana replied.

Later that night, the team met at a newly constructed fire pit about fifty meters from the facility. Nick had been in charge of the evening meal. He ordered pizza, The Driver's favorite, as a sick sendoff to his twisted friend. While the team gathered around the fire, The Mentalist was sulking as she was doing the evening's dishes. She was grateful Nick had bought pizza and not made another roast. She only had to wash a few plates with tomato sauce stains and a few forks. Nõn would have thought it ironic the Asgarda now regularly used napkins at dinner. When The Mentalist was finally done with what would be many weeks of dishes, she finished up and went outside to the fire. Svetlana had been waiting patiently and quietly in an adjacent room. It was time to put her plan into action.

Before the fire and dinner, Bexx had approached Buffy and handed her the envelope that concerned her future as The Driver had envisioned it post Cachibaché mission. Buffy was stunned. Then she read the plan for her after the Izadi Mission. She paced and cursed on the far end of the fenced area surrounding the facility.

Finally, she asked, "What are your plans, Commander?"

Bexx answered, "I first want to know if you're able to understand this has to end... and now?"

"I agree. What about the rest of the team? Did he have similar plans for all of us?"

"Some are similar. Some are not as kind as yours were," Bexx replied.

"Do they know? Does the team know?"

"Not yet. We're planning a dinner and then a fire afterward. While I hand out the messages that correspond to each team member, Svetlana has asked to be the one who confronts The Driver. Afterward, I'm hoping the two of you will be able to work together. Svetlana will be assuming The Driver's online identity and continuing the communications with The Director. Do you think you'll be able to do that?"

"Yes, I believe that would be best. Now that I see what they both had planned for me, I cannot imagine what they had planned for the rest of us. I'm even more motivated now to pursue The Director."

As they gathered around the fire, Bexx had called each of the Asgarda members by name and handed them an envelope. Some were larger than others. Bexx explained all contained messages sent and received from The Driver and The Director concerning each of them. First, the plans that had been made for the survivors of the Cachibaché mission, and then again for the survivors of the rescue of Svetlana or the Izadi mission. She asked each of them to wait until she instructed them to open the envelopes.

She nodded, acknowledging their astonished faces. "Yes, The Driver has been against us from the beginning."

In the Bat Cave, The Driver was messaging The Director about the latest developments in the facility. The DVD was having the desired effect.

The team was questioning their commitment to Nick's quest. As he typed, Svetlana knocked at the door.

"Driver, are you in there?" Svetlana said quietly.

The Driver said, "Yes, hold on."

A moment later, he opened the door. Svetlana smiled and asked seductively, "May I come in?"

"Sure, come on in. What's up? What can The Driver help you with?"

Svetlana did her best shy girl routine and said, "I heard you being disciplined earlier by Buffy."

The Driver was slightly embarrassed but only momentarily. "Yes, I don't know what got into her," he said, laughing.

Svetlana laughed and began in her most coy and shy little-girl voice, "Yes, I wondered that myself. But I found the idea intriguing. Driver, I was wondering while everyone is at the fire tonight if you would like to discipline me. I've been a very bad girl."

The Driver grinned. "Of course. I mean, it'll be our secret, right? No one has to know, especially Buffy."

"Of course. We wouldn't want her to know about our little secret." Svetlana smiled shyly. "You should probably close the door and secure it just in case someone comes back."

The Driver jumped out of his chair and ran to the door to secure it and returned to Svetlana. "Tell me, what have you done to deserve to be punished by The Driver? How bad have you been, little girl?"

"Just to be safe, Driver, let's lock the inside lock as well." Svetlana ran her index finger down the front of his shirt.

The Driver agreed. He turned and bolted the door from the inside and turned around.

Outside the door, Special K had been tasked to back up Svetlana just in case things went south. She was waiting just out of sight when the door closed, and she heard the locks being engaged. She had keys to each of the locks. Bexx had provided them just in case.

Inside the room as The Driver turned to face Svetlana, the scene switched instantly. Svetlana had dropped the seductive schoolgirl ruse and assumed a fighting stance. When The Driver eagerly spun to face her, he was met with a left jab to the throat. Svetlana began her extraction of a pound or two of flesh from The Driver. Someone definitely would be disciplined tonight, and it wouldn't be Svetlana.

The Driver dropped to the floor, choking, gasping for air. Svetlana drove her foot into his groin, kicking him repeatedly until he passed out. She kept at it. When she was done with his genitals, they were black and blue and effectively crushed to a pulp. It would be a long time before The Driver would be able to play with his favorite toy. Svetlana was just getting warmed up.

Special K heard the fight begin and tried to open the door. All the doors' locks were unlocked in moments, and still, the door would not open. She panicked. She began kicking on the door, calling out to Svetlana, and then to The Driver. No one answered.

Ten minutes later, the door opened, and Svetlana peeked out, smiling, covered in sweat. She said, "Hey, sis, I thought Bexx might have tasked you to be here as a backup. Sorry about that, but not today. This was mine. I locked the door from the inside until I was finished. Now, would you help me drag this piece of shit to the silos? Silo number one is open and will be The Driver's new home. Bexx has it all ready."

Special K looked at The Drivers' bloody, purple, and swollen face. "Um, yeah, I think I can do that."

Outside, Bexx had begun to have the team open the envelopes, one by one, and read the messages out loud to the rest of team. By the time they were done reading them, the team was done with The Driver. When all the girls had finished, Nick stood up and walked over to where Diamond Dave was standing by the fire.

"Sorry, brother, but no one is immune today. Here are the messages about you from The Director, advising The Driver that you would be coming, and you were secretly working for him." The group was silent, the girls glaring at Dave. Nick continued. "You'll find the fourth paragraph particularly interesting. That's where The Director admits his good fortune in your offer and reveals he'd planned to have you killed until you called to offer to infiltrate us."

Dave said nothing; he was genuinely terrified of what would happen next.

Nick smiled. "No worries, Dave. I knew you were working for him. There would be no way he'd let you come here otherwise. The fact that you made it here in one piece, unharmed, confirmed you were a spy. But you see, as soon as you're done, he's told The Driver you'll be 'removed from the equation,' so there was no need to involve you in their larger plan; just let you distract me and Bexx, and if I didn't kill you, he would have a team ready to do the job once The Asgarda and I were destroyed. Wonderful to have such good friends, huh?" Dave was silent and looked at each team member, one at a time.

JT snickered as he watched the scene unfold. He looked at Diamond Dave. "Nick asked me to keep an eye out just in case you or The Driver decided to make a move before he was ready. You wouldn't have succeeded." He nodded to Bexx. "That was the conversation you asked about. I was the insurance policy, just in case."

Just then, Svetlana opened the facility door and, assisted by Special K, dragged the limp body of The Driver to silo number one. They dropped the body into the silo. There was a brief pause, and then a sickening thwack as the body of The Driver hit the floor thirty-five feet below. Svetlana closed the door and began walking to the fire.

Fearing he was next, Dave asked, "So what now?"

Nick nodded. "Exactly. What now, Diamond Dave? The decision is yours. Work with us, or should I put your ass outside of the gate and let The Director have his way with you? Seems pretty clear to me what your decision should be. Either way, The Director will kill you if he survives. Seems you have a definite interest in working with us. Kind of caught between a rock and a hard place, huh?"

Dave nodded. He was caught; Nick was right. It was very clear the road to survival had only one path—to work with Nick, Bexx, and the Asgarda against The Director.

The next morning, Nick opened the door to silo number one. The Driver was sitting upright and looked up into the bright sunlight with the one eye that wasn't still swollen shut from Svetlana's revenge beating.

"Driver, is that you?" Nick called out. "What the hell are you doing down there?"

The Driver started to cry out as he stood up, "Hey, brother, am I glad to see you! Help me. The girls... the girls went crazy. Svetlana tried to seduce The Driver! She wanted some of The Driver's legendary BDSM discipline. Then she just snapped and attacked me in the Bat Cave. I think I must've broken my arm when they dropped me in here. Help me, brother! Please!"

Nick lowered a bucket with a piece of twine slowly to The Driver.

The Driver looked in the bucket. "What the hell is this? The Driver isn't in a position to make proper use of this at the moment, brother. Get me out of here!"

Nick laughed maniacally. "It puts the lotion on its back," he called out over and over again, laughing so hard, he could hardly breathe.

The Driver slid back down the wall and sat down, realizing now he was truly screwed.

Later when Nick returned to the facility, Bexx looked at him. "Where have you been?"

"Just spending some quality time with The Driver."

Bexx rolled her eyes and looked in the bucket. "What are you doing with my lotion?"

Nick laughed until his face was bright red, and he was gasping for air. He repeated in-between gasps for air, "It puts the lotion on its back." He laughed harder, tears rolling down his face. He began coughing and gagging until he nearly threw up.

Bexx rolled her eyes. Shaking her head, she thought silently, *Nick can be so incredibly juvenile sometimes.* "What do you think we should do with him?" she asked in a more serious tone a few moments later.

Nick stopped laughing for a moment. "I don't know. Maybe I should make a trip to Grand Forks and prepare a war bag."

"A war bag?" she asked, confused.

"Just a few items to make his passing more memorable. Until then, let's give him hope—just a small glimmer of hope. Let him think you may take pity on him, and he has a chance. Then when the time is right, I'll pull the chair out from under him."

"I thought you wanted to leave this to me? That is what you said, remember?" Bexx reminded him.

Nick nodded slowly. "Yes, I remember. That was before I read the e-mails Svetlana recovered. In particular, the one that mentioned how he would enjoy breaking you. I'm no longer interested in letting him pass easily or without pain."

"You seriously think I'd go easy on him?" Bexx said, astonished.

Nick laughed. "No, but I don't think you'd be as enthusiastic."
"

CHAPTER THIRTY-SEVEN

The next day, Bexx and the Asgarda began the devious task of slowly convincing The Driver he may have a chance at surviving his betrayal after all. It was a lot easier to accomplish than they expected. The Driver actually believed he deserved to survive and that in some way, all of them secretly envied Buffy and her relationship with him. Apparently, his ego knew no limits. By the end of the week, his arm was set by The Mentalist. He was back to his old, cocky self, making barely veiled references to his sexual prowess and hacking skills. Finally one day, Bexx came in to check on him.

Bexx nodded. "Driver."

"Commander," he replied, "I assume you're here to ask me a few questions."

"No, not really. Just checking on your recovery. Do you feel ready to return to the Bat Cave yet?"

Stunned, The Driver smiled. "Yes! Definitely yes, I feel up for it. When do you see that happening?" Already he was plotting his communications with The Director and imagining the many different ways he would pay the Asgarda back for their treatment of him. They'd beg The Driver for mercy when he was done breaking them.

Bexx thought. "I'm not sure. We'll have to talk it over, I guess."

"We? You mean you and the Asgarda?"

"No, me and Nick."

The Driver felt a chill run through his body, and he noticeably shivered at the thought. "How's Nick doing?"

"He's gone to Grand Forks today. He should be back tonight sometime. I'll talk to him when he returns, and then we'll let you know what the plan for your return will be."

The Driver smiled and nodded. "Thanks. Let me know."

Bexx nodded. "Rest now. I'll have someone bring you dinner tonight."

The Driver nodded. "Could Buffy bring the meal? I mean, we need to talk. I need to apologize and explain."

"Explain? Explain what? Apologize for what?"

"Um... my indiscretion with Svetlana."

Bexx said nothing. She realized The Driver had no idea about the cache of emails Svetlana had given them describing what he planned to do with each of them if and when The Director defeated them.

Bexx shook her head. "No, I don't think so. She isn't as forgiving as she should be. That may take some time, I'm afraid. But I'm sure eventually she'll come around. I mean, you are The Driver, after all."

The Driver nodded, smiling, unaware she was being sarcastic. He thanked her as she walked to the metal staircase that hugged the circular concrete tube that encased the missile silo he'd called home for the past few days.

Nick returned from Grand Forks later that afternoon with a few boxes, some tools, an ATV battery kit, and a wooden chair. Bexx met him at the parking garage.

"Did you find everything you need?" she asked.

"I did, and I had an idea on the way up." He pulled out a small ATV battery and then pointed at the wooden chair. "It needs to be assembled, but it'll do the trick."

Bexx nodded. "I don't want to know, do I?"

Nick smiled a wicked smile. "Not this time, no."

She nodded. "I spoke to him today and realized he has no idea about the cache of e-mails Svetlana gave us. He thinks this whole thing is because of some sexual indiscretion he had at Svetlana."

Nick laughed. "Of course he does. Don't you realize every woman born secretly wants The Driver?" Nick laughed and laughed. "Classic Driver move if there ever was one."

Later that day, The Mentalist brought The Driver dinner and sat with him while he ate. He assumed she missed his company as well. As they sat, he tried to make small talk, asking about how things had been going outside the silo. She answered in vague terms, watching to make sure he ate the entire meal. As they talked, The Driver began to drift off to sleep. Her task had been completed. He'd consumed the entire narcotic-laden meal. He'd be out for hours while Nick made his preparations.

The next morning, The Driver slowly awoke. His head hurt, and he felt foggy. He had no memory of what'd happened the night before. The last thing he remembered was speaking to The Mentalist while he ate... and then nothing. He struggled to open his eyes and moaned deeply. He was very thirsty. His mouth was dry, and his tongue felt thick and burned. He tried to lick his lips and was vaguely aware of the sick, sticky sound his mouth made when he tried to open it.

Nick had been waiting, watching for hours. The chair had been assembled, and all the items he'd bought were set up. He'd duct taped The Driver to the chair while he slept and then sat back, waiting patiently. He got up as The Driver started to move and picked up a small bottle of water.

"Drink, brother. I need you to be in top form today. Lots of unanswered questions. Most of the answers, I already know, but a few I want to hear for myself, straight from the legendary Driver himself."

The Driver lurched back to reality at the sound of Nick's voice, suddenly very awake and afraid.

Nick pressed the bottle to his mouth and said, "Drink? Or no?"

The Driver paused for a few seconds, looking terrified into Nick's calm face. Finally, he nodded and managed to whisper, "Yes."

Nick let The Driver drink as much as he wanted and then sat back down and looked at him quietly, patiently.

Several minutes passed, maybe even an hour. Neither said a word. They just looked at each other. Nick, lost in thought, remembered the conversation they'd had in the original Bat Cave and how The Driver had found the information about the drone strike on his home Nick hadn't realized, there had been a survivor. Nick remembered he'd been so stunned at the realization he'd dropped his guard and chose to believe in The Driver. Now looking back, it was crystal clear. The Driver had been hiding in plain sight for so long, lying, evading, and eluding, that when he was faced with Nick and the painful loss of a fingernail, he just played the part he'd been born to play. Nick bought it.

He smiled, thinking to himself, *Yes, he was pretty convincing and continued to be for a long time.*

Nick was startled as The Driver finally spoke. "Are you waiting for me to say something, brother?"

Nick smiled. "Nah, just thinking about how we met, our Tinder date. You remember that day in the Bat Cave? You found Jay had survived the drone strike and used it to prove to me you were the hacker you claimed to be. An amazing feat of hacking there, brother."

The Driver nodded uneasily. "Thanks. It wasn't much, really."

Nick nodded. "No, no, it wasn't. I should've realized there would be no path to that information. The Director would have made sure of that. You pulled it up because you had inside knowledge of the event. You work for The Director."

The Driver said nothing. He made no verbal denial but shook his head no.

Nick smiled. "Don't shake your head, brother. We both know it's true. Verbally, you don't deny it. Physically, you try to deny it by shaking your head. See, that's called a conflict, a nonverbal cue that tells me you know I know. Time to be real, Driver. Time to be honest. I value honesty, remember?"

The Driver managed to speak in a small voice. "I don't know what you're talking about, Nick. We were friends, remember? We were in this fight together."

Nick shook his head and sat down, staring at the floor, not making eye contact with The Driver. He continued. "Then I went to see Jay and obtained the information on Cachibaché, really only the post office box where the bills were paid from. A forwarding address was all. Remember how you were stunned? Then you asked how I was able to obtain it. Sloppy seconds, you called it. Now I wonder what address you would have sent me to if I hadn't been able to get the real information. I probably would've died in some shitty ambush set up by you and The Director." Nick looked up at The Driver and asked, "Yes? Am I right? That's why you were so stunned. You had no expectation of me finding any information at all, and then when I did, you had to backpedal. Switch to a new plan."

Again, no denial from The Driver.

"I asked you a question, Driver," Nick said menacingly.

The Driver said nothing.

"Do you understand the rules here, Driver? I ask a question, and you answer honestly." Nothing... silence. Nick shook his head and picked up the Hitachi NR90GR2 gas operated framing nail gun. "This is the most powerful gas operated nailing gun I could find online. I picked it up on my trip to Grand Forks. It has hundreds of four and five-star reviews. Let's see how well it works, shall we?"

Nick turned the gun on, walked to The Driver, and dropped the gun onto his left hand and pulled the trigger. The nail pierced the back of the hand and drove into the wooden chair's armrest, securing the hand brutally. The Driver screamed. The pain was unbelievable. He was too panicked to realize Nick had moved the gun to his right hand. The explosion of pain in the right hand instantly cleared his head of any doubt. Nick meant to get the truth, and he would do whatever it took to make The Driver talk.

Nick stepped back. "Are we clearer now, Driver? You backed the wrong horse, brother! Time to pay the piper. Time to come clean and cleanse your soul of all your dirty little secrets. Spill it!"

The Driver screamed for a few more moments, eyes wide as he stared astonished at the sight of the nails piercing the backs of his hands. Meanwhile, Nick had sat back down calmly and began again.

"Am I correct in my assumption you had another more devious plan in mind when I was at the burn unit?"

The Driver finally nodded. "Yes," he said, breathing heavily.

Nick nodded. I thought so. "And you've been in constant communication with The Director this entire time, correct?"

The Driver nodded.

"It was no accident we took Cachibaché. When I changed the plan at the last minute, you had to as well, and that was why..." Nick paused. "That was why we were successful and why the sniper team waited until the entire team was all present before they engaged us?"

The Driver said nothing.

Nick sighed, picked up the nail gun, and began to walk back to where The Driver was sitting.

"Yes! Yes! I had to change plans. And when we found out about the gas station incident, I wanted to make sure you were dead first."

Nick stopped and thought. "Tell me, Driver, why didn't you just flip the script? Change sides and join us? I mean, do you really think it was wise to cross me? Did you think I wouldn't figure you out? Seriously?"

The Driver tried to explain. "It seemed like the best bet at the time, brother. I mean, you were convinced I was legit, or at least I thought you were. The Director had been a thorn in my side for so long, using me, threatening me. Finally, you just kind of fell into my lap, and he wanted you badly. He promised if I delivered you, I'd be free again."

"So my life, Nõn's life, and the Asgarda for your freedom? That was the deal?"

The Driver nodded.

Nick spoke quietly, "So tell me what his plans are now."

"I don't know," The Driver replied.

"Wrong answer, brother." Nick brought the nail gun to The Driver's right shoulder and fired a nail into the joint. The nail brutally wedged in-between the ball and socket. The Driver's eyes rolled back in his head, and he passed out. Nick spoke out loud. "Not yet, brother. We're just getting started. I have many more questions for you to answer." He went to the medical kit and retrieved the smelling salts. Breaking one open, he waved it under The Driver's nose, snapping him rudely back into consciousness. "No naps," Nick said and laughed out loud. "No naps! Driver, did you ever see that show? Some guy shrinks his kid and then makes the kid huge, and the kid hates naps. I forget the title."

The Driver didn't answer.

"Anyway," Nick continued, "let's move along. Next question."

CHAPTER THIRTY-EIGHT

O utside the silo, Bexx and Buffy were walking while Nick and The Driver began their Tinder date part deux. Bexx asked how Buffy was doing since the emails Svetlana had recovered had been distributed to the team.

"I'm okay, I guess. I mean, when I look back, I knew something wasn't right. Too many unanswered questions and coincidences, you know?" Buffy answered.

Bexx nodded and replied, "I believe we'll have our answers now," she said as the muffled sound of The Driver screaming rolled over the dry North Dakota ground.

Buffy nodded and said, "Can we go back in? I don't want to listen to this. I know what he was, but still it's fresh, and honestly, it hurts."

Bexx nodded. "Sure. Let's go in."

Inside, Nick had decided to let Bexx and the Asgarda finish off The Driver. He had one final question.

"Driver, tell me something I don't know. I've asked what I already figured out. Tell me what I missed."

"Fuck you!" The Driver spit out venomously.

Nick rolled his eyes. "Okay, man, I'm leaving now."

Nick started to pack up the war bag and gathered up all the tools. He started toward the metal staircase when The Driver finally spoke.

"I'll have the last laugh, you fuck," The Driver spit out. "Wait and see. When The Driver sets up a plan, it's flawless. Remember, you never saw it coming when I set you and Nõn up. You won't see it coming now. Your precious Bexx will wish she was dead before The Driver is done pounding that ass. She'll beg for the release of death! Did she ever mention to you the time she got down on her knees, begging The Driver for a taste? I bet she didn't mention that one."

Nick stopped. He'd walked fifteen steps. "What did you say?"

"You heard me, asshole. She begged me. 'Please, Driver, let me taste you,'" he said mockingly. "And when I'm long gone, my plan will still be in effect. You'll watch her be violated, tortured, and in pain and be able to do nothing, but while you watch, I want you to remember she begged The Driver, licked her lips and begged me."

Nick erupted from the stairwell. In one move, he hurtled the handrail and landed on his feet with the war bag in hand, fifteen feet below. "That's more like it, brother. Keep talking. Tell me all about your plans to harm Bexx. Tell me how she begged the legendary Driver for some of his amazing dick. Keep talking. You're on a roll. Go, brother, go!" Nick ripped the war bag open and removed a cordless drill, a pack of Dewalt titanium drill bits, and the ATV battery.

The Driver kept spewing details about how he'd bent Bexx over in the barn and fucked her in the ass while Nick had been on one of his ridiculous walks. "She screamed when she came for The Driver," he said. "Has she ever screamed for you? Doubtful! Oh, and by the way, Nick, how does my cock taste? She's sucked it so many times and then went to your room. You must have tasted it nearly as much as she did."

Nick pulled out the battery and removed the water that accompanied it. He matched the water hose to a drill bit that would be about the same size, secured it in the drill, and tightened the drill chuck.

Nick turned to The Driver. "Now I see why The Director is sacrificing you so early. You lack imagination. Your replacement at least has some imagination." Nick pulled the trigger on the drill, making sure it would operate. "Shall we?"

The Driver screamed as Nick drilled a single hole in each of his knee-caps and then opened the ATV Battery water bottle. "Acidic water, my friend. You may want to prepare yourself, this is going to really hurt." Nick put the hose into the freshly drilled hole in each kneecap and poured the acid water straight into the joint.

The Driver discovered pain he would have thought impossible to survive, but he kept describing the sexual encounters he claimed to have had with Bexx. Finally, he said, "This is something you don't know. Are you ready, Nick? Think you have it all covered? Got it all figured out? Bexx, your precious Bexx, works for The Director! She has from the start. Did you really think she came all the way here because of some stupid fucking wolf story? Oh no, asshole, she's been in on the big picture the entire time, and when the time is right, she'll..."

Nick picked up the nail gun and loaded it. He turned to The Driver and began firing. He fired it until all of his nails were gone. Finally, the room was quiet, and The Driver was silent.

Nick breathed heavily. Listening to the claims The Driver made had flipped a switch in his head. Nick thought he could deal with nearly anything The Driver said; he was wrong. The Driver had found his Achilles heel.

Nick climbed slowly out of the silo, one metal step at a time. It seemed to take hours to climb the stairwell, and eventually he came out into the nighttime air and walked toward the main above-ground building. Nick grabbed the door handle and waited a moment and then pulled it open, going inside.

Bexx and Buffy were sitting at the kitchen table, still talking, when Nick entered the room. They both stopped when they saw him. He looked at them and then through them. He looked much older than he had when he entered the silo and began the interrogation of the Driver.

Bexx looked at Buffy and nodded toward the door. She whispered, "Go now!"

Nick walked to the sink and turned on the water and began to wash his hands. They were sticky with blood and ooze from The Driver's wounds. Bexx waited silently.

Finally, Nick spoke. "That didn't go well. I'm sorry. I'm afraid I made a mess. I lost it, and well, I made a mess."

Bexx nodded. "Is he dead?"

"I assume so. I doubt anyone could survive that," Nick said.

"What did he say?"

"He said you were one of The Director's people and that... and that you and he... that you begged him."

Bexx said, "Stop now! Don't let it in. Don't let him poison you with these ideas. I'm not one of The Director's people, and I would never beg anyone, ever, not even you. You know this. Don't let this infect you. This was his last defiant act, and he made it count. Don't let it work."

Nick nodded. "He knew just what to say... exactly what would hit me the hardest. If he knows me that well, then so does The Director, and so will his spies."

Bexx nodded. "Let's get you cleaned up, and then you go get some rest. I'll take care of the cleanup of The Driver."

Nick nodded and left the room to shower.

Bexx asked Svetlana and Special K to follow her to the silo. As they walked out, The Mentalist said, "Do you need me? I can grab my med bag."

Bexx replied, "Doubtful, but come anyway. We can use the extra help."

When they arrived at the base of the stairwell, they were all silent.

"What happened?" The Mentalist asked in a whisper.

Bexx told them what The Driver had said to Nick, adding, "Nick said he snapped."

The Mentalist said, "Snapped? Jesus, you think? The Driver's head looks like..."

Bexx cut her off, irritated. "We can all see what it looks like! Let's get him out of here and disposed of, and then we need to clean this mess up."

A couple of hours later, Bexx came into their room. Nick was standing at the dresser.

"How are you doing?"

Nick said nothing for a few seconds and then turned to her. "Tamriko, I want you to finish this now. If you are one of The Director's people, just finish it." He handed her his loaded Para Ordinance, GI Expert .45 caliber. "Don't talk. Don't deny it. Just do it. End it. If you're one of The Director's people, just finish it now."

Bexx took the gun and unloaded it. The impact The Driver's final words had on Nick was disturbing. He looked beaten down, and his hands trembled.

Bexx thought silently, *Every dragon has a chink in his armor... somewhere, a weak link. The Driver has found yours.*

"The Driver has been removed from the silo and disposed of. Special K and The Mentalist helped, and so did Svetlana. It's done. Tomorrow, we start again without The Driver. Now let's go to sleep. You need some rest."

Nick nodded. The Driver's words echoed in his head, circling back around every so often like aftershocks from a devastating earthquake. Nick wouldn't sleep for several days, listening to the echo's painful repetitive return.

CHAPTER THIRTY-NINE

It had been three days since Nick had slept. He sat outside on the ground a couple hundred meters from the missile facility's buildings. He hadn't sat in one place for three days. Sometimes he walked, and often he talked to himself, replaying conversations he'd heard, some he'd participated in, and others he hadn't. Checking his memory of the reactions Bexx had with the context of what had been said. His mind replayed every single betrayal of his entire life. Every memory came back and waited to be replayed, examined for similarities. Previous mistakes replayed, times he'd trusted another person and shouldn't have. When he was done examining a memory, it was discarded, and the next one brought up, and the process began again.

This was how he made the connections to the seemingly random events in the recent past. He used the same process to check The Driver's claims of Bexx being one of The Director's spies. The claim had shaken him to the core, no point in denying it. Betrayal had always shaken him deeply, deeper than it should have, maybe, but this was who he was. The Driver's claim of her sexual betrayal had been easy to put aside. Yet, he admitted he did examine it carefully on the first day, running every moment she and The Driver had been present together past his mind's eye, checking every expression and body gesture they shared in each other's presence. That kind of thing wasn't easy to fake... and harder if you were looking for it. Eyes dilated when a lover walked into the room, a seemingly insignificant brush of a finger or hand, hair tucked coyly behind an ear, sudden preoccupation with your personal appearance or cleanliness. It was impossible to hide. He looked again in his memories and found nothing. Nada.

Much to his surprise, he did find something he had missed though. He rechecked it... twice. Yes, it was definitely there, no mistaking it. In hindsight, he realized he'd missed it because he'd been unsettled at the appearance of the Asgarda when Nõn returned from Ukraine. Playing it over and over in his head, he smiled. No wonder she'd been so contentious from the beginning. He made a mental note to bring it up with Bexx when he was done. Now Nick needed to sort out the rest of The Driver's final desperate message.

Bexx stood at the facility doorway, watching as Nick paced and ran his hand along the chain link fence. It had been two days, and he hadn't let up. Pacing until he could no longer walk in a straight line, he would stop and hang on the fence. She could see his back and torso heaving as he tried to catch his breath. He breathed heavily, not from exertion, but from exhaustion.

While she watched, she heard the familiar footsteps of Special K approaching from the kitchen area. "Is he still at it?" she asked.

"Yes, two days now, no sleep, and he hasn't stopped," Bexx said nothing for several minutes, watching. Finally, she said, "I wish I could take back the decision of letting him deal with The Driver. Double crossing prick really got into his head with those last few comments."

"I'd say so," Special K agreed. Special K waited and sighed.

Bexx's eyes hardened. "Out with it. I can always tell when you have something to say. You do that long pause and then sigh. Spit it out!"

Special K erupted in a barely-contained and yet controlled burst. "Is this what you envisioned when you decided this direction? I mean, we were doing fine in Ukraine until Nõn arrived. She goes down memory lane and begins her story of Baroota, and as soon as you hear the whole 'wolf thing,' it was like you snapped. I know you left it up to each of us whether or not to follow you, but honestly, what did you expect? Of course, we'd follow."

Bexx said nothing. Nick had finally let go of the fence and begun to walk again. "I made my decision, and you made yours. We can't go back, and I wouldn't go back. Period. The discussion is over. If you want to leave, I made it clear you're free to go. I'll think no less of you."

Special K nodded and turned to walk away.

Bexx returned to her silent watch and wondered how long it would take for Nick to work through the mental virus The Driver had planted. Later that evening, in the early morning of the third day, Nick sat in the dark, exhausted, dirty, smelling like a transient living on the fringes of society. Rocking back and forth, his eyes closed, he worked through the final details of the last scenario. He stopped rocking, opened his eyes, and stood up. He'd finished the mental Google search of every detail of every day since Bexx had arrived in Spokane, Washington, and stood in his path as he walked around the van. He remembered feeling the heat coming off her in waves. He smiled. Nick turned and walked back to the facility. Opening the door, the bright lights of the entrance area stung his eyes. He stopped to let his eyes adjust. Walking to the fridge, he grabbed a cold water and tore off a generous portion from a roast chicken that had been left inside. He ate the meat ravenously and then tore off another piece. When he was done, he went to shower.

Bexx listened as the footsteps came down the hall. She had heard the unique cadence of Nick walking in the hallway many times. This time was different. She wondered what conclusion he had come to. Would he believe The Driver? If so, the next few moments could prove to be very interesting. She lay in bed, facing away from the door as she heard it open slowly, and Nick entered the room. He was silent as always, his footsteps always carefully placed. She smiled as she remembered how that had struck her at first. He walked quietly like a wild animal very aware of the space surrounding him. Not like a domesticated animal, clumsy and heavy as it plodded along. But much like her wolf, silent and light, his feet seemed to barely touch the ground. She heard the door close, and Nick stood for a moment looking at her. If the attack was going to come, it would be now. She realized she was vulnerable, but she felt she had to be. To be on guard would send the wrong message and more likely than not start a new round of Nick reflecting on every detail of their time together. She had decided. Trusting in his process mattered more than ever. She waited.

Nick looked at Bexx after he closed the door and waited for his eyes to adjust to the darkness. He guessed if an attack was to come, it would be now. If he'd missed something, this final pause would cause her to come unraveled. If she were one of The Director's spies, now would be the time she would be unable to contain the anxiety. He waited and watched. Finally, his eyes adjusted, and he could see her arm slowly rise and fall as she breathed. No anxiety, no increase in her breathing cadence, no change in rhythm. Nick started to undress and carefully climbed into bed. He lay there motionless for some time and then rolled over and put his arm around her.

"Are you awake?" he asked.

"Yes, of course. You aren't the only one who's had a few sleepless nights the past little while," Bexx replied.

The words stung. Nick nodded. "Sorry. Couldn't be avoided. Had a lot to work through, but I'm back."

Bexx nodded and pulled her arm out from under his and pulled him closer.

Nick breathed in and out slowly. "Svetlana mentioned she knows who The Director is. She has his name. Sorry I didn't mention that. I was a bit preoccupied, I guess."

Bexx listened, her eyes opened. He was back, truly back and refocused. She listened as he paused.

"Bexx, I have a question. Something did come from the last three days... something I missed. It's personal. You don't have to answer if you'd prefer not to."

Bexx replied. "No, go ahead."

Nick began, "I know we never spoke about monogamy or exclusivity. I don't expect it. I never have. But I do expect honesty."

Bexx rolled over. "Listen, there was nothing between me and The Driver, period, ever."

Nick nodded. "I know that now. That isn't what I was speaking about."

Bexx stared at him, puzzled. "What, then?"

Nick dropped his gaze from hers. "Special K. How long were you together? I mean, I realize it must have been over before you arrived in Spokane, but for her, there's still something there. You do realize that, right? Please don't pretend I'm wrong. I'm not. We both know I'm not."

Bexx sat quietly, letting the implication of the question settle in her thoughts. He'd really examined every conversation, every moment, every gesture of the entire team. She nodded and whispered, "Yes, we were together in Ukraine. The relationship had run its course and ended long before Nõn arrived. What else would you like to know?"

Nick nodded. "Nothing. Thanks for being honest. I'm very tired now."

His final question answered the weight of The Driver's last toxic, verbal infection had been lifted. The demon had been exorcised. Nick closed his eyes and instantly was asleep.

Bexx, too, fell asleep soon after as she watched his eyes twitch. He was dreaming almost instantly.

The next morning, there was a slight knock at the door. Bexx quietly got up and answered it. It was The Mentalist. Slightly upset, she spoke rapidly.

"Commander, Nick is gone. I've looked everywhere, and he isn't outside."

Bexx nodded and walked into the hallway. "He's inside, asleep. Let's let him rest. Is everyone awake?"

The Mentalist nodded and replied in a relieved but smart-ass tone as she recovered, "Oh, damn it! I thought maybe he wandered off and was walking aimlessly toward Canada, looking like some worn out homeless man off his medication."

Bexx smiled. "I'm glad he's back, too. Let's get some breakfast."

~